D1531779

THE
DYNAST

Also by Paul Erikson

THE MONEY WOLVES

THE DYNAST

A NOVEL BY

PAUL ERIKSON

WILLIAM MORROW AND COMPANY, INC.

NEW YORK   1979

Library of Congress Cataloging in Publication Data

Erikson, Paul.
    The dynast.

    I. Title.
PZ4.E67Fl   [PS3555.R46]   813'.5'4   78-12194
ISBN 0-688-03418-7

BOOK DESIGN   CARL WEISS

Printed in the United States of America.

First Edition

1   2   3   4   5   6   7   8   9   10

To My Dearest Cyn,

Who Has Stood

the Midnight Watch

Living a nightmare is a curse straight from hell. There is no chance to awaken from the dream, and flee the savage night.

JOHN VINCENT SALISBURY III LOOKED OUT AT THE DARK-
ness spreading its fingers up from the surface of the Atlantic,
which was now almost black in the absence of the sun.

They were at forty-six thousand feet, hurtling their way
from London to New York.

John was always fascinated by the way the earth darkened
first. The deep shadowed blues, then the mauve, then the rose-
orange tints on the underside of the high-altitude cloud deck
below. He knew darkness would come swiftly now, would
possess the earth completely as they flew west.

He sat not quite alone in the large high-backed swivel chair,
his cheek resting against the palm of his right hand, but he
was alone in his thoughts.

His staff was always alert to his moods, especially his principal aide, Carter Lawton. There were only four of them on
the plane other than the flight crew: John, Carter, Douglas
Dowding, president of the First Manhattan Bank, and Daniel
Bernays, executive vice-president and head of the bank's commercial operations, both foreign and domestic. They watched
John, carefully, not obviously, but were sensitive to his need
to be alone.

The aircraft could hold up to nineteen people, so there was plenty of room to give John every opportunity to be by himself.

Though John Salisbury spent most of his waking hours in the company of other people as chairman of the First Manhattan Bank, he was not by nature a gregarious man. In the press and on television he was usually with leading world figures, so one thought of him as convivial. Actually, he was the kind of man whose natural inclinations were to withdraw into himself. In spite of his courtly, gracious manner and his quick, almost professional smile, John lacked the natural warmth that would normally make his relations with other people truly relaxed and friendly.

There was about John a core of inner reserve that was the result of a protected childhood, and of the unease with which he carried the burden of the family name.

Now head of the only true dynasty in the United States, John had been brought up with the awareness of the family's turbulent and troubled past, and also the knowledge that its future reputation, which was by far the most important element in the life of the senior members of the Salisbury family, was his major responsibility. The family had spent nearly two billion dollars within three generations to eradicate the stigma of the family's early money and power. It was this responsibility, and the tenuous grasp the family had upon the affection and respect of its fellow Americans, that caused John to be always aware. He was always somewhat remote, and for those who were closest to him, there was something about John Salisbury that seemed removed, even sad.

That was why Douglas Dowding and Dan Bernays were chatting quietly with Carter in the forward section of the aircraft, glancing occasionally at John, who was lost in thought, staring out at the swiftly approaching night.

The cabin lights came on, but softly. They had become their own separate hurtling star above the black forbidding sea. The door of the flight deck opened, and the copilot came out with a message in his hand. He walked over to Carter Lawton.

"This just came through, sir, on the emergency frequency." He handed the slip of paper to Carter.

Carter, who the top echelon in the bank knew had been handpicked by John, not only for his fluency in five languages, his unfailing knowledge of international protocol, his ability to orchestrate John's murderous worldwide schedule of meetings, dinners, and transportation, but also for his trustworthiness, his tact, and his taste.

Carter looked at the slip of paper and saw that it was in code.

"Would you excuse me?" He smiled at Doug and Dan Bernays. "I've got to get this to John."

They looked at each other, realizing the message must be terribly important. They traveled frequently with John, and had never before known him to receive a coded message on the bank's emergency frequency.

Carter went to his seat, opened his briefcase, and extracted the code book. There were only two copies of this book, one in John's office in New York and the other always in the briefcase of Carter Lawton.

Carter switched on his overhead light and spent several minutes decoding the message. As its content became clear, his face became grim. He finished, put the code book away, and walked back toward John.

"I'm sorry to disturb you, sir, but this just came in. I'm afraid it's not very good news."

John turned slowly toward Carter. He had been so deeply immersed in his own thoughts that he was startled at the tall, poised figure of Carter Lawton standing beside him.

"I'm sorry. What were you saying? It's the sunset and the noise of the engines. They make me sleepy."

"You've had a difficult week, sir. I'm sure you can use

some rest." Carter paused. He was distressed at having to give John this kind of news.

"I'm afraid this won't help you relax." He handed John the piece of paper.

John read Carter's thin, precise handwriting: *"Bond inventory overevaluated by 12 million dollars. Internal auditors suspect amount could be substantially higher."*

It was signed by Robert Dwyer, Senior Vice-President and Controller.

John's mind had been too far away for the impact of this to register as it should. He held the note while Carter took a chair beside him to await instructions. John put on his glasses, absentmindedly brushing his dark brown hair from his forehead.

Slowly it came to him. Forty-six thousand feet and nearly six hundred miles an hour above the Atlantic, the thing that John dreaded most had happened. His bank, or at least what the world thought of as his bank, had suffered a smashing blow at the institution's integrity, and therefore at John's.

If it were anyone else, or any other bank, this calamity would be just that, but for John it was a disaster. As chairman of the First Manhattan Bank, he was responsible. But more than that, the old specter of tainted money would rise to haunt him. All the years, all the philanthropies, would be washed away in cries of ineptitude, deceit, and foul play.

It was one thing for a bank to show losses, but this was an outright fraud against the stockholders, directors, and even the depositors of the bank.

They would be screaming for his scalp. There was enormous pressure to rid the bank of Salisbury and Doug Dowding, and this might prove to be one debacle even John Vincent Salisbury III couldn't surmount.

It was such a personal thing. His association, and that of his family, with the First Manhattan Bank was inseparable. The legacy of the family's money and early misuse of its power had never left the consciousness of his generation. This would tear open all the old wounds, and the pain for him and for all the family would be unbearable.

But how was John to know that three people he had never heard of, a greedy Arab, a suspicious Englishman, and a frightened woman awaking from a nightmare, would have a more disastrous effect upon his life than all the righteous bellowings about his bank?

John looked at Carter, his face ashen. "Would you ask Doug and Bernays to come back here, please."

When John handed Doug the message without saying a word, Dan Bernays knew that something terrible had happened in New York.

Doug read the message swiftly. He was a big man, nearly six feet four. Everything about him was large: his head, his face, his hands, even his voice—a deep bass, almost theatrical in quality.

Doug was the opposite of John: commanding, authoritative, quick to show his reactions. He lacked John's reserve, and he lacked his capacities and depth.

Douglas Dowding was a mirage. He had been picked out of the Manhattan District, where he successfully handled some of the bank's largest customers, but he had been picked because John thought he saw in Doug qualities that weren't there. John thought that Doug, if properly groomed and given the chance to grow within the bank, would develop what John perceived to be Doug's natural qualities as a leader. Except that Doug lacked those qualities; that was the mirage. He couldn't conceptualize or initiate imaginative policy, and he lacked the administrative capability to oversee and follow through. It was as if one projected an authoritative image at a mirror and then turned on a recording of a deep voice. It would lack substance, reality, as did Doug Dowding, at least in his capacity as president. Many in the bank were aware of this; several of the bank's outside directors, especially Frederick ("Dutch") Dernberg, were pressing hard to kick Doug upstairs to vice-chairman, but John didn't see it. He didn't see it in the beginning, and he didn't see it now, and the more they urged him to dump Doug the more that stubborn pride that John had in abundance manifested itself. Doug was John's protégé, and as such he was inviolable. But perhaps not for long.

"Jesus Christ, this is awful. How the hell could this happen? We both told Gallagher to reduce that bond inventory. What the hell has happened to him?"

Doug handed the message to Bernays. Dan read it quietly. He made no reply. His lips were pressed together and a hard, uncompromising look came into the appraising hazel eyes.

Dan was tall, good-looking, with a normally quick smile which exposed large, even white teeth. His smile wasn't infectious, for if you watched his eyes, they rarely smiled.

Dan held one of the most powerful positions in the bank. He was the natural successor to Doug. He was head of both the international and domestic commercial areas of the bank, which, except for the retail and treasury functions, comprised about everything that really counted. He had climbed the slippery rungs of the bank's promotional ladder by a combination of luck, political adroitness, and a contrived social skill.

Dan Bernays was the kind of man whose wife might very logically ask one night in bed after nearly thirty years of marriage, "Who are you?" She might turn toward him and see in the darkness only the brilliant smile of those gleaming white teeth. She might reach for him, but only the smile would be there.

Dan shook his head and handed the note back to John.

As THEY SAT TOGETHER, DOUG SUDDENLY GOT UP, RE-membering to lower his head. "I need a drink. Anyone want one?"

Dan Bernays glanced guardedly at John. John was a notorious abstainer. He occasionally had a cocktail, but more normally it was a fine wine with dinner. John smiled thinly, putting the message in a folder in his briefcase.

"I think I'll pass."

Dan paused. He really wanted a drink, but he disliked having one if John was declining.

"Me too, Doug. I think I'll skip it."

"Suit yourself."

Doug walked over to the bar, his mind absorbed by a variety of thoughts that seemed to have a momentum of their own.

This bond thing might wind up getting him canned. Though John had the ultimate responsibility as chairman, as president, Doug had the responsibility for the bank's opera-tions, and he was damn well aware of how some of the board members felt about that.

He poured himself a Jack Daniel's and water from the

liquor cabinet. He stood in front of it, slowly sipping his drink, his eyes now and then capturing the cold spark of light from a passing star. The blackness of the night and the brilliance of the pale distant dust specks of light were only vaguely impressed upon his mind. Doug was not a contemplative person. He noticed things in quick surface impressions, and he reacted viscerally, emotionally.

Doug tried to keep his mind on the bond scandal, but his thoughts drifted into a montage. He thought of Karen, of how he was looking forward to seeing her after this trip. He had even phoned her from London to see if she could fly down this weekend to Oxford, Maryland, with him. He could hear the hesitation in her voice. He knew that she wanted to break things off with him. She had been trying to tell him that for months, but he knew, too, that their sexual appetite for each other would not let them go.

His wife was beginning to suspect that he was seeing another woman, but Doug felt she hardly expected that woman to be Dr. Karen Lockhart, the assistant to her own doctor, Dr. Stanford Harding.

Doug poured himself another drink. The whole damn thing was crazy, he thought. It could wreck his marriage with Bardia, and if that happened, he was through at the bank. John and Margret Salisbury were very fond of Bardia Dowding, and if John found Doug involved in an illicit affair, it would be the ultimate breach of trust, not just with Bardia but with John too. John sometimes thought of Doug in some subliminal way as the son he never had, and because of this psychic connection, any break in the ethical bond between the two of them would hurt John deeply. Doug was more than just a protégé; he was John's creation, and though John would and was defending him against the winds that were beginning to tear at them both, John's pride was too great to see his trust and confidence so terribly misplaced.

Then why the hell did he risk everything to see a woman who really didn't turn him on that much?

He told himself that it was because he and Bardia couldn't
have a normal married life together, because Bardia's illness
made sex dangerous for her, and almost unpleasant for him.
But he knew that wasn't the real reason. Being with Karen
on these quick flights to Oxford somehow gave him the
separateness he needed from the pressures of the bank. Deep
within Doug there lurked the suspicion that his whole life
had really been a play for which he had been miscast. He
was fine when he ran the Manhattan District, because that
was mainly a marketing and relatively narrow administrative
role. That was the happiest time for him at the bank.

When he was graduated from Dartmouth and entered the
bank's training program, he was happy. When he married
Bardia and he was making his way in the bank, both of them
couldn't have been happier. When John tapped him to work
closely with him and made him a senior vice-president and
then an executive vice-president, he knew his moment was
coming. It was then that things started to fall apart. If he
had to choose the point in his life when he had begun to
have those hidden suspicions about his own capacities, that
would have been the time. Then Bardy came down with this
damn respiratory thing, and nothing ever seemed to go right
after that.

He put his glass down and lit a cigarette and looked at his
watch. He had set it on New York time. It was eight o'clock.
They should be at Kennedy between twelve and twelve-thirty,
depending on winds. Jesus, it was going to be one hell of a
tough day tomorrow, he thought. That son of a bitch Gallagher. He'd like to strangle that bastard. This would be the
most embarrassing thing that ever hit the bank, and everyone
would ask how it could have happened. And it was his direct
responsibility. Gallagher was no minor employee who ran
away with some dough. No one could blame him for the
actions of some nut like that. But Gallagher, that son of a
bitch, was a senior vice-president in charge of the bank's
bond-trading operations. The bank had in inventory several

billion dollars' worth of bonds, and they traded millions of dollars in these mostly government and state obligations every day.

"And you've got some crazy bastard like Gallagher responsible for an operation like that?" they would ask. Only Gallagher wasn't crazy. He was one of the best bond traders in the businenss. What happened to make him go off the deep end? Doug shook his head. He didn't know, but a part of his mind understood that Gallagher's incredible behavior was not far removed from his own.

Why was he still tied up with Karen? Neither of them seemed to be enjoying it that much. Karen was racked with guilt, and each weekend at Oxford seemed to make her more pensive, more withdrawn. Besides, he wasn't sure that Karen was the kind of woman he could really be happy with even as a mistress. She was too independent and self-assured. Like the few other woman doctors he had known in his life, she had a certain false masculinity. Maybe it came from having to prove to all those guys in medical school that she was really one of the boys; that she could take anything they could, and probably do what was required more proficiently. She was smarter than hell and damned attractive. When you got past all that doctor stuff, she was even good in bed, but their relationship was strained for a thousand reasons, and it wasn't making either of them very happy. And for him it was extremely dangerous. He made a weak resolution that he would break it off, but he knew in the part of his mind where the truth refused obfuscation that it was more likely that Karen would call it quits than that he would.

It was all part of what was wrong with Doug, and part of what was wrong with the bank. With John acting as a goodwill ambassador to the rest of the world, the running of the bank was left to Doug. This was hardly the role for an emotionally weak personality who lacked the intellectual abilities to conceptualize and the organizational powers to see that his ideas were properly executed. He sighed, and walked back to Dan and John.

"Is anybody hungry? How about a steak?"

Dan looked at his watch. "That sounds like a good idea to me." He looked at John, who sat grim-faced, lost in thought.

"How about you, John? Can we get you some dinner?"

John's eyes came back to them.

"What time is it?" He looked at his watch. "Well, I must say I didn't realize it was so late. These time changes. No matter how often I make them, though my mind seems able to adjust, my body never does." He stretched and got up. "That sounds like a good idea."

Carter had been watching John and came over to see if there was anything he could do.

"You might get us some steaks, if that's all right with everyone." Both Doug and Dan knew that the choice filets from John's ranch in Wyoming would be more than satisfactory.

"And how about some wine?" They knew John's fondness for fine wines and Carter's ability to select them.

"Sounds good to me," said Doug.

"Good. Carter, would you see to it?"

They sat down again, John taking the swivel chair and Doug and Dan seating themselves on the long couch opposite him. John spoke first.

"Now, what are we going to do about all this?" He looked at them intently. The somewhat long, pointed nose and dark brown eyes gave his face a sharp, incisive expression.

"I think the first thing we have to do is send a message suspending Gallagher temporarily, and get him the hell out of that bond room. Gallagher reports to Gaven Fuller," Doug said, shaking his head. "I wonder where Gave was when all this was going on."

"In Europe, unfortunately," said Dan Bernays. "Gave has

been spending a lot of time in Europe and the Middle East. I'm sure if he had been on deck this never would have happened."

"And why do we have a man who has the ultimate responsibility for our bond trading in Europe and the Middle East?" It was a good question. It was the kind of question that the directors and the shareholders and the authorities would ask, but the key to the whole problem was that it was being asked after the fact. The three men who should have been able to plan things so that this kind of gross foolishness couldn't happen in a major United States bank were sitting together on that plane. The real answer was that the bond scandal had been another example of flagrant administrative ineptitude. These three men, John, Doug, and Dan Bernays, about to eat a succulent dinner, speeding high across the Atlantic, had dropped the ball through a very wide crack at great expense to the shareholders of the bank.

Dan Bernays' thoughts were rapid and self-serving. He too would be tarred with the brush of ineptitude, but if he played his cards right and kept out of the main line of fire, this might prove a blessing in disguise. This might be the last straw for Doug, maybe even for John, but that could be stretching things a bit. It would be damned hard to get John Salisbury out of that bank. He had five years to go before he had to retire, and he would have to be dragged feet first if they tried to force him out.

As he ate slowly, Dan Bernays kept his eyes averted from Doug's. That was the bird who would get it in the neck, Dan thought. If there had to be bloodletting, if it came to a choice between Doug and John, there was in fact no choice. Doug would be sacrificed, probably kicked upstairs to vice-chairman if John was still in control. But if he wasn't, Doug was through. This might just be the time to stay low and hang on tight, Dan thought, and he was usually accurate in judging the winds for such a balancing act.

He would stay in town tonight, of course; it was too late to make any train for New Canaan. He thought of his middle-aged wife with the trim figure, the carefully set hair, the right clothes for country and town, her quick smile and ready hand in reception lines, and the despair he saw at the back of her eyes on those rare occasions when they actually looked at each other.

"I'm going to call a meeting at eleven tomorrow morning. That should give us time to catch up on a little sleep," John said, and turned to Carter. "Would you try and call Tom Gallagher at home and tell him to be in my office at eleven. Also have Bob Dwyer there and Gaven Fuller as well." He turned to Doug. "We'll have to get a message out to the directors as soon as we've talked to Gallagher. We'll also need a statement for the press. I'll leave that to you and Dan. Get up something as soon as possible. We can fill in the details when we know them. I want something to give the press as soon as the directors have been notified."

WHEN JOHN ARRIVED AT HIS HOUSE ON SEVENTY-THIRD Street between Lexington and Park, it was nearly one o'clock.

Margret Salisbury knew that he was coming home, and she couldn't sleep until he was finally in bed beside her, where she could feel his exhausted body, and comfort him, and do whatever she could to bring him a little peace.

One of the blessings of John's life was Margret, the eldest daughter of Silas Cummings, a former governor of Rhode Island, who represented one of the oldest families in the state.

Margret and John fell in love very quietly. They first met when John was working in the bank's London office one summer while he was getting his doctorate at the London School of Economics.

They were almost instantly attracted to each other, for reasons that they initially sensed and more fully comprehended as their marriage matured under the pressures of John's life. In this crucible, they learned to appreciate the qualities of character that each could contribute to the other.

On that scale, however, Margret stood far heavier than John. Not because he wouldn't give to her; he would have given her his life. He adored her, but there was never enough time. He was committed to his work eighteen hours a day and often on weekends. His schedule was one of his biggest problems. Between his commitments representing the family and those of the bank, he had little time for anything else. Margret's secretary had all she could do to coordinate Margret's schedule with John's so the two of them could spend some meaningful time together. John became Margret's vocation. She protected him, soothed him, took care of him; she ran their houses scattered about the world, and accompanied him on his endless trips just so they could be together. This had become her life, and although she didn't complain and wasn't unhappy, she felt guilty about what this had done to their only child, Jane.

Jane had grown up without really ever knowing her father, had been denied that relationship that is particularly important for a daughter. There was between Jane and her mother the normal hostility that is usually beneath the surface in such relationships, but in some not altogether inaccurate way Jane construed her father's life and her mother's protection of him as a betrayal of their affections toward her. She felt less than abandoned, but not less than deferred, held off, kept too remote from her parents; she was not really a part of their lives. She felt cheated, and she was. It was an unhappy approach to her twenty-first birthday, which was only three days away. That birthday would cause John as much anxiety as his problems at the bank.

Most of these thoughts ran through the mind of Margret Staunton Cummings Salisbury as she watched her husband get wearily into bed.

She was fifty-three years old, and still attractive. She had never really lost her figure. Through disciplined, purposeful exercise and diet, she still wore the same size dress she did when she was at Radcliffe.

"Darling, you look terribly tired." She sensed more than just the usual fatigue in his manner.

He got into bed and flicked off the lamp on his side. Despite all the pressures of both their lives, they insisted on sleeping together. It was one of the few comforts their marriage gave them.

John sighed. "Something terrible has happened, Marge. Tom Gallagher has rigged the bond inventory so that the bank will show at least a twelve-million-dollar loss, and probably a lot more. The worst part about this is how it looks for Doug and me. It makes us look like idiots. We'll never be able to explain the lack of supervision or controls that could permit a thing like this to happen." He paused as he looked at her, his eyes filled with fatigue and despair. "No one will realize that the only way a thing like this can happen is through the breakdown of integrity within one very human being."

Margret listened with great sympathy and found herself agreeing with her husband's theory of human fallibility, but what she found harder to agree with, in that silent part of her mind that sifted sympathy and support with her New England pragmatism, was how it could be that whatever control mechanisms the bank needed to protect itself against this kind of manipulation hadn't caught a Tom Gallagher and put a stop to what he was doing. Margret kept this to herself.

"Dearest, that's absolutely awful." She knew what the effect could be on John and on the family. All the old ghosts coming back. She moved closer to him and put her arms around him.

"John, listen to me." Her voice was now strong and determined. "All this may create a terrible fuss, but if it does, even if it should mean your having to withdraw, darling, it could be the best thing that ever happened to you, to us! You have enough interests for ten men. All that bank has ever done is come between Jane and you and me. It's too much, John, representing this family and that bank. One man can't do it." She was trying to talk both of them into believing that, and they almost did.

EARLIER THAT EVENING HENRY CANNON WAITED AT THE bar of Le Cirque for Joan Hopkins. This was the first time in the three years that Joan had worked for Henry that they had been out together socially. Henry hadn't dated much since his divorce three years ago, especially women who worked for him.

As Henry sat at the small bar, sipping thoughtfully at a Dubonnet, he thought about the propriety of all this. Henry was fairly old-fashioned; a lot of Lancaster, Pennsylvania, was buried deep within the urbane and well-traveled Henry Cannon.

Henry was one of three children, the only son of James and Martha Cannon, who owned one of the largest dairy farms in Lancaster County, Pennsylvania. The farm had been in the family for over a hundred years, and its soil and heritage were an inalienable part of the consciousness of James Cannon. Even at seventy-eight James had never really forgiven Henry for breaking the chain. Henry was the first male Cannon to disavow his tie to his own land. His sisters had married; one lived in the Midwest, married to a small-town lawyer, and the other was on the West Coast, divorced, and living on the money she earned as a secretary. Her two children were helped by the monthly checks that came from the old man as regularly as clockwork. But Henry was the great disappointment. His fame had never touched his father; it was meaningless. When Henry's mother died, while he was still at Cornell, he lost his only intermediary between himself and the silent hostilities of the rock-hard man who could only see in Henry a repudiation of everything James Cannon felt was precious in his own life. To have lived to know that the homestead of the Cannon farm and property would fall into the hands of professional managers or, worse yet, real estate developers embittered the old man and drove a wedge between Henry and his father.

Henry was happy to leave the silent censure of his father, the brooding, dark house that was emptied of the love of his mother and sisters, the constrictions of that island of discipline, whose only gratification was work.

But a lot of those rural attitudes of his early life had stayed with Henry. He was never really the free spirit, the international cosmopolite that his career of globe-trotting and world reporting might have made him. He was quiet, self-controlled, with an ingratiating modesty that depreciated his obvious talents.

Often, when he looked at his own life and thought about the death of his only son, James, killed in Korea, of his divorce from Katherine, or the lonely hours spent away from his only real joy, his daughter Claire, who had become, like Henry, a constant traveler and successful free-lance writer, it was only the thought of Claire that gave him any real comfort. He often thought his father was right; perhaps he should have stayed with his roots, for without them his life had been that of a lonely spectator, observing the insanities of his fellowmen, and like his marriage, which ended in failure three years ago, had left him unfulfilled.

As he waited for Joan, he wondered about the wisdom

of this meeting. He knew that all of this would get back to NBT, where he was director of television news. He had been around long enough to know how quickly the ground fire of office gossip swept through a place like NBT. He had already begun to hear the Mutt and Jeff jokes that started circulating when he made Joan his assistant. She was nearly four inches taller than Henry, and if she wore any kind of heels at all, she seemed to tower over him. To many men this would have been embarrassing, but not to Henry. He had hired Joan for her brain, not her body, and he had talked her into coming over to NBT from the "other" network, where she had been doing a first-rate job in their news department.

Henry was neither threatened by the fact that Joan was a stunning redhead with the body of a movie starlet, nor intimidated by the knowledge that she was a Phi Beta Kappa graduate of Wellesley, had been president of her class, and had been graduated summa cum laude. The fact that she also held a brown belt in karate didn't bother him either.

Henry was one of those men who simply weren't threatened by women, any woman, not even one with the awesome background of Miss Hopkins.

Joan was one of the winners in life's roulette. She was the daughter of Chip Hopkins, who was a successful executive with a major food company, and both Joan and her brother had been raised in New York by loving, interested parents who happily shared their active social lives with their children. Almost everything came easily to Joan, who seemed to be a natural leader. She was strikingly attractive, with large bright green eyes, a full, ripe figure, and legs that came straight from her mother, who was known around Sutton Place, even at fifty-eight, as "Legs Hopkins."

Joan dated constantly, and had had enough proposals to keep in a rotary file, but she held everyone at a distance, with an adroitness that many of her admirers and would-be suitors found exasperating.

Her sexual life was surprisingly sparse. It wasn't that she wasn't interested; it was just that she wasn't promiscuous and had the rather old-fashioned belief that she had to feel deeply for a man before she would make love to him or allow him to make love to her.

It did seem a bit strange that while Henry glanced at his watch and realized that she was now twenty minutes late, Joan was rushing from her apartment, where she had spent a lot more time than usual making herself look especially attractive for a man who was nearly four inches shorter than she, and old enough to be her father.

She had put on a long, low-cut black gown that she had bought in Rome, and had draped across her shoulders and over her forearms a burgundy-colored silk shawl. She wanted to be particularly attractive for Henry.

In the three years that she had worked for Henry Cannon, he had been the only man she had ever known who hadn't tried to get her into bed.

But more than that, Joan saw in Henry a quiet, urbane man, who had covered three wars and most of the other important events that had struck at this distressed planet in the last couple of decades.

Through the cloud of cigarette smoke that continuously hung about Henry's face, she saw his large dark brown eyes that seemed quietly appraising, often preoccupied, compassionate, and sad. It was those eyes that had told Joan that Henry was going to be her man.

In three years she had had ample time to come to know Henry; they were together on assignments he chose to supervise, and she was in daily contact with him at the office. She had even begun to know Claire, that dark-eyed sensitive daughter of Henry's whom he adored. There was a special bond between Henry and Claire, and Joan felt that Claire, with a woman's instincts, had discovered Joan's interest in her father.

Henry saw Joan as she stood looking for him in the restaurant. Her eyes swept to the bar, and he could see the light come into them, the broad smile as her face lit up at the sight of him.

If Henry had never seen her before, he was most certainly seeing her now. As she came toward him, her hand extended, with that smooth, fluid motion which was her stride, he was literally struck with her youth and beauty. It never occurred to him that she could be seriously interested in him. He could easily be her father. He was too old, too worn; he had seen too much of the human condition. The only thing that kept him from being a cynic was the generousness of his nature. Henry was incapable of thinking everything was bad.

"You look absolutely marvelous."

"Why, thank you, sir." She radiated toward him.

"Do they really let women like you out alone? You ought to be arrested. Anybody that beautiful is a traffic hazard. You could cause an accident."

She laughed, a full, throaty laugh, and lightly kissed his cheek.

"A girl doesn't often get compliments like that, you know. Especially from her boss."

He took her arm.

"Joseph has been holding a table against the wall for us."

"Lead on, sir."

"Not on your life. I'm going to let you follow Joseph, and I'll cover the rear. The way these fellows are looking at you, that's the only way you're going to make it to the table."

She laughed heartily at that one and followed the shaved head of Joseph to a corner table.

They talked mainly about the office, skirting around the corners of each other's mind, avoiding what interested Joan most, and what was slowly beginning to interest Henry in spite of himself—the relationship between the two of them.

The warm, intimate ambience of the restaurant and a

bottle of good French wine helped take the edge off things a little for Henry. He still felt slightly guilty, no matter how often he told himself that this was a business dinner, about being with this smashing young woman who could be his daughter. That's what really bothered Henry. At the back of his mind there was the suggestion that things might develop with Joan if he wasn't careful. How would that look to Claire, and even to his former wife, Katherine? Katherine was French and very European, so she would be more likely to understand; she wouldn't necessarily approve, but she might understand. But Claire—that was his real concern. He could never do anything if Claire totally disapproved; or perhaps more accurately, anything that would harm what they had between them as father and daughter. He dismissed what Lionel Emden, his boss, the president of NBT, would say. Lionel would kid the pants off him, perhaps be even more than just a little envious. But these thoughts were ridiculous, he told himself; this was ego. This girl wasn't interested in him. She would probably want some young buck who could bodysurf and ski, someone her own age. She didn't need a broken-down news director who was a little tired of it all.

Henry put down his wine and looked at her carefully.

"You know, this really is supposed to be a business dinner."

She feigned seriousness. "I assumed nothing less, sir. Shoot. What have you got in mind, boss? You want to fire me? Is that what this is all about—the golden handshake?"

"Be serious."

"Sorry, sir. Just a little macabre humor there." She brushed back her long red hair that hung to her shoulders.

"You do look serious, Mr. News Director, so let's get on with it." She blotted her lips with her napkin.

"Joan, I've been playing around with an idea about you, and I'd like to try it out on you."

The green eyes focused on him. "Go ahead."

"Well, it goes something like this. Although you have had

little training or experience in front of a camera, I don't think that should be a problem. You've got looks, brains, and you can think quickly on your feet. I've watched you in meetings. Your thought processes are logical and direct. You seem to know how to reach for the core of a problem." He paused to crush out his cigarette.

"Want a brandy or a liqueur?"

"I'll have a brandy with you."

"That's my girl." He motioned to the waiter.

"What I'm trying to point out to you is that you have all of the attributes of a successful television reporter; you lack only one qualification, and that is experience. But we can fix that up. Your previous background, which has been mostly in research and administration, should have given you—and I believe it has—a good grounding in the overall business." Henry's voice was always professional: low, resonant, sonorous. If Joan had been old enough, she would have recalled that voice during the blitz on London. Millions of Americans sat glued to their radios while that same serious, concerned voice told of the valiant defiance of a small island standing alone against the Nazi onslaught. But that was before Joan was born.

"What I'm taking a rather long time to say, Joan, is that as well as fulfilling the role of my assistant, I would like to start having you cover special selective assignments, if you think that's something you'd enjoy."

She looked at him carefully, knowing that there was more to come.

"Sounds challenging, Henry."

"It is. At times perhaps more than you'd like." He paused, and she could see his thoughts drawing inward, searching the film of his mind, reviewing his own career.

"The problem of covering the news, Joan, is what Malraux referred to as *la condition humaine*. It isn't always very pretty. That's not to suggest that there aren't some aspects of the human scene that make you glad that you're part of it, but one of the unfortunate parts of the news is the morbidity of people." He paused. "Just think of how many times you've driven on a turnpike or expressway and watched a whole caravan of cars slow down and tie everyone up just to pause and see some poor guy who's parked off the road with a motor problem, everyone wondering if there's some spilled blood somewhere. Call it the ghoul syndrome. Unfortunately, it's that almost universal attraction for the catastrophic that makes up a lot of our news. But it's not the morbidity that's the hardest to get used to." He paused again, making abstract impressions on the tablecloth with the edge of his butter knife. "The hardest part of this game is when you have to report news that you know is going to hurt someone, maybe someone you know and like a good deal. But it's news, and a reporter's job is to bring that back to his editors and re-write people, and let them make their evaluations. That's the tough part, Joan."

She watched him intently as he spoke. His voice was quiet, coming to her from someplace far back in his mind.

"Sounds ominous, boss."

He heard her, but he was far away. He was walking through the dark streets of London, the shattered skeletons of torn buildings lifting their dark, broken teeth to the sky. He saw the glow of fires, heard the clanging of bells and the tormented howls of sirens as the emergency vehicles lurched crazily over the broken rubble. He remembered the hollow-eyed expression of men along the muddy roads in France and Italy, the exhaustion, the fear, the smell of death, and the moans of misery of the crippled and dying.

"Boss, are you leaving me?" She knew he was far away, going deeper into memories that were wounds that would never heal.

"Sorry, Joan. Just combat fatigue, I guess." He looked at her closely. "Well, what do you say? Want to give it a whirl?"

She hesitated. "I don't want to disappoint you, Henry. I don't know how good I'll be."

"If I thought you would disappoint me, I wouldn't have suggested it."

She smiled. "If you're willing to risk it, Henry, I'm game."

"Good." He looked at his watch. "Say, it's getting late. We've got work to do tomorrow, you know. Shall we leave this den of iniquity?"

"I'm ready, boss. Let me make one little trip to repair the ravages of this sumptuous meal and I'll be right with you."

The cab stopped at the corner of Seventy-ninth and York. He told the driver to wait.

"You don't have to bother, Henry. I'm a big girl."

"My father always told me to see the lady all the way home. Come on, I'll take you up to your apartment."

He took her up to the door and watched her fumble for the key. She got the door open and turned to him, looking almost unbearably beautiful.

"Want a fast nightcap?"

He hesitated. He knew that if he entered her apartment it would be the beginning. "Joan, it's late."

"I think I can be relied on to get you back home in time to satisfy the warden, sir."

"O.K. One quick one. Then we'd both better turn in."

"Make yourself comfortable, boss. What'll it be?"

"Just a light Scotch with a splash of water. No ice, Joan."

"Coming up."

Henry looked around her living room. The room reflected Joan. It was bright, colorful, tasteful; expensive period furniture was skillfully blended with a few choice oriental pieces. A beautiful Japanese screen was hung as a wall covering, opposite the Lawson sofa on which he was sitting. The paintings and etchings that hung on the walls and the scattered pieces of sculpture reflected her taste and her refusal to own reproductions. What she did have was original and good, carefully selected yet affordable. There were freshly cut Japanese irises on the low oriental table in front of him.

"Here you go, sir." She handed him his drink. She sat down beside him. They each drank quietly, knowing that this was a beginning.

Henry for the first time in more years than he could remember felt the nearness of a woman stir him. He could smell her perfume and could see the flecks of light from the low lamps reflected in her eyes. He saw that she was looking at him intently.

"In case you're wondering, sir, not many men get to see this apartment."

He didn't answer. He was struggling to find the resolution to get up and leave. He knew this was what he should do.

"Joan, I think I'd better leave."

He stood up and she rose with him. They stood looking at each other, standing very close together. Henry put down his drink.

He started to move, but found himself moving toward her, not away from her. Suddenly she was in his arms. They kissed each other slowly. She moved so that her breasts, which were now rising and falling with the more rapid increase of her breathing, seemed to pulsate toward him the scent of her perfume. Henry felt her press very close to him. Her mouth reached down for his, and suddenly he felt her fingers with great delicacy touch him so very lightly. The electricity shot through him.

They were locked together. It became an eruption for both of them. There was no thought of leaving now.

"Henry. Go down and take care of the cab. Here's my key. I'll slip into something more comfortable."

Henry seemed to be gasping for air. He knew he should get into that cab and just keep going, but he couldn't, not any more.

When he came back into the apartment, she was in a nightgown covered by a peignoir. She moved toward him. He could feel the smoothness of her gown and the softness of her body.

They sat down on the couch and kissed each other passionately.

Henry slipped his hand into the deep V of her gown to feel her full, warm breast. There was no turning back now.

"Henry, take those things off."

She began to help him undress. She was impatient, excited to find Henry as hard as a rock.

"It's beautiful, Henry, beautiful." She played with him until he thought he would go right through the ceiling. She kissed his penis, gently, slowly, using her tongue expertly.

"Let's go into the bedroom, Henry."

Their lovemaking was made more intense now by Henry's experience. It was Henry who kept slowing her down, drawing out the essence of their passion, making her wait, building her hunger and desire until she was on fire. She began to dig her nails into him and to bite him; she could wait no longer. She thrust herself on top of him, her large breasts with their distended nipples hung toward his mouth like ripe fruit. She moved her large, full hips down upon him, thrilling at the size of him. She pulsed faster and faster, her ecstasy beyond anything she had ever known.

It was Henry who had orchestrated their passions, until he too was no longer in control. They exploded inside one another. Again and again she thrust herself on Henry, moaning, sighing. It took far longer for Joan to expend her passion.

As they held each other panting in their exhaustion, alone with their separate thoughts, Henry wondered where all this would take them. His experience was so much greater than hers that it led him to doubt. She, with the assurance of youth and with the certainty of her own determination, was far more assured as to where they were going. Perhaps she didn't know their final destination, but she was sure, whatever it was, they would approach it together.

At Seventy-first and Park, Doug opened the door of his apartment. It was quarter past one. He was exhausted from the long flight, but as was usual with him, the time difference affected his body rather than his mind. His mind was alert and sensitive to the darkness of the apartment. He knew the servants would be asleep, but he wasn't sure about Bardia. She slept restlessly, and often got up to read if she couldn't sleep.

He hung his coat up in the hall closet and left his briefcase near the umbrella stand in the foyer so he wouldn't forget it in the morning.

He walked softly through the living and dining rooms, half hearing the ticking of the tall standing clock. He saw a light under Bardia's door. He opened it carefully. She was reading in bed.

"Aren't you up a little late?" He stood tall and somewhat stiffly in the doorway.

"Oh, not especially. When you're on my schedule, day or night makes very little difference."

As he looked at her, he couldn't help think of how much

she, and they, had changed. He had not gone over to kiss her, an indication of how different everything was from what it used to be.

She was sitting half up in bed, propped up by several pillows, looking at him with cool detachment. Her attitude was one of indifference. She had her reasons.

Bardia had married one man, and found herself very gradually married to someone else. They both had been so different in the beginning.

She met him the first time at Sweet Briar when he was in his senior year at Dartmouth. She was a warm, intelligent girl, full of life. Her eyes sparkled with her own internal satisfaction and optimism.

Her parents had provided a fun-filled, loving, and interesting home, with their liberal ideas and many vital interests. The house was often filled with noisy, charming people, especially the fellow artists and writer friends who lit up in the company of her famous mother, one of America's leading painters; and there were also the quarrelsome but affectionate friends of her father, who was a professor of English literature at N.Y.U.

Their house on Bleecker Street was full of light, sound, and warmth. It was to this house that she introduced Doug Dowding, who was foreign to its environment but not unwelcome.

As a commercial banker, Doug was accepted as the nihilist from Wall Street, but always with a touch of generosity; there was nothing offensive to Bardia's family in the difference of Doug's background and interests.

Doug's family was the antithesis of Bardia's. Doug's father was a partner in a Main Line Philadelphia investment banking firm. His mother, Sally Hart Dowding, was from a socially prominent Philadelphia family and had entrée into all the right clubs in that insular city, but her fortune had been irresponsibly dissipated by her husband's desire to buy his own way into his wife's social position, in a society where money couldn't purchase that. Doug's father was big, affable, and ingratiating, but an incorrigible snob.

Doug's values were pointed always in the direction of "making the right impression," being with the "right" crowd. It had turned his two younger brothers into impossible bores who sought their own successes through carefully contrived marriages. It had directed Doug toward the importance of "projecting an image," in a world where "form" often passes for substance.

There was little emphasis by either of Doug's parents in filling the vacuum behind the bass voice with any real sense of purpose. It was assumed that his "natural" talents and the careful guidance of his parents would keep him close to the right people.

They were visibly shocked when they learned the background of Bardia's family, and they were embarrassed to have to invite their Philadelphia and Boston friends to the wedding, held in Greenwich Village. They smiled thinly as they drank their champagne, and they used the expression "quaint" a lot.

In the beginning Bardy was attracted to the image of strength and direction that Doug seemed to have. She was as much taken in by the deep bass voice, the air of authority, as was John. But she only came to discover this much later.

During their early happiness she forced away from her mind the little suspicions that surfaced, but as the years passed, as Doug became more burdened with responsibilities, the pressures that grind away in the trials of marriage began to expose characteristics she had only begun to suspect.

When she became ill, that seemed to cut them both adrift. Doug needed an escape from the forces and pressures of the bank that were stretching his capacities, and Bardy could no longer give him that. After a while, with some special instinct that women have, she sensed he was seeing another woman. In her own guilt at not being able to be the wife or the woman he needed at that point in their lives, she didn't bother to question him. But as her suspicions grew, it put an even greater strain on their relationship.

Bardia was a woman of great integrity, and to think that her husband was breaking their vows of mutual trust was a condition of their marriage she couldn't tolerate. She lacked the pragmatism of the European; she was imbued with a particular brand of American puritanism that could not tolerate this kind of thing. Bardia wasn't petty; she wasn't lacking in understanding or compassion. She had simply meant it when she had pledged to love him "until death do us part," and to find his commitment less than hers was something that she couldn't accept.

"Was your trip terribly tiring?"

He still stood in the doorway. His eye saw the cylinder of oxygen and the face mask on her night table.

"No more so than usual." He shifted his position. "We have had a rather interesting development," he said dryly. He told her about the bond problem. He saw the concern come into her eyes.

"What will you and John do?"

"Well, the first thing we'll do is get together with Gallagher in the morning. We'll grab every file and piece of correspondence he's got, and then we'll fire the bastard. Of course, since there are potential lawsuits in all of this, we'll have to be guided by counsel, but Tom's through."

"What on earth would make him do such a thing?"

"We've all been asking ourselves that, Bardy. It's not that he profited by any of this personally. He didn't. If he had embezzled a couple of million dollars, that would at least be understandable. But the guy has crucified himself, and John and me as well, I might add, and he doesn't have a damn thing to show for it."

He saw the confusion in her eyes.

"To make matters worse, those real estate properties in Florida and Puerto Rico are giving us a hell of a problem,

and I've got to go down there on Friday to see what, if anything, we can do."

Her lips tightened. Her voice lowered. "Then you're not
going to be home this weekend either?"

He felt a shaft of guilt at her question. He didn't really
have to go to Puerto Rico. He wanted to go to Oxford with
Karen. But, he rationalized, he really should take another
look at those properties, and he could fly back late Saturday
afternoon on the bank's jet, meet Karen at Westchester
airport, and fly down to Oxford in his own plane, the little
white Bonanza that Karen had come to know so well.

"Gay will be disappointed. She was hoping we could all be
together for the weekend. She sees so little of you as it is."

This cut at the heart of him. Gay was his youngest child,
and was in her last year at Barnard. Gay was what mattered
to him in their marriage. It was not that he didn't love his son,
Craig, but their interests and values, even their characters,
were so different that there was little ground for any real
understanding. Craig was like his mother and her side of the
family. Money or status had no attraction for him. His real
concern lay in the history of man, and after he received his
Ph.D., he would stay at Yale and teach. He had been a brilliant student, and they wanted him on the faculty, and that
life suited him. His direction was away from his father.

"If things get much worse at the bank, Bardy, I'll have a lot
more time to spend with Gay."

It was lame and flip, and he felt a further shrinkage in his
own self-esteem for making it.

He stood there watching her, but trying to avoid her eyes.
He felt vacuous, adrift, as if someone had cast off his mooring
lines one by one in the dead of night, silently, while he slept.

Bardy, too, felt without purpose. She felt unwomanly, unable to be a wife or a true companion to her husband. If it
weren't for Gay, she would just as soon stop fighting this
damn thing inside her that wanted to cut off her air, and just

go; instead of renewing her life each time with oxygen, why not just let it run out? But there was Gay, and there was still some spark left within her that didn't want to go out. She still longed to recover her life, to make it a meaningful life if she could, with or without Doug.

"I hope things go all right for you and John tomorrow."

"Thanks. Is there anything I can get for you?"

"No. I'm fine."

"You'd better try and get some sleep."

"You too."

"I'll do my best, but these damn time changes raise hell with me. I just can't ever adjust as quickly as I'd like to."

She turned out her light as he left her room. She stared at the doorframe where he had stood, now deep in shadows. She had an almost unbearable desire to have him come to her, to comfort her and hold her.

There was no one left except Gay. She had tried to keep the news of her disintegrating marriage from everyone. Most people thought, if they did at all, that it was her illness that seemed to take the edge off what she and Doug once had together. But as she lay in the semidarkness, really alone, she could feel her heart breaking into small pieces. It was only her own grace, her own courage, that kept up a public façade. She and Doug were like two performers who embraced heatedly onstage, and when the curtain lowered, immediately turned away from each other and walked toward separate exits.

She wondered in the shadows of the room if this was the way it was meant to be for her. Would she simply run out of air like some limp balloon—in the light or in the darkness? Is that what she had come through forty-seven years for? Is that all there was?

She knew she had to guard against these depressions, not let her isolation overwhelm her mind. She could recover with care and rest—if not completely, at least enough to be granted more time. She turned over and determined to fall asleep. She had come up to this a thousand times in her contemplations of her life, and she always returned to the same question: Was it worth fighting on for, if just to be granted more time? More time for what? To *live*, she decided. Whatever that means.

She heard the ticking of the living-room clock as she was at last granted the peace of a few hours' sleep.

THREE THOUSAND MILES AWAY IN CALIFORNIA IT WAS A magnificent night. From the house in Hillsborough, Peter Tennant could look down at San Francisco Bay. He could see the ribbon of lights which was the San Mateo bridge, and just the edge of the San Francisco airport. His eyes moved northwest, to the yellow coals that were the lights of San Francisco disappearing into the velvet darkness of the September night.

The large screened patio faced the bay. The cypress and eucalyptus trees, dramatically lit, became pieces of sculpture as they ascended into the darkness. He sat sipping a gin and tonic, the glow of his cigarette a small coal, fanned more brightly by his occasional inhalation.

Peter Tennant was chairman of the board and chief executive officer of the Tennant Corporation. He was the successor to his father, Malcolm Tennant, who founded the company, but it was Peter who had carried it to its present size and complexity as one of the world's largest design, engineering, and construction companies, specializing in mining, power, petroleum and pipeline, and commercial construction. The corporation was acknowledged worldwide. Its people were tough, intelligent, tenacious competitors. So was Peter Tennant.

Peter's peripheral vision caught the soft glow of lights from both wings of the sprawling single-floored house, with its flat, gently sloping, overhanging roof that formed a sharp edge of black triangle against the night sky.

It was the home of Sayed Saif Ibn Abdul Ageel, known to his Western friends as "Ali." Peter was pursuing a very special contract with Ali. In fact, it was the largest contract his firm had ever bid on: FOURTEEN BILLION DOLLARS. He was trans-fixed in silent awe as he thought of that number. FOURTEEN BILLION DOLLARS. It was mind-boggling. It was preposterous. He continually had to tell himself that the whole thing was real. The first part of the contract alone was worth nine billion. He sat there thinking of this once-in-a-lifetime opportunity to build.

It was nearly three years ago when Ali came into his office to propose to the Tennant Corporation the creation of a complete plan for developing the infrastructure for the southern portion of his country.

The Tennant Corporation was well known to his king, and if Ali could swing this deal he would charge and receive over the life of the contract a fee of one hundred and forty million dollars, which would amount to one percent of the total transaction.

For three years the Tennant Corporation's team working on the plans to be presented to the king and his advisers' had shuttled back and forth to the Gulf, enduring the murderous temperatures that could rise to 120 degrees in the shade in summer.

Peter Tennant was, like all men, more and less than he seemed. His crew cut, his steel-framed glasses, the wide Western belt with the heavy silver buckle, gave him a distinctly southwestern appearance, rather than the more casual, sophisticated look of the San Franciscan he was.

Peter's quiet manner and encompassing gaze hid the banked fires that burned inside him. He was a builder, not for money, not even for power, but for the sheer creativeness of construction.

Peter's real satisfaction came from the knowledge and the presence of the physical grandeur he created. An enormous project of one kind or another: a dam, a pipeline, a bridge, something he could look at for hours on end. Something he could walk or drive on, touch with his hands, feel cold steel or concrete, and remember that before him, nothing was there. He had built it, and it would stand, if not forever, at least for his lifetime and that of his children. That was enough for him.

Slowly, the plan had taken shape for financing the vast project; for developing ports, roads, cities, towns, schools, hospitals, homes, office buildings, power stations, water supplies, storage facilities, irrigation systems for vast areas of desert. The king had decided to do in one generation what it had taken nearly ten generations for Western societies to evolve: to establish a modern industrial state.

What the king couldn't buy with his petrodollars was the instant education of his people to run such a society, so the Tennant Corporation had to plan for primary and secondary schools and universities, for teachers; in fact, in order to meet the king's requirements, Peter Tennant's planners had to consider importing an entire technocratic society from Europe and the States. There were a few problems.

Very few Western families wanted to live where the temperatures rose to 120 degrees in the shade; where women were separated from men; where there was no liquor, no theater, no concerts; almost nothing to do but work.

Peter could hear the muted sounds of servants in the house.

Ali was almost forty minutes late. This was not unusual, as Peter had come to accept. Part of Ali's inability to be anywhere on time was his incredible schedule. He held conferences in the VIP lounges of airports, in limousines, in restaurants; in fact, anywhere, at any time.

He had recently purchased a Boeing 737 with special long-range tanks, which had become a flying office and conference room, so he could continue his worldwide deals even in flight.

But to really understand Ali you'd have to understand the desert; the nomadic, fiercely independent masculine environment that made Ali, for all his Western education and experience, a free spirit of those timeless sands. This was one of the reasons why Ali was rarely on time. He felt inhibited by the restraints of the schedules of his Western friends. He had to show his independence, his freedom, even if he didn't realize his reasons for doing so.

On this particular night Ali was lucky to have arrived at all. He had just come from Houston after a murderous three days and nights of showing twelve of his fellow countrymen, all prominent businessmen, the wonders of American technology —everything from the manufacture of oil-drilling bits to the port facilities for handling the enormous shipping traffic that flowed in and out of Houston.

As always, Ali was trying to compress time. Right now he was trying to herd his prospective clients into his Boeing 737 that was his flying office, while his chief lieutenant, Noel Aragon, stood quietly by, watching these time-consuming proceedings with stoic British reserve.

It was not an unusual scene for Houston.

The aircraft, waiting on the commercial aviation ramp, was flanked by several long black limousines. Short, dark men with spade beards were shaking hands with tall Americans. All were laughing, clapping each other on the back, shaking hands vigorously. Revolving emergency lights from several police cars slashed repeatedly at the soft light of the late afternoon.

Aboard the aircraft ties came off. Feet slipped out of alligator loafers, and the hostesses, carefully selected by Ali for this occasion, began to pass drinks to dark-eyed men who looked at them greedily. Men who were glad to be away from the restraints of behavior of their king and country, and the conventions of American business routine.

Now, it was time to relax, with Middle Eastern style and imagination. Ali knew how to orchestrate this kind of affair down to the last erotic detail.

The big plane was still reaching for its cruising altitude of thirty-eight thousand feet over northwestern Texas.

The girls, who came straight from several chorus lines in Las Vegas, knew what to do and did it.

Soon, accompanied by whoops of delight from these Arabian knights, full, bare-breasted Anglo-Saxon women were bending pink nipples toward the mouths of hungry, laughing Arabs, feeding them, among other things, whiskey and caviar. This goddamn Ali knew how to entertain!

Now the girls were stark-naked, so were the men. The only ones with clothes on were the pilots, Ali, and Noel.

Ali laughed and drank moderately. He was the host, the impresario. Besides, this kind of bacchanal was not his style. He had his own thing planned for this evening. He occasionally glanced at Noel, laughing loudly at the discomfort of his British aide as Noel dodged flying hors d'oeuvres and spilled drinks. Ali roared when Noel frantically sought his last refuge, in the lavatory.

As this airborne debauch sped through the gathering darkness toward San Francisco, all constraints of behavior were blown away by the liquor and the sexual hungers now released by men who wanted just this kind of excitement.

Dark bodies writhed with soft white skin. Mouths searched and groped. It was a montage of soft round white buttocks. Blossoms of pink nipples. Erect cocoa spears bobbed up and down the aisle of the Boeing as Arabian stallions hunted their mares with shrieks of delight from the pursued as well as the pursuers. There were no longer any sexual fantasies; they were being enacted by minds that had freed themselves from any restraint.

At 547 miles an hour, thirty-eight thousand feet above the

earth, these sons of the desert poured liquor over the women, over themselves. They sprawled on chairs, in the aisle, in Ali's bedroom. Only the advent of physical exhaustion and their arrival in San Francisco had ended a bacchanal that was truly Middle Eastern in extravagance. That was the real reason Ali was late. It was a miracle of will and endurance that allowed him to keep this engagement with Peter Tennant.

PETER HEARD THE SOUND OF A CAR, THEN THE SLAMMING of the car doors, laughter, and scattered voices. He remained seated, quietly.

"I'm so terribly sorry, Peter. I really apologize. We were delayed at the airport in Houston, and then again here. We couldn't make up the time." Ali winked at Noel. "You know my vice-chairman, Noel Aragon."

Noel stepped forward, a middle-aged, somewhat round, very soft Anglo-Saxon with thinning dark hair, a pale face, and dark, unfathomable eyes—obviously weary from the long flight.

"Yes, we've met," said Peter. "How are you, Noel?"

"Somewhat fatigued at the moment with having to keep up with this young rascal." Noel glanced at Ali with the look of a resigned schoolmaster.

They all laughed.

They shook hands, standing in the semidarkness of the patio with the slim, taciturn Westerner, whose reserve and steady calm Ali had never seen broken.

Sayed Saif Ibn Abdul Ageel was dark, short, and trim, with

a mustache and spade beard. His movements were well coor-
dinated, like an athlete's. When he spoke, his accent was a
combination of his British-style boarding school in Alexandria, Egypt, and the faint singsong of the Arabic of his native
speech. He was hospitable, as is traditional with Arabs, peripatetic, devious, secretive, with one foot in the world of a
culture that was exploding from a seventeenth-century languor and the other gingerly placed in the technological societies of the West.

His usefulness was his ability to translate one to the other.
His king and countrymen, as well as his Western and Far
Eastern clients, were willing to pay handsomely for this Arabian connection that could bridge the cultural gaps between
the desert and nuclear power.

Peter and Ali had grown to know one another, and they
had become friends, but with a wary respect. Now, both were
ready to make the Tennant Corporation's presentation to the
king, and the stakes were enormous.

It was past midnight. They sat in the cavernous living room
of Ali's house in Hillsborough, whose decor was a blend of
East and West. As were all of Ali's homes throughout the
world, this house some twenty miles south of San Francisco
was not a home but an oasis; a watering place reached by
Mercedes instead of camels, but an oasis nevertheless. It was
without charm, without any sense of permanence. It was without a hostess.

Ali's wife and four children were rarely with him on his
continuous rounds between the Gulf, Europe, Japan, and the
United States.

His son was a junior at Cal Tech. His other three children,
daughters, were kept carefully at home with their mother, who,
in the tradition of Islam, raised her daughters alone and was
not disturbed by the continual absences of her husband.

Ali and Noel were at least two centuries apart, yet although
their cultures were as different as the sun and the moon, their

strange alliance worked because of what each was able to contribute to the other.

Ali was the product of a professional family, without hereditary royal connections. His father, through a series of fortunate circumstances, had been trained in London as a physician, and chose to return home to those arid sands and dispense whatever help his skills and training would permit. His reputation as a compassionate healer had reached the ears of the king, and after learning of his Western training acquired at the best schools in England, the king chose to have Ali's father as his personal physician. This role gradually expanded to that of confidant, and Ali's father became a valued adviser to the royal family.

As Ali reached adolescence, his father made sure that a Western education and contacts would be afforded his eldest son, who at an early age displayed a restless energy and a bright, retentive mind. After school in Alexandria, and later Stanford and MIT, Ali had acquired the technical background and a nucleus of contacts, especially in the United States, that he wished to capitalize upon as quickly as possible.

Ali, unlike his father and younger brother, was driven. There ticked within him some inexorable time clock that kept pushing him ever faster, telling him for reasons he couldn't fathom that time was running out.

After MIT he put together a company called, appropriately, East-West Trading, Ltd., and sought to form a bridge between the technologies of the West, so desperately needed by his country, and the feudal society of the royal family to which his father had access.

He had married for appearances. He needed an obvious and permanent familial stake in his country, so that he wouldn't be regarded by the king as a potential expatriate. He had little time or affection for his family. Rather, he provided for their material needs, and saw them infrequently, both through choice and as a result of his incredibly peripatetic activities.

Ali was a true nomad, a Bedouin. Deep within was an ancient pride and masculinity. He loved everything that moved quickly—fast planes, cars—and some things that did not move very quickly at all—women. Ali thought of women, in the traditions of the Middle East, as objects that gave him great pleasure. His Western veneer hid that effectively, but not from himself. He was circumspect and careful. He didn't want any touch of scandal reported back to his king. But when he could, he reveled in their soft arms and their bodies. It was a release for his enormous energies.

He could be understanding, but not compassionate. He could be attentive, but not loving. He was always somewhat humorously cynical; just a little aloof. No one, not even his current mistress, who waited patiently in his bedroom for her Bedouin to finish his business, ever really got to the volatile dark core of this mysterious son of the desert.

Noel, on the other hand, was more superficially obvious, but equally hard to uncover.

He came from a well-known banking family who controlled one of the City's most prestigious merchant banking firms, and his alliance with Ali was applauded quietly by his family as an entrée for the bank into the bursting coffers of Middle Eastern oil money.

Noel was particularly suited for this role. At Eton and at Oxford he had remained a loner. His interest was in Middle Eastern studies, he spoke Arabic fluently, and had a quick, perceptive mind. Through his family, he had access to Western European capital and the right contacts to admit him to the more important boardrooms; he seemed uninterested in both men and women sexually, and appeared to be one of those upper-class English gentlemen whose chief interest in life seems to be their own physical comfort. His association with Ali gave his life some of the color it would otherwise have lacked, and their rapport further deepened as they gradually discovered that they were both completely amoral human beings whose vocabulary did not include the word "integrity."

"My sources tell me, Peter, that the German and Japanese consortium are ready to present their plans to my king." Ali's dark eyes reflected the lights from the oversized crystal chandelier that hung gaudily, like a fat, bejeweled madam, from the center of the ceiling.

Ali leaned forward toward Peter.

"What we must have is an *edge*. The plan is fine. It's professionally done—carefully and, I believe, effectively conceived. But as you know so well, Peter, in my country decisions are made on the basis of personal relationships, and although you are known to my king, we do not have the kind of rapport between you and the king that is essential."

He handed Peter a cigarette.

"What we need is a presence—if you will, a sponsor or possibly an advocate, Peter, who is known to my king and who has his admiration."

Peter looked at Ali, his mouth forming a wry smile. "Would you suggest we call the President?"

Ali laughed. "I don't think my king would respond too warmly to a man who so openly supports Israel."

Peter exhaled smoke, his legs crossed. His whole aspect conveyed a studied nonchalance. Peter needed this reserve to deal with people like Ali, whose sudden explosion of wealth, coupled with their memories of an exploited colonial past, gave them an arrogance that badly needed to be blunted by an ambience of cool indifference.

"My connections with God, Ali, leave something to be desired."

Ali laughed heartily. "I would have assumed that someone as composed and serene as yourself had easy access to God."

Ali got up to pour himself a drink. When he was in the West, he did as he pleased. He smoked, drank, gambled, made love to women. But as soon as his Boeing touched down on his own turf, he would step out into the blast of humid

heat fully dressed in the traditional black gossamer wool robe
with its gold borders that was a luxurious representation of
the ageless Bedouin garment that had protected his ancestors
for a thousand years from the extreme variations of heat and
cold of the desert.

"Your lack of access to God may be a just punishment for
your intransigence, Peter." Ali waved his drink with bantering
sarcasm. "But if we are to win this contract, my dear Mr.
Tennant, we have to come in with an *edge*."

"You have a suggestion, Ali?" Peter glanced at Ali with a
raised eyebrow that seemed to indicate his suspicions of tonight's meeting.

"Let us say I have a few ideas."

Peter grunted his acknowledgment at his own intuitiveness.

"If I may say so, Peter, I think the solution is before us."

"It may be for you, my friend, but I can assure you I haven't
the faintest idea of how to please your king."

Ali reached for a cigarette.

"Do you know John Salisbury, Peter?"

Noel looked at Ali with just a suggestion of surprise. Noel
was not often privy to Ali's plans until they were formulated
and ready to be implemented. He wondered if Ali was about
to hit him with another of his unexpected plots.

"I've met him on a few occasions, but I would hardly say I
know him."

Ali walked back to the sofa, sat down, stretched, and
loosened his tie.

"Let me tell you a quick story, because it's getting very late
and I know you don't share my disdain for sleep or lack of
food.

"When the king's father was trying to unite my country by
subduing a group of fractious tribes, he needed economic aid."
Ali smiled. "Money, if you wish me to be blunt.

"He naturally turned to the oil companies, who were making
enormous profits from the crude that was being piped out

of our wells at very low prices. The oil companies were cautious, because they didn't know who was going to win. I should say for brevity that the father of my king could find only one friend with the courage and the foresight to help him."

Ali cast a dark-eyed glance at Peter.

Noel was blandly curious.

"Would you care to hazard a guess who helped to rescue my country—from behind well-devised screens, of course."

"Not John Salisbury. He would have been about ten years old at the time."

"Quite right—and wrong, my dear Peter. It was a Salisbury, only not this one. It was the present Salisbury's grandfather who, as they say in Houston, 'bellied up to the crap table' and threw in his chips with the father of my king. This little tale is not often told, of course, Peter. It might even be denied in some quarters, but it is true.

"The royal family have never forgotten their obligation to the Salisburys. Does this suggest anything to you?"

"I'm afraid I lack your facility for Byzantine thinking."

"Well, I will enlighten you, my unimaginative friend. If you will let your engineer's brain play with some suppositions for a moment. As I said earlier, we need an *edge*. If John Salisbury III could be such an *edge*, it would put us over, Peter. I'll guarantee it."

Peter sat quietly, digesting what had just been told him. It was provocative. In fact, a fourteen-billion-dollar contract was more than just provocative—it was irresistible. "About the closest I can come to Salisbury is Dutch Dernberg. Dutch is an old friend of mine. He's a member of John's board, and chairman of their executive committee. I know John thinks very highly of Dutch."

Ali seemed to leap from the sofa. "Now, that's inspiration, my friend, true inspiration. Could you call this Mr. Dernberg and ask him to talk to John for us?"

"I could. I don't know if he'll do it, though I don't see why not."

Ali's eyes sparkled with the energy of his thoughts. He turned to Noel, who had been sitting quietly, trying to divine Ali's real purpose. He knew Ali well enough to know that he would hardly get excited because a board member might telephone John Salisbury for him.

"Peter, you have your friend Dernberg call Salisbury and put in a plug for us. Noel and I will take it from there."

Ali got up and looked at his watch.

"I'm sorry to have kept you so late, Peter, but I think this meeting was terribly important. Why don't we let you get some sleep? We'll carry on from here."

Both Peter Tennant and Noel knew that Ali had something in mind he wasn't telling them.

As they walked Peter to his car, Peter felt that whatever machinations Ali's Byzantine mind was concocting, he'd rather not know about them.

The night air was soft and cool. The sky was a panoply of stars, and the breeze that blew in from the bay was damp and carried the hint of fog.

"Let me know as soon as Dernberg has talked to Salisbury."

"Will do."

The red taillights of Peter's car disappeared down the curved drive.

Ali motioned to Noel, who was obviously tired and ready for bed.

Ali grinned. "The night is still young, and we've got work to do. Then you can go to bed, my English friend, and sleep until noon. No wonder you British lost your empire." He looked at Noel with a baleful, patronizing glance.

"Come. A quick nightcap, and I'll tell you of my plan. How about some champagne, eh?"

Ali thought about the luscious Nancy Keating, who was waiting for him in bed. She would be naked, he thought, probably asleep. She didn't have to fly tomorrow, which was lucky for him; otherwise she would have been furious with him for being so late.

He thought of the lovemaking that awaited him after he finished the one more job he had to do tonight before he could release himself to the delights of his planned predawn debauch.

Noel waited with mounting impatience as Ali poured them both a glass of champagne.

"I didn't feel it necessary to go into any of this with our friend Peter. Peter has too much business tied up with American government contracts to feel sanguine about what I intend to propose to you, Noel."

"I wish you'd get to the point, Ali. I don't share your enthusiasm for these all-night meetings. I also have to fly back to Houston tomorrow, and I'd prefer not to fall asleep at my meeting with American Oil."

Ali laughed. "All right, my impatient friend, here goes, as the Americans say. I got a call from my father yesterday. He tells me that the Germans and Japanese are going to make their proposal very soon. From what he hears, they have an excellent plan, which has the backing of Bonn and Tokyo. My father tells me that the backing of the two governments is regarded as very important by my king. He fears that unless we can come in with some kind of *edge*, the fact that Washington will not lend the kind of political support to the project that Tokyo and Bonn will may decide against us. He thinks we need some kind of *edge*, and fast."

Noel was showing his boredom and impatience.

Ali took a special delight in breaking the reserve of his British lieutenant.

"My friend, our timing is auspicious. Some of my contacts in New York tell me that Salisbury's board is hardly thrilled with the bank's performance. They are pushing very hard to get rid of Dowding. I'm told some of them would even be glad to see Salisbury step down, but my sources regard that as not very likely. Even better, I hear that Dowding has woman trouble. Don't look so surprised, my friend. I've gone to a great deal of trouble to learn as much as I could about Mr. Douglas Dowding."

"And I'm sure you will enlighten me as to why you think all this is helpful."

Ali laughed heartily.

"I have always said, Noel, your only deficiency is a lack of imagination. Now, let's analyze what we are trying to do, and how best we can do it, eh? We need Salisbury to get us the approval of my king, eh?"

Noel nodded.

"We have a beleaguered Mr. Dowding who I have reason to believe is being pressed very near the breaking point—psychologically, I mean."

Noel shook his head. "I'm afraid I still don't have a clue."

"You will. Be patient, my obtuse friend. Listen carefully. I believe great pressure will be exerted upon Salisbury to do something quickly about replacing Dowding. We can offer Salisbury an opportunity to participate in a fourteen-billion-dollar financing that could take the pressure off Salisbury that his board is exerting. But Salisbury is plagued, probably because of his background and personality, with what I call a certain curious myopia. He seems to see things only on a national or world level. He's not concerned about the day-to-day details of running a business, which, by the way, is what is chiefly wrong with his bank. He might not even be concerned with a project of this magnitude, because now his myopia allows him to see only his present problems at the bank."

Noel was still in the dark. He got up to refill both glasses.

"Now, to carry on. Salisbury is the only man who can truly influence my king in our representation of Tennant's bid. Who would you suppose is most likely to influence Salisbury in our behalf?"

"Not Dowding."

"Precisely, Dowding."

"But Dowding looks like he's batting a sticky wicket."

"And so, my friend, is Salisbury. But, you see, Dowding was selected by Salisbury; he's Salisbury's protégé. If Dowding can be saved, Salisbury looks a lot better."

"But I thought you said Dowding was on his way out."

"And so he may be. It's a matter of timing, Noel. Eventually I think Dowding will go. But I ask you this: Can you picture any board firing a man who has a good chance of helping put together a fourteen-billion deal?"

"And just how does Dowding do that?"

"Ah, my friend, now you are beginning to touch the robes of wisdom." Ali laughed and lit a thin black cigar. "By ensuring the interest of Mr. Salisbury in Peter Tennant's proposal to my king."

"And how can we be sure Dowding will do that?"

Ali got up and began to pace nervously about the room. He finally turned to Noel, a wide grin on his face.

"By placing eleven million nine hundred thousand Swiss francs in a numbered account for Mr. Douglas Dowding."

Noel Aragon nearly dropped his champagne.

"My God! That's five million dollars!"

"Exactly. And though the dollar may devalue, my good friend, I hardly think the Swiss franc will do so in proportion."

"Are you telling me, Ali, that you are going to bribe the president of one of the world's largest banks?"

"Not exactly—you are!"

"But Dowding will never buy it, Ali. There are some things that are more important than money. Besides, if this got out , we would be finished in the U.S."

Noel got up, his eyes averted from Ali's.

"You simply can't be serious, Ali. That would be like trying to bribe Salisbury."

"Not quite."

"But Ali. You're talking about the president of one of the

world's most powerful banks, in one of the most tightly regulated countries in the world. Would you try this in England or Germany or Switzerland with a major bank?"

"Of course not."

"Then why, for God's sake, in the U.S.? Why in the biggest, most important market we have? If we're found out, Ali, you'll be through, and so will I. We'll both be lucky if we don't wind up in jail."

Ali seated himself before the fire and stared into the flames.

"Our fee for securing this project for Mr. Tennant over the approximate fourteen years of the contract is one hundred and forty million dollars; less five million, of course, for Mr. Dowding. I do think it's worth the risk." Ali paused. He turned to Noel. "Do you realize our fee is only one percent of the total project? Are we working too cheaply, my friend?" Ali roared with laughter.

"Consider two things, Noel: (a) one does take risks when a hundred and forty million is at stake, and (b) you confuse the institution with the man. You are not going to tempt FMB, my dear Noel, you are going to stimulate the greed of one man. You will be his salvation, a savior in a bowler hat." Ali's face became serious.

"Noel, you have never been in the desert without water. You have never felt the heat tear at your soul until you drink the blood of your camel for its fluid, and crawl into its gutted belly to be shielded from the sun, or from the cold of night. My ancestors knew what that was like, Noel. I, thank God, have never known these things, but the terror is in my blood, and my instincts tell me that our Mr. Dowding is walking in the desert without water. You can buy a lot of water with five million dollars, Noel."

Noel's brain functioned differently from Ali's, but he was beginning to see the cunning behind the psychology of Ali's proposal.

"I am willing to invest—not gamble—five million dollars

that Mr. Dowding will ensure Mr. Salisbury's participation in our bid. If Mr. Salisbury supports us, my king will look favorably upon our group, and five million dollars is a very small premium to pay to insure a fourteen-billion-dollar contract."

Noel Aragon was always fascinated by the Machiavellian thought processes of Ali's mind.

"So what you're really saying, Ali, is that under certain circumstances everyone has his price, even the president of the First Manhattan Bank."

"Exactly." Ali turned his dark eyes toward Noel's. "What's your price, my dear Noel, for perhaps betraying me, eh?" He laughed loudly into the shadows of the room.

Noel looked at him harshly. "I don't see a bloody thing funny in that."

"Relax, my friend. You are my brother. You have proved your services to me and your trustworthiness a hundred times. Now all you have to do is to convince Dowding. Believe me, Noel, he'll listen, the desert winds tell me so."

Ali laughed heartily again and swallowed the last of his champagne.

Noel continued to pace the room deep in thought; his instincts for self-preservation were acute. "What I don't understand is why we have to go through all this. Why not just make a straightforward approach to Salisbury?"

"Because what I know about Mr. Salisbury's current problems and how he operates tells me he'll turn the thing over to Dowding to get the details, and it could very easily end right there. I want to ensure Dowding's interest in seeing that Salisbury follows through."

Noel thought about this for a moment, and shook his head. "I'm sorry, Ali, but I can't afford to be mixed up in anything like this. I not only have myself to consider, but if this ever got out it would affect my family and the firm. I don't have to remind you that I still have a major financial interest there—"

Ali looked at him coldly; his eyes now snapped with the black fire of the desert hawk.

"And I don't think I need to remind you, Noel, of how much business your association with me has brought your family's merchant banking firm. Through me they have gained an access into the petrodollar area that they could never have gotten on their own, and would lose tomorrow, I might add, if you and I severed our very profitable and, I hope, mutually agreeable relationship."

Ali had a furious temper, and Noel was aware that Ali was going to great lengths to control it.

"But there has to be another way, Ali. If this thing blows up in our faces, we will have lost more in the long run than we could ever hope to gain."

"It will take us a very long time, Noel, to lose a hundred and forty million dollars." Ali was beginning to look at Noel with those fierce, piercing black eyes that were burning bright with anger.

"And if I refuse?"

"Then we part company."

Noel continued to pace back and forth. He stopped and remained thoughtful for a moment. His hesitation had nothing to do with morality; he was simply weighing his chances of getting caught.

"I think it's a mistake," he sighed, "but I'm willing to give it a go."

Ali's face immediately brightened. He walked over to Noel and put his arm around the soft, slightly rounded shoulders. "Now, that's more like it. It's a risk, true, but one that is worth taking in a project of this magnitude." He paused and looked seriously at Noel.

"Dowding will buy it, Noel—you'll see. He'll rationalize that it will be good for the bank, and good for Salisbury as well, in his present difficulties. I know something about Dowding's finances. They are not as substantial as one might suppose. This can be a way out for Dowding. With that kind of money he can be independent. Tell everyone to go to hell. And think about it: What are you really asking him to do? I see nothing that Salisbury should have the slightest qualm about; talking to kings is perhaps his greatest talent."

Ali's eyes lost their edge and he laughed loudly at that.

"Now suppose we both get some sleep, eh, Noel. Peter will let me know when Dernberg has spoken to Salisbury, and I'll call you. And now, if you don't mind, I still have something to do, but this"—he smiled slyly—"will give me pleasure." He thought about the exceptionally long nipples of Nancy Keating, and he hurriedly turned out the lights.

THE FAMILY ATE BREAKFAST IN A SMALL ROOM ON THE second floor on the rare occasions when the three of them were together.

Jane knew that her father had returned late last night from London, but that was nothing unusual; he was always returning late from somewhere. Her mother took one look at the tight-lipped expression on her daughter's face and knew the storm signals were up. Jane had her mother's temper, but she lacked the maturity of her mother's restraint.

John came in, white with fatigue, and dreading what the morning would hold for him at the bank. He thought particularly of the telegrams that would go to all of the directors about the bond scandal, and the news release he would have to make to the press. John looked forward to this morning as he would have looked forward to shaving with broken glass.

They ate almost silently; any conversation was forced. The air of tension hung like a blanket of damp fog.

"This is certainly a jolly group." Jane jabbed with annoyance at a stubborn piece of bacon.

Her mother looked at her. "I don't see you adding any particular ray of sunshine, do you?"

"Oh, shit," Jane said, and slammed down her knife and fork.

"Watch your language, young lady."

"Oh, Christ." Jane started to rise.

"Jane. Please sit down. Your father's very tired. He has a horrible day ahead of him today, and he's just come back from an exhausting trip."

Jane thrust herself back in her chair, her eyes fixed on her plate. Her head was bent forward as if she were examining something intently; her long dark brown hair was partially draped on the table.

"What's so unusual about that?" Jane seemed to grind the words between her teeth.

"About what?"

"About Father coming back from a trip. If he weren't coming or going somewhere, what would he do?" She toyed grimly with her fork. "It's like always looking at the back of someone's head. That's how I see Father; I only see the back of his head."

"Jane, please."

"Margret, let her talk. She certainly has a right to her impressions of me." It hurt John deeply to hear her say these things to him, but he knew she was terribly upset about her coming birthday; it had become an obsession with her.

Her mother tried again. "Since we're all here for breakfast at the same time, which is at least something of an occasion, maybe, Jane, we can discuss your birthday, which I've been trying to do for nearly a month now."

Jane's lips tightened. She had the same dark brown eyes as her father; his same thin, pointed nose; she had her mother's figure and her temper.

"I've told you now, Mother, for the hundredth time, that I don't want any celebration of any kind. What for? What am I going to celebrate? That the newspapers will all be writing about my thirty-one-million-dollar trust fund from Grandfather that I'll get when I'm twenty-one? How much my annual pretax income will be? Oh, Jesus, how I hate that money!"

Her father colored. He put down his knife and fork and looked hard at his daughter.

"And just what makes you so ashamed of the money you're inheriting? Is it your great-grandfather? Are those the old ghosts you're so afraid of? Jane, more constructive things have been done with this family's money than by any other private group of people in the world. Why can't you think of that for a change? Why can't you prepare yourself to use your money constructively, as all of us have done?" He paused. "Is it the responsibility you're afraid of? What is it about our money and our family that makes you treat your mother and me as strangers, or worse than strangers? Interlopers in your life?"

She kept staring at her plate, making abstract designs on her place mat with her fork.

"We're freaks. That's what we are, freaks. We live in this freaky house that's always filled with freaky people. We hardly ever have a minute alone." She looked up, the mist coming into her eyes.

"I can count on the fingers of one hand, Father, when you and I have had any time alone together."

This cut him like a knife. His voice was hushed. He had paled visibly.

"If I've failed you in that, it's not because of any lack of love. You should know that. I just have never been able to figure out how to be in two places at one time."

She looked first at her mother and then back at John. Her voice was choked with emotion. She fought to hold back her tears—and then it ruptured. Her whole anguish, the repressed torments and aggressions that the weight of her twenty-first

birthday posed for her—having to step forward and receive
her money, take her place as an adult member of the family,
assume the burden of the name publicly, forever—it all ruptured. Her entire twenty-one years of rebellion against her
family, her class, her status burst like one great infected boil
that had blown open its tissue.

She stood up, tall, slender, vibrating like a young sapling
in the wind, her hair flying violently like dark brown whips
as her head jerked her mouth's vituperation, first at her father,
then at her mother. She was screaming at them. "You talk to
me about being in two places at one time. All right, then, I'll
tell you. You made the choice, Father. It was me or that goddamn bank or your committees or some other horseshit—"

Margret stood up. "You stop this right now, Jane. Who
do you think you're talking to?"

The tears were streaming down her face. Her eyes were
wild with rage, sorrow, and frustration.

"Who am I talking to? Who am I talking to?" She stood
on the opposite side of the table screaming at her mother.
"I'm talking to you, my mother, and I'm talking to you, my
father. Can you hear me? For once, just for once, can you
hear me? Can you hear me when I tell you I don't want to
celebrate any birthday—for what! Celebrate my coming of
age as a freak. People starving all over the goddamn world
and little Jane Salisbury gets thirty-one million dollars as a
birthday present. Jesus Christ! Doesn't that strike either of
you as insane? Not five blocks from here there are kids being
bitten by rats, and if they're lucky, they're having a Coke
for breakfast—"

"What your father's trying to tell you, Jane—"

"What's he trying to tell me? To take that stinking Salisbury money and do more good with it, make it purer, launder
it. Isn't that what the Mafia does with dirty money—launder
it?"

"Jane, stop it! You're behaving irrationally." John was on

his feet, his face flushed with anger. "What your grandfather did was generations ago. And I might add that he started a new method of philanthropy that has—"

"I know," she said, whirling to face him. "The Salisburys have been one great big public tit for everyone to suck on. We all have to justify how we live and how we look every day so that when we give away our money through those fucking foundations—"

"Jane, stop it! I won't hear another word."

"Oh, yes, you will. If this is going to be my coming of age, the two of you are going to hear me even if it's for the last time. You want to talk about my brithday. Well, then, let's make this my party. One big, happy family party—"

All three of them stood confronting one another. Both Margret and John were overcome with her vehemence. She had struck each of them in different ways, but it was John who was affected the most deeply. Jane had scored him with guilt as if she had whipped him with a hot iron.

The tears were streaming down her face; the heart inside that was broken and confused spilled out of her eyes.

"Well, happy birthday, Daddy. When was the last time you saw me, can you remember? Do you remember, Father? When the hell was the last time you ever really looked at me and saw me? Now that I'm twenty-one, now that I'm rich, now will you take a look, Father?"

"Jane, please—"

She whirled on her mother. "And you, Mother! My warm, tenderhearted mother. You want to make it a big deal, my coming of age—great, huh, as long as it fits in with Father's schedule. Oh, if he has to be away Friday, we can switch things around. You're a great arranger, Mother. Anything to protect Father. Well, lucky him. But what about me? When was the last time, Mother, you switched something around for me?"

Margret felt the spear of Jane's judgment, and it seared

through her, because a good part of it was true. As she stood facing the wrath of her daughter, her hands began to shake so that she had to hold on to the edge of the table.

"Well, happy birthday, both of you, because this is it. I'm moving out of this goddamn museum, and if I can't do anything about the dirty Salisbury money, then I'll give it away. Every dime I get." She threw her napkin down and fled from the room.

John was so unnerved by the explosion of his daughter that he sat down staring straight ahead, his eyes fixed, seeing nothing but the mist that clouded his vision, that began to break up the light in the room into a thousand tiny radiances. His voice was so choked that he couldn't speak. He tried, but no coherent words would come out.

Margret sat down, her face ashen. She wanted to reach for John's hand to comfort him and be comforted by him, but her feeling of guilt at Jane's accusations about their affection for each other, which she felt had excluded her, made Margret hesitate. She acknowledged that there was a degree of truth in what her daughter had said.

John realized that he had to leave for the bank. He didn't know what to do. He wanted to go upstairs and put his arms around his daughter and tell her how terribly much he loved her, how sorry he was if he had helped, through seeming indifference, to make her life unhappy. But the damn bank was in a crisis, or would be when the news got out. They were all waiting for him. He had to go. The hell with them, he thought. He got up shakily.

"Where are you going?"

He looked at Margret, not really seeing her. "I'm going to Jane."

"She'll—she'll be all right, John. It's—"

He shook his head in immense weariness and started for Jane's room.

* * *

"Let me in, Jane. Sweetheart, please open the door, I want to talk to you." He could hear her crying. He heard the lock slide, but the door remained closed. He tried the handle and it opened.

As he came in, she threw herself facedown across her bed in abject misery, her thin body convulsing with heartbreaking sobs. He sat down on the bed beside her, wondering how all three of them could have seemingly been so close and yet were torn by this dissension.

He searched back to his own childhood. Was he ever this unhappy? He was lonely at times, frightened by the great brooding house at Salisbury, and by those ferocious gliding swans that as a young child he found so threatening. He remembered always being afraid of the dark, and being lonely at school. He remembered his frustration at being so shy. He remembered the cool, watery blue eyes of his grandfather, and being held in those thin arms. He might not have been lighthearted or overwhelmingly happy as a boy, but he was never as distraught as this. What had he done, or perhaps not done, that could make his own child so unhappy? Why was the money so onerous to her and not to him or his brothers? Had his father prepared him for the responsibilities of his heritage better than he and Margret had prepared Jane? Or was it the different attitude of this generation toward wealth and position?

"Darling, listen to me—please." He found his own voice trembling. "Jane, if you are this unhappy, then somewhere your mother and I have failed you." He hesitated, and bent down to kiss the back of her head. "Sweetheart, I can't make up for all the years that have gone by, and I wouldn't be truthful if I told you I can spend the time with you that we both would like. Besides, I suppose it's too late for that now; you're a grown woman, or at least a grown young woman about to be twenty-one." He stroked her hair.

"Can you turn around and look at me?"

She shook her head and remained lying facedown on the bed.

"Perhaps it was wrong for your mother and me to assume that your only alternative was to carry on in the family as we all have done. I can see now that it was. But we all can't get too far away from what we really are, and you're a Salisbury. Nothing is going to change that, even marriage; even a new name." He hesitated, trying to collect his thoughts, to bring some logic and common sense to what he was trying to tell her. He sensed that this might be his last chance to reach out and touch her, really touch her, and he silently prayed for the wisdom to find the way.

"Maybe what we can try to do together, Jane, is to find out how you can be a Salisbury your way, to discover some approach to your life that will be right for you. I promise you, sweetheart, that I'll do anything to help you achieve that. Do I have to tell you, Jane, that your happiness and your mother's mean more to me than anything else in my life?

"All the rest of it has been service. That's what I was trained for—to be utilitarian, to try and steer the family in a direction that would do some good. I've lived with the stigma of our money, darling, but I've also been very proud of what we've done with it."

He bent over and kissed her again.

"Jane, please get up."

She turned and slowly sat up to face him; strands of her hair stuck to her face that was wet from her tears. Her rage had subsided, but her slim body still trembled with the residue of her despair.

He took her in his arms and held her as he had done when she was a small child. His own tears mingled with hers.

"Jane, baby, give me a little time. We'll go somewhere together and we'll figure out an approach to your being part of this family in a way that you can live with, that will make you happy. Will you give me that chance?"

She looked at him with deep, serious, searching eyes.

Suddenly she was in his arms. He could feel the rapid beating of her heart as they held each other, and for the first time in such a very long time, they reached out and found one another.

As he held her, he felt her stiffen, her body grow rigid. He turned and saw Margret standing in the doorway. Her face was pale as death. She watched them silently, not entering the room, just standing there feeling terribly alone.

THE EXPLOSION OF THE NEWS OF THE BOND SCANDAL HAD been even worse than John anticipated.

Two sets of telegrams had to be sent to the directors when the internal auditors dropped the other shoe; Gallagher had overevaluated the bond inventory by an incredible *twenty-two* million dollars. When this news hit Dutch Dernberg's desk in Seattle, the big ex-marine who headed the board's executive committee went right through the ceiling.

Dutch was the tough-as-leather head of PTM Pacific and head of a family that controlled enormous private wealth. On a personal basis, Dutch had more money than John. He had been brought on the board and elected chairman of the executive committee by nervous outside directors who wanted someone who would stand up to John. Dutch sure as hell wasn't intimidated by anyone. He had called for a meeting— insisted upon a meeting—of the executive committee to be held no later than Friday. He wanted Dowding left out of it.

They had all agreed to fly down to Dutch's place at Delray Beach, Florida, as they wanted as much privacy as possible, and it was getting very difficult to escape the media and the stockholders, who were all howling for blood. The bank's switchboard was lit up like Manhattan at night.

John had flown down to Delray on Friday morning, and had sat through one of the most sulfurous, critical meetings of his life.

As he returned to New York on the bank's jet, alone, for a very private birthday dinner for Jane, his mind was scored by the blasts of Dutch's criticism.

This had been a pivotal week for John Salisbury. He had been forced to take a hard look at his life by his daughter, and now his business life, his whole career, had been scorned by that son of a bitch from Seattle. The plane's engines droned their background noise at a part of his mind.

"How the fuck do you expect to run a goddamn drugstore, much less one of the world's major banks, John, with you spending more time in a plane on your way to kiss some king's ass than staying home finding out how some crazy bastard like this Gallagher can tell you he's got twenty-two million more in bonds than he has in inventory! How the hell does that make us all look, John? We're supposed to be protecting the stockholders as responsible businessmen elected to represent their interests. We're gonna get our asses sued off, every damn one of us. We all look like a bunch of jackasses."

John thought about the others with their grim expressions, letting Dutch do all the talking. He knew Dutch was speaking for all of them.

What defense did he have? What could he say to them? He had questioned Gallagher for hours to try and find out why he had done it, and all he could come away with was some quirk in Gallagher's mind that led him to want to cover up his actual losses in his bond-trading operation. For some unfathomable reason, Gallagher thought he could outguess the market and that his inventory would adjust to the values he was reporting, but that didn't happen; the systems that were supposed to control a Tom Gallagher hadn't worked.

That was what made Dutch so mad, what seemed to him to be sheer incompetent management.

"Jesus Christ, John, where would any of us be if we ran our companies like that? And you're running a bank! At rock bottom, what you're really selling is safety and integrity. If this can happen to the First Manhattan Bank, who the hell is going to want to put his money in an institution like that?"

John felt the plane begin its long letdown for New York. He recognized Delaware Bay and realized they were approaching the southern tip of New Jersey. Dutch's eyes and voice hammered at his mind.

"John, this bond business strikes us as just plain old-fashioned lack of systems and controls, and in my book that means one thing—operating management.

"John. There's something else. The boys feel that the relationship between you and Doug isn't working. To be specific, it's their feeling—and I concur—that you overshadow Doug to a degree that affects his efficiency as an administrator.

"No one expects you to run the bank yourself, even though that happens to be your ultimate responsibility. But they do expect the president of FMB to fully utilize his authority to run the place, and Doug isn't cutting the mustard."

John watched the industrial haze of Philadelphia develop far off to his left.

"John, I think I know what part of the trouble is with Doug. He's under the shadow of you and your family. The whole history of your family weighs down on him. Even if he had the capacity to run the bank, the man is too damn much in awe of you, your brothers, your late father, your grandfather. It's too much for him."

Then it came. John hadn't expected it to take this form, and it disturbed him. And it hurt. It hurt his pride and his estimation of his own capacities.

"The committee feels that an outsider should investigate the main problem areas of the bank, and then report to you.

If our suspicions about Doug are verified, we'll recommend his being moved to a spot that would take him out of the senior administrative role."

John rested his face against his right hand, his elbow on the thick, padded armrest. He only half saw Lower Bay and the tip of Manhattan, the blue-shadowed vertical slabs momentarily hidden from a setting sun by scattered clouds whose rose-mauve masses burned at the edges with a searing orange light.

The main objective of his life and career was to prove to himself and to the world business community that he had the capabilities to turn this bank around. If Dutch was right in his assumptions, he wouldn't let his own personal feelings stand in the way.

He remembered himself saying, "I'm not sure I like the idea of an outsider going through the bank, Dutch."

"He won't really be an outsider. The man I would pick runs my oil group. He's one of the best men I've got. I hate like hell to take him away from my own operations even for a short time, but I think he'd be first-rate for what we're trying to accomplish. He's smooth. He won't ruffle any feathers, and he has both the domestic and international experience needed to take a hard look at the bank. He's one first-class executive officer, John. I think you should meet him."

"What's his name?"

"Mike Giles."

As John's plane entered the New York area and made the wide turn over the tip of Manhattan, flying over the Hudson River now shimmering with splashes of color from a dying sun, John could still see the cold blue eyes of Dutch Dernberg boring into him. "John, I hate to say this, but either we get a commitment from you that Mike comes in for a look around, and that you take charge of that goddamn place until we can get a first-class operating manager in there, or I'm going to resign, and these birds are going with me." Dutch had swept his arm to include the rest of the committee.

But John Salisbury had his own stubborn pride. No one in his entire life had ever spoken to him the way Dutch had, and he refused to buckle under the onslaught of this enormous Westerner.

It was unthinkable to allow all of the outside directors of the bank's executive committee to resign; even John couldn't stand in the face of that. But he wasn't going to be rushed into a humiliating capitulation, either. He was going to fight for some time.

He had stood up quietly, looking at all of them.

His whole demeanor throughout this meeting showed the inborn class of the man. Whatever truth there was in Dutch's accusation, he had to admire the balls of this Salisbury. When his prong was in the fire, that's when you could judge a man, and this Salisbury was a man, Dutch decided. It was John's coolness and balance under fire that kept this hanging party from using the rope. They all admired the way John took it, and they gave him what he needed most: time.

"I'll give you my decision on Dowding and your man Giles within a week," he said, and that's where they left it for the time being. But John knew that only a miracle could save Doug, and a phone call to Dutch by Peter Tennant over the weekend would turn out to be just that.

John heard the scrunch of the tires and watched the runway lights flash by. He thought of Jane, and wondered why at sixty years of age his life seemed to be coming apart.

As Doug packed a small bag, Bardy watched him closely.

He hadn't told her that John had gone down to Florida to meet with Dutch and the executive committee.

She could see the pallor of his face and the anxiety in his eyes.

He knew what was going on down there. He knew there was a good chance that this would be *it* for him. He had no way of realizing the proud, stubborn defense John would put up; his inner fears had discounted John's support. After all the years together, Doug still didn't really know the mettle of the man who was his sponsor.

All Doug wanted to do now was to get away. He would do it the hard way. John had the jet, so he'd have to fly down to Puerto Rico by commercial plane. He'd spend the day there looking at those empty properties the bank held, and then he'd get back to New York tonight.

He had talked Karen into another trip to Oxford, and that was his major preoccupation right now. He wanted to get away, if only for a few hours. He wanted to get away from the searching glances of his wife, from the caldron that the bank had become. He wanted the incredible sexuality of Karen. He only wished to hell he could leave the whole damn thing and go away with her. But then there was his daughter, and there was Bardy. How could he leave them?

Bardia should have been used to his going away. Sometimes it was all right, but now she felt depressed. But Gay would be home. Perhaps if she felt up to it, the two of them could go to the theater.

Bardia was beginning to feel depressed about her appearance. She had lost so much weight that it had affected her figure. She couldn't exercise, so she felt tired and listless. Her skin was pale and dry. Her hair seemed lifeless, without luster.

How could any man be attracted to me, she thought, and she determined that she would make an appointment at Arden and get the works. But she knew she lacked the physical strength for this, and she became even more depressed as she thought of the confinement that her illness had forced upon her; it seemed to be draining her of life.

"Must you really go away again, Doug?"

He tried not to let his eyes betray his thoughts.

How much she's changed with this damn thing, he thought. Where was the girl full of life that he had known on those weekend dates at Sweet Briar in 1949? The girl he could remember holding in his arms at the Roanoke Country Club, looking at him with those luminous, adoring eyes.

"I really have to go, Bardy. You know that."

She nodded disconsolately. She didn't know that he would return tonight and that Karen would meet him again at Westchester and they would fly down to Oxford for another weekend.

She didn't know any of that until after she got two phone calls that would change her life.

It was six-thirty that evening when Gay answered the telephone.

"Mother. It's the bank. They want Daddy. They're calling from Puerto Rico."

"I'll take it, honey. . . . Hello. This is Mrs. Dowding." She hesitated, instinctively knowing something was wrong. "Ah, isn't Mr. Dowding down there?"

"He finished here around five, Mrs. Dowding, and went back to New York. When he gets in, would you have him give me a call? George Bottomly. He'll know what it's about. He can get me any time until midnight."

Bardia's eyes were far away. She felt suddenly old and abandoned. She knew Doug, and she knew that if he had changed his plans, he would have called her. What really had formed a knot in her stomach was the suspicion that her husband was with another woman. That's why there had been no phone call, and there would be none.

She felt physically sick. She tried hard to control her voice. "I'll have him call, Mr. Bottomly, if it's not too late."

She hung up and almost staggered to the sofa.

Gay saw that something was very wrong.

"Mother, are you all right?"

She sat beside her mother and put her arms around her. "Mother. Please. What's the matter?"

"Nothing, dear. It's all right. I just don't feel very well, that's all."

Gay paused. "Do you want to cancel the theater?"

"No, dear. I'll be fine. I just want to rest for a minute."

Bardia hadn't been lying down for more than ten minutes when the phone rang again.

Gay picked it up. "The police! Yes, my father is Douglas Dowding. No, Officer, I'm afraid he won't be back until late Sunday. Whose apartment did you say? Well, why should that concern my father? Oh, I see. Yes. Well, thank you, Officer." Gay hung up the phone and looked at her mother, her expression one of complete confusion.

"What was that all about, Gay?" Bardia had sat up from

her reclining position on the sofa, and looked inquiringly at her daughter. "Did I hear you say the police?"

Gay quickly reassured her mother.

"It's nothing, Mother. Karen Lockhart's apartment has been broken into."

"Oh, my Lord!" Bardia looked startled. Her hand went to her breast in surprise. "Is she all right?"

"She's fine, Mother. She's not there."

Bardia was equally confused. "Then how did the police come to call here?"

Gay's very quick mind had been frantically computing the implications of this phone call from the New York Police Department. The conclusions she had come to she didn't want to reveal to her mother.

"Well, don't just stand there. How did the police come to call us?"

Gay hesitated until she saw the look of annoyance come into her mother's eyes.

"They talked to the superintendent of the building, and he had a phone number to call in case of emergency. They called, and it turned out to be a house in Oxford, Maryland. When they checked with the local police, they found the house was owned by Daddy. The lieutenant that the officers report to wanted them to check to see if it was the same Douglas Dowding who was president of the bank."

Bardia's face had gone dead white. She couldn't breathe.

Gay took one look at her mother and ran to the secretary, where a bottle of oxygen and a connecting face mask were always ready. There was a cylinder of oxygen in every room.

She twisted the valve and clamped the mask over her mother's nose and mouth. Slowly a regularity returned to Bardia's breathing, and some color came back to her face. She inhaled the oxygen for approximately three minutes and then removed the mask from her face. She looked at Gay. "Darling. Call Angus at the bank and tell him to go to the box office and pick up the tickets. I'm sure he can sell them at the theater. I hate to think of them going to waste."

Gay looked at her mother. She fought hard to keep back her tears. She wanted to fling her arms around her mother and be comforted by her. She felt like a lost little girl again. But this time it was she who would do the comforting. She would hold her mother in her arms and the two would share their agony together in silence.

Gay held Bardia, rocking her gently, as her mother had so often done with her, and both women felt soiled and betrayed.

Silently Gay wept for her mother. Not my Daddy. Please, dear God, not my Daddy.

THEY WERE BOTH VERY TIRED BY THE TIME THEY GOT TO the darkened brick cottage on Batchelor's Point that caught some of the silvered moon slipping between passing luminous clouds. He could smell the river and the bay.

It was a warm night on the Choptank, and the dark silhouettes of the trees at the edge of the lawn blocked out their view of the river.

They had said little on the flight down. Karen's mood was a mixture of apprehension at the chances they were taking, and the primitive sexual attraction she felt for Doug that kept their affair going.

She had tried a hundred times to tell herself how stupid all this was. She knew that Doug was attracted to her for all the wrong reasons; that they were temporary and superficial; that his wife and daughter had a far stronger hold on him than he realized. They both knew what they were risking, and yet their mutual lust for each other had prevented them from breaking things off.

They lay together in bed, listening to the wind from the river, and the occasional sound of a squawking gull.

She wanted him inside her, and when they both were spent,

she waited until she could make him hard again. She wanted to go to sleep that way.

Karen knew what a physical woman she was, and she had always guarded against allowing her full passions to control her. She did it mostly through work—first in medical school, now in practice.

Those who thought they knew her well thought that she was some incredibly motivated workaholic, with a freckled nose and auburn hair. Her manner seemed austere, almost masculine. Her physician father had despaired of her ever marrying and having some kind of life outside a hospital. She had plenty of chances, but she had never met the right man.

God knows Doug wasn't the right man, but a part of her responded to the illicitness of their affair. Somehow it excited her sexuality, and though it also filled her with dread for the consequences of discovery, her carnality made her go on with it.

She would only go to sleep if she could feel him inside her. After the arid plain of Doug's wife, the open sensuality of Karen Lockhart was a temporary oasis.

Saturday morning they slept late. The sun that poured through their bedroom window and the noise of the gulls from the river finally awakened Karen. She put on her dressing gown to go down to cook breakfast. Doug was still asleep.

In New York, John had decided to talk to Doug about yesterday's meeting. He called, and when Bardia answered, he was delighted to talk with her; she was one of his favorite people.

"Forgive me, Bardy, for calling so early, but I have a very full day scheduled, and I do want to see Doug around six tonight if that's not too inconvenient."

Bardia sounded strange to him on the phone, guarded. He thought it peculiar that Doug wasn't there, and that she was hesitating to tell him where Doug was.

"It's important that I see him, Bardy. I've left some time this evening around six for us to get together." He paused. "How are you feeling?"

She tried hard to control her voice, shaking with the emotions this call aroused.

"I'm fine, John, thank you." She hesitated. "John, I believe I can locate Doug for you. I'm sure six will be all right with him." She hung up, her body trembling. Somehow she had to find the will to hang on.

Doug awakened, aware that Karen was not in bed. He rubbed his eyes sleepily and heard the sounds of her moving about the kitchen of the small cottage; the aroma of cooking bacon told him that Karen was preparing breakfast. He glanced at his watch; it was eleven-fifteen. He had slept far longer than was usual for him. The traveling and tensions of the last several days had exhausted him.

He had started to get out of bed when the phone rang downstairs. Just the sound of the phone startled him. They got very few phone calls in Oxford, except perhaps from their caretaker, or the grocer.

He heard Karen answer, and from the sound of her voice he knew that something was very wrong.

He took the stairs two at a time to see Karen holding the phone, her face scarlet.

She held her hand over the speaker as she handed him the phone. "It's Bardy," she whispered. It cut through him like a knife.

The voice on the other end was as cold as the dark side of the moon.

"Doug?"

He could hardly speak. "Yes."

A very long pause.

"John wants to see you at six this evening."

Before he could answer, she hung up.

JOHN HAD JUST HUNG UP FROM BARDIA WHEN HIS PHONE
rang on his private line. Very few people had that number.

"Sorry to disturb you, John." It was Dutch.

After the meeting in Delray their relations would never be
the same. John's voice had all the warmth of an Arctic
winter. Dutch couldn't have cared less.

"Peter Tennant called me about one hell of a big contract
he's bidding on in the Gulf. I think this could pull our tit
out of the wringer, John. Peter's talking about a fourteen-
billion-dollar deal. He says that his company is leading the
American group, and that their main competition are the
Germans and the Japanese. He's being represented by a guy
called Abdul Ageel—I believe they call him Ali. You know
the guy, John; he's got that big goddamn Boeing that he
flies all over the place in—"

John could be like ice when he disliked someone. One of
his responses was to say very little; in this case he said almost
nothing, and Dutch found it very irritating.

"Are you still there, John?"

"I'm here."

I thought the fucker had gone to sleep, Dutch said to himself.

"Well, anyway—this guy Ageel is very close to the king. Peter says he can do more than anyone else in the Gulf to close a deal— You still there?"

"I'm still here."

"The problem is that Peter is really competing with Bonn and Tokyo. Our guys in Washington as usual have their thumbs up their ass and don't want to show any so-called favoritism. Peter says that Ageel tells him you can be very helpful because of the king's feeling for what your grandfather did for his father." Dutch paused.

"John, are you interested in any of this, or am I wasting your time?"

"Go on, Dutch, I'm listening."

"There's fourteen billion involved, in the richest area on earth. If you could help Peter swing it, the bank would be in the best position of any foreign financial institution in the Gulf; the business could be enormous. It might be just what we need to cool everyone off, until you can find someone who can really run the place for you."

This stung John. The unmitigated gall of this garrulous, offensive bastard, who just happened to be proposing something that might bail them all out, irritated him beyond patience. He had everything he could do to keep from telling Dernberg to go to hell.

"Ageel's got a guy working for him who would like to call you to set up a meeting. His name's Aragon, Noel Aragon. Will you see him?"

The logic of Dutch's conversation was irrefutable, but his offensive implication regarding the bank, and inferentially John, enraged John. John was also angry that this Ageel, whom he knew only by reputation as a Middle Eastern broker of influence and guile, was not himself proposing to call him, but was having an aide do it. John Salisbury wasn't accustomed to dealing with people's aides.

"Tell Mr. Aragon to get in touch with Doug. I'll let him get the details, and then I'll see if I can be helpful."

"Doug!" It was like waving a red flag in front of a bull. "Aragon wants to talk to you, not Doug!"

John knew if he didn't hang up soon he would explode. "I appreciate what you're doing, Dutch, and I'm sure it will be helpful. Have Aragon call Doug, then I'll take it from there."

Dutch for once in his life was speechless; he couldn't believe it. Was this playboy Salisbury, who couldn't run a fucking kiddy car, pulling his leg?

"Doug! Are you serious, John?"

"Very. One other thing, Dutch." The empirical part of John's mind knew that there had to be some concession. "Have your man Giles give me a call." John paused. "Enjoy your weekend, and thank you for calling."

John sat there shaking with fury. It was a miracle that he had been able to retain his control. His breath came very rapidly. His face flushed with emotion. He leaned back in his chair, exhausted by the strain of the phone call. But his mind had begun to work again.

That son of a bitch may just have given Doug and me what we both need—a small miracle.

John couldn't help but smile at the thought of Dutch staring into an empty phone. Not many people hung up on Dutch Dernberg.

Joan and Henry made little effort to conceal their relationship, which grew closer each day. Henry missed Joan when they were separated by their jobs. If he had to be away on a trip, he couldn't wait until he got to a phone to call her, to get back to her.

With her youth, her vitality, her body, and her mind, she had reawakened his life. More than that, she seemed to reach back, far back to his youth, and extract some part of the essence of when he was young, and she would hold it up for him to look at, and convince him that it was still there. She would shine it all up with what she was, and hand it back to him, and he could see it, feel it. He couldn't remember being happier.

On this Indian summer Saturday in September, when the trees in Central Park had yet to flame, Henry was walking with his topcoat over his shoulder, holding the hand of the smashing redhead who could easily have kissed him on the top of his full, dark hair; she swinging her handbag like a young, adolescent girl, and he alive to the motion, color, smells, and sounds of the Sheep Meadow as they felt the soft grass underfoot.

"Got a surprise for you," he said.

She stopped him short and held on to his arm, turning him toward her. Her eyes sparkled with their own light.

"I love surprises, darling. Come on. What is it?"

She looked radiant to him. He studied her carefully with those observing, quiet brown eyes; then a slow smile emerged.

"Your first assignment as a reporter."

"Are you serious?"

"I sure am."

She watched him to see if it was something he had devised that would test her. She knew that Henry had a very professional side to him; he could be all business, even with her.

"Do you know what is going on at First Manhattan?"

"I've read about it in the papers."

He took her hand and they started to walk.

It was the kind of day when the grass flicked with the movement of late summer insects stirred by the warm sun, and puffs of clouds cast blue-gray shadows on the shafts of tall buildings at the edge of the park. There were sounds of children laughing, and the colors of flying kites and lost balloons.

"I'd like you to interview John Salisbury or Doug Dowding. If it's possible, I'd like to tape a five-to-eight-minute slot for the evening news, if you can get it."

"You can't be serious."

He kept walking now, almost pulling her along with him. She wanted to stop him and to look at him and tell him he was crazy.

He pulled her along.

"Henry, you really can't be serious. My first assignment, and you want me to interview John Salisbury. What do I know about banking? I wouldn't know what to ask him."

They came to some benches and sat down.

"You don't have to know anything about banking. What I want you to find out is how something like that could happen to one of the biggest banks in New York."

"But why me?"

He turned and looked at her, his eyes smiling. "Because I think you can do it, probably better than anyone we have. Because I think the bank might respond to your youth and obvious lack of experience in finance, where they might be very reluctant to talk to an experienced reporter they knew would dig for the hard answers." He paused. "Joan, this is an important story. Maybe it's not World War Three, but something challenging enough to cut your teeth on."

MORE THAN ANYTHING IN HIS LIFE, DOUG DREADED THIS
meeting. He dreaded seeing the look of accusation of his wife
and daughter. He dreaded the futility of trying to explain to
them what was unexplainable.

It was four o'clock when he entered the apartment.

Bardia was lying on the sofa. Gay was reading to her.

His heart nearly broke when he saw them.

"Hello, Daddy."

Of all the people on earth Gay was closest to him. He
knew that nothing could rupture the bond that had been
forged by time and love, and that special feeling that most
fathers have for their daughters. She would forgive him anything; he knew that. She would bend over backward to make
allowances for him, but he had hurt her mother irreparably,
and this she would find difficult to forgive.

"Hi, honey." He took off his coat and hat and laid them
on a chair, putting his overnight bag beside them.

"Honey, can you leave your mother and me alone for a
few minutes?"

She forced a smile and started to walk out of the room;
then she stopped. She turned and walked toward him, put her

arms around him, and kissed him lightly. He could tell she
was fighting to hold back her tears. She patted his shoulder
and left the room for the library.

Bardia sat up. Her hands automatically smoothed her hair
and straightened her dress.

She looked at him, her face pale, her expression a mixture
of hostility and sorrow.

He went to her and sat beside her.

"Bardy, look. I'm not going to make any more excuses, or
lie to you."

"That will be refreshing."

He paused. "Bardy."

The tears came to her eyes and ran silently down her
cheeks. Only her eyes were crying. Her voice was strained
but steady as she spoke to him. She sat very erect, her hands
folded in her lap.

"I've been lying here waiting, wondering what I would
say to you. How I would put into words the way I feel about
all the years we've been together."

Her tears had formed two narrow streams which glistened
in the reflected overhead light.

"I've been going over and over it in my mind, all of it.
Before we were married, college, you starting at the bank,
the children, and how it all quietly slipped away. It's like
trying to clutch at fog."

He watched her, feeling waves of remorse and misery.

"I knew we were drifting away from each other." Her chin
tilted upward in just the slightest gesture of pride. "I don't
blame you, Doug. I can't compete with a woman like Karen
Lockhart." Her lips trembled, but she remained sitting erect,
her whole bearing reflecting the thoroughbred she was.

"Bardy, I can't explain this rationally. I don't think it's just
a middle-aged man's infatuation with a younger woman, but
whatever it is, Bardy, I want you to believe that neither
Karen nor I ever wanted any part of hurting you." He saw
the look of hostility in her eyes, the disbelief.

"It's true. She's told me fifty times that she couldn't be a part of breaking up our marriage, and that we'd have to call it off."

Bardia's eyes flashed at him. "Am I supposed to feel grateful because my husband's mistress condescends to let him go? How do you think that makes me feel toward you?" She paused, looking away from him. "Most women begin to feel vulnerable as they grow older. The lucky ones have men who don't seem to notice what the years have done; they grow old together. They share a love that is strengthened by the events in a marriage, so that they are bound more closely together." Her voice faded for a moment as she half whispered to herself, "But I don't know too many people like that." She straightened and turned to look at him.

"The only happily married people I can think of, at least given my definition of what a happy marriage should be, are my mother and father, and John and Margret."

She looked right through him as she said it, and he knew the weapon she held if she wanted to use it. If John Salisbury learned that he had been unfaithful to Bardia, for whom John had great affection and respect, Doug would never have John's confidence again. That would be devastating for the president of FMB.

"Don't worry, Doug, I have no intention of letting John or anyone else know of our sordid little life together, I have too much pride for that. I also have no intention of forcing on you a relationship you're obviously unhappy with. And I'm not going to become a shrew whose only life is to make yours more miserable." Her voice was almost inaudible. "Evidently it's miserable enough."

"Bardy."

"No, Doug. Whatever time is left to me, I'm not going to spend it here with an oxygen mask clamped on my face waiting for you to return from your mistress of the week."

"What are you going to do?"

She remained silent for some time before she spoke.

"I haven't got an answer for that yet, but when I do, all I'll ask from you is your financial support. I won't ask you for a divorce because that will ruin you." She looked at him steadily. "But you can have one if you want it."

He started to put his arm around her, but she recoiled from him.

"Don't touch me, Doug. Just go." She raised her eyes that were filled with tears. Her voice was racked with the pain of her emotions. "It's all over, Doug." She paused. "I'm simply too old-fashioned to forget this and try to find what we once had." She thought for a moment, trying to explain how she felt.

"Maybe it's because I still have the example of my mother and father. Maybe I see the love that they've shared for half a century, the respect and affection they have for each other. Maybe I thought our life would be like that." She shook her head sadly. "Perhaps it was a dream, but it was my dream, and I won't settle for pity or patronizing. I may not be much to look at any more, Doug, but if I can't have the dream, I can live with the reality."

He started to speak; he had to say something to her. She was killing him with her nobility. It wasn't an act. It was the way she was. Perhaps for the first time in his life he realized the full depth of character of the woman he had married twenty-five years ago. But it was too late. He had failed, and the real tragedy was that he didn't know why.

"I WON'T TRY AND TELL YOU IT WASN'T ROUGH AT DEL-ray—it was rough as hell. Those birds wanted blood down there, yours and mine, I might add." John's face clouded. "Dutch was very direct, I'm afraid." He sighed as he looked at Doug. He saw the fatigue and pallor, the deep rings under Doug's eyes. But even in exhaustion Doug seemed to project force and authority. It was his natural camouflage, and John had still not been able to penetrate it.

John told him about Mike Giles. Doug was less than enthusiastic about an outsider looking into his area of operations.

"Dutch says he's the best man he's got. My guess is Dutch will make him president of PTM one day."

"But you say the guy runs Dutch's oil group? What the hell does he know about banking?"

John waited a long time before replying.

"It's Dutch's theory that a first-class administrator from the outside will give us a more objective critique. He's suggested one of his own men as a discreet way of handling things." John knew that these remarks would be interpreted by Doug as an indictment of Doug's failure to do his job.

Doug got up. He lit another cigarette and started to pace the oriental rugs that covered in part the waxed wooden floor of John's library. His face, his whole manner, reflected worry, consternation, and antagonism. He turned to John.

"John, if the board has that little confidence in me that it has to send somebody in here to look at what I'm doing, then perhaps I'm not helping you or the directors by staying on." Doug paused, his face stern and resolved. "If you or they want my resignation, you can have it."

John held up his hand; his voice was more nasal, higher in pitch. "Now, don't start talking like that, Doug. That's not what Dutch is saying at all. He heads the outside directors, and with all the problems we've had lately, some of them are becoming restive. This is as much an attempt to protect themselves as it is any criticism they might have for either you or myself."

Doug sat there grimly, his wide mouth now one straight line. He almost didn't catch the full implication of John's next sentence. His mind had strayed too far away, back to when everything was so much better, so much easier. He was thinking of a time when he and Bardia really had something, and the bank was a glorious mountain whose peak was bright, brilliant, and he was climbing it successfully. Now there was nothing. He felt as empty and hollow as a steel drum.

"I told Dutch to have Giles come and see me. But what I didn't tell him was that I've already made up my mind." John paused, his head slightly bent forward, looking directly at Doug. He saw his misery, and felt it deeply.

Most of what John was saying was just "voice" to Doug; in his intense preoccupation he missed its implications. He felt as if he were standing with his feet nailed to the floor. He couldn't move, and those who might help him—who were they? Why did they seem to stare at him, wordless, with cold, fixed eyes?

Doug had completely discounted the paternalism that

existed between them. He had also forgotten John's stub-bornness, his pride, and his belief in his own judgment. Doug was one of the most important products of John's selective process, and John still thought he had not made a mistake. It was part of what Ali called "a certain curious myopia," and John's response to the threats he faced at the bank was fitting all too accurately Ali's assessment of how John would react.

"Doug." John watched the glazed eyes come slowly back to him, but still not seeing. "Doug. I've made up my mind that we're going to fight this through together. Dutch called me about a major project in the Gulf. I'm going to turn the initial phase of it over to you."

Doug was now very slowly beginning to hear that there was a reprieve, another chance, even if it seemed like a long shot; but his depression was so deep that his relief would be a long time coming.

John's strategy was to move Doug temporarily farther away from operations; John would get closer to that. He would blunt Dutch's criticism of his spending too much time away from the bank and ease Doug's vulnerability for the moment.

John had no real confidence in the Gulf project; he was too familiar with the mind-boggling complexities of trying to get anything substantial accomplished in that part of the world, even for him. The Arabs were known for envisioning enormous plans, and for their timeless attitudes in seeing them carried out.

John was behaving exactly as Ali had guessed he would; he was distilling his anxieties into an intense preoccupation with his bank. Ali's "insurance policy" would be needed.

"Doug, a Noel Aragon is going to be in touch with you on this Gulf thing. See if there really is anything solid in all this. It could be very important for us, and for the bank." He was so right.

*   *   *

On an impulse Joan had picked up the phone and called Douglas Dowding at the First Manhattan Bank. When his secretary had told him she was from NBT, he had taken the call. He had agreed to meet her in his office for a brief interview at two-thirty that afternoon.

She thought for a minute and then dialed Henry Cannon's extension. Her voice was throaty and excited.

"Suppose I told you, sir, that I'm meeting Mr. Douglas Dowding at two-thirty this afternoon."

"What?"

"Yes, sir, you heard right. FMB has finally decided to let someone in."

Henry chuckled. "When Mr. Dowding sees who he's let in, you may have a hard time getting out."

She laughed. "Seriously, Henry, isn't that great?"

"I think it's terrific. I want to hear all about it when you get back."

She was anxious to get out in the sunshine, to feel the pulse and movement of the city. She was unfamiliar with the downtown financial district, but the thrill of beginning her first important assignment had sharpened her zest for the day.

Joan's cab stopped in front of the First Manhattan Bank Building, which was fully exposed to the wind from Lower Bay. The wind was vigorous, and as she paid the driver, she felt it whip at her long hair. She was glad to gain the protection of the lobby.

Joan looked for the elevator bank that would take her to the sixty-seventh floor and the executive offices of FMB. When she got out, a guard in a brown uniform asked her whom she wanted to see, and then pointed her toward one of two reception desks, where a pleasant woman with a very British accent smiled at her and called Mr. Dowding's secretary to let her know that Miss Hopkins was waiting in the lobby.

Joan was escorted through clear plastic doors. She didn't realize they were bulletproof, a precaution against threats the bank had received, directed specifically at John Salisbury, a worldwide symbol of capitalism.

Another set of clear plastic doors and she entered the softly lit aerie of Douglas Dowding's office; its walls of glass windows looked out on the bases of scattered clouds and the light-reflecting surfaces of a green-gray bay.

The effect of Doug's office was often felt by visitors to the sixty-seventh floor. Joan might be some fledgling bird stand ing on the top of a giant nest, waiting to launch herself into space.

Doug got up from behind his desk and walked toward her with a tired smile and a large outstretched hand. He was taller than she had imagined, larger in almost every way, including his head and hands. Douglas Dowding was a big man.

As he moved toward her in greeting, she was interested in what she thought she saw in the appraising, searching eyes. She saw great fatigue, that was obvious, but she also felt she detected a certain projection of theatrical authority.

"I appreciate your coming down, Miss Hopkins." His voice was deep and resonant. He pointed toward the sofa or the chairs that flanked a low glass table on which was a professionally arranged bowl of fresh flowers.

Joan was smart enough to take the sofa. She knew her legs would look better from there, and Doug couldn't have agreed more. She was the best thing that had happened to him all day. In a way she reminded him of Karen. She seemed to have that same natural latent sexuality, though Joan was even more attractive, and on first impression more gregarious, more feminine, and not as serious as Karen.

He offered her a cigarette.

"I certainly appreciate your giving me this time, Mr. Dowding."

"Not at all, it's my pleasure. Now, what can I do for you? By the way, am I on the record?"

"Not at all. As a matter of fact, I didn't come here to interview you in any formal sense; rather, I hoped that we could talk about how, from your point of view, to tell the public what happened here, so that our viewers can gain some perspective, and possibly some knowledge of how something like this could happen to a major bank." She paused. "In a way, Mr. Dowding, so few people—" She smiled at him, her voice trailing away. Her full red lips glistened in the soft light. Doug stared at her long red hair, at her incredibly lovely face and body, at those bright, intelligent green eyes that never left his, and at those unbelievable legs. Joan knew that she had Mr. Dowding's full attention.

Jesus Christ, he said to himself, she's the most beautiful woman I've ever seen. He didn't even hear what she was saying, not really. He allowed one small portion of his mind to retain whatever it was she was telling him, and the rest of him wanted only to look at and absorb this magnificent woman.

"What I am trying to say, Mr. Dowding, is that I'm like so many of our viewers. What's happened at FMB seems scary to me and to a lot of other people who don't know anything about how banks are run. I'm sure they feel the same way I do; a little frightened and confused—"

Doug was well aware of his attraction to beautiful women. As Bardy's illness separated them physically, this latent sensuality of his became more pronounced. He found himself often thinking of women, of Karen in particular, whose own sensuality seemed more intense than his; but when he was confronted by a woman like Joan Hopkins, Doug found his susceptibility even more acute.

As he heard her voice, his mind fixed itself on one idea: He wanted to get away with this woman, to go anywhere. He wanted someone, a total stranger that he could open up to, someone with whom he could share the nightmare that had become his life. He wanted some relief, perhaps even a little solace, maybe even to get laid. He smiled at that.

She watched him looking at her, knowing that sometimes —in fact, quite often—she was glad she was a woman.

"Do you agree with that, Mr. Dowding?"

Joan knew he was faking interest; she could see it. It was an occupational hazard with her where men were concerned. She wanted to talk business, and they wanted to talk about her. But in this instance she didn't mind; as a matter of fact, she had hoped it would turn out this way.

"About the bond problem."

He was brought back. "The problem, Miss Hopkins, is, if this is off the record, that we had a breakdown in the judgment of one of our senior vice-presidents; perhaps it may have been some psychological flaw; I don't know. But when you deal in any sensitive area of activity—money, intelligence gathering, even politics or the military—you have to depend in the final analysis on the integrity of people. We've got nearly forty thousand people around the world, Miss Hopkins, and we can't climb into the heads of any one of them."

She wasn't going to press him on this. Not now. That was not why she was there. She was there to let him see her, to have him come to her, instead of her, as a member of a news staff, having to chase him.

She had begun to sense there was something locked inside Douglas Dowding that wanted desperately to break out. Her instincts as a woman and her intelligence told her that within this troubled man might be the key that could unlock many doors. Through Doug Dowding she might be able to get behind a cold institutional explanation of what went on in a place like FMB, and find out how people hunted and were hunted in the softly lit beige corridors of that tower of money and power.

She didn't doubt whether she could get to him. She smiled

inwardly; she already had. Doug Dowding had grabbed the bait, but as yet he hadn't felt the hook.

Doug looked at his watch. "Miss Hopkins, I'm terribly sorry about this, but there are four men I have kept waiting now for over fifteen minutes. I'm afraid you'll have to excuse me, but I have a suggestion for you if you think it would be helpful. Suppose I have my secretary call your office and make an appointment for lunch. You're far too attractive to invite to eat here at the bank. I'd never hear the end of it. Suppose we say the Côte Basque when our schedules permit." He got up and shook hands with her.

She smiled and thanked him for his time.

Before leaving, she turned and looked at him closely. She found him curiously attractive. There was something about him that seemed to her like a big awkward boy playing games. She sensed some particular vulnerability that perversely she found appealing. There was something about the big frame, the bass voice, that reminded her of the Wizard of Oz, hiding behind an enormous screen, flashing lights and making noises, trying to frighten everyone, when in reality it was the Wizard who was frightened.

They stood looking at each other. Of the two of them, she was far more intuitive and perceptive. She felt his quick, strong physical attraction for her, and she wondered if he were capable of feeling more than that. As she walked out, she could feel him watching her, his desire like warm sun at her back.

He needed someone right now. He knew that the wounds of guilt Karen felt were too deep, too new; she needed some time to heal. The pragmatist in him told him that this woman needed him—as a source of information, if nothing else.

He realized, of course, that instead of a solution Joan might very well turn into another problem. He was beginning to suspect his own ability, even desire, to steer a course away from the rocks. But what the hell, what was one more problem in the life of Douglas Dowding?

* * *

When Joan returned to NBT, she reported back to Henry. They sat together in Henry's office. Henry was clouded in the fog of his continuously present cigarette smoke, obviously aware that Joan was concerned about something.

"He's asked me to lunch, Henry. He hasn't set a time yet, but it will be soon."

Henry watched her closely. He saw that her eyes were far away, her thoughts probing areas that weren't entirely all business.

"This is a vulnerable man, Henry." She paused. "This may sound ridiculous to you given the fact that I've spent all of about half an hour with Dowding, but—chalk it up to woman's intuition if you want to. I feel there's—" She shook her head, surprised at herself for saying it. "There's a touch of tragedy about Dowding. My God, anyone that's human would bend under the load he carries. Henry, I simply can't imagine what it must be like to manage fifty billion dollars' worth of anything." She stabbed her cigarette and sighed. "But that's not what's bothering me." She looked directly at Henry, her green eyes locked into his. "Henry, this man is very attracted to me."

"What's so unusual about that?" Henry's voice was quiet and reserved.

"I mean not just physically attracted. I can't explain it, but it's something I feel. This could get to be too personal."

His eyes narrowed. "For you or for him?"

"I mean that I don't want to take advantage of his confidences." She hesitated, looking thoughtfully at Henry. "And then turn them over to twenty million people."

Henry watched her for a long time. He admired her concern for the ethical conflicts she was beginning to realize were inherent in their profession. He looked at her, feeling the differences between them, the differences in the years lived.

"Joan. Level with him right from the beginning. Tell him that nothing is ever really off the record. If he doesn't want something publicized, he shouldn't talk about it. That way you've warned him and you can live with yourself. You can't give him protection, but you can offer him perspective and some objectivity."

She thought about that for some time, then got up slowly and sat on the arm of Henry's chair. She kissed him, and then as she got up to leave his office, she turned. "I'm beginning to believe that this can get to be a lousy business sometimes, Henry. Do you know that?"

His voice sounded sad and very tired. "I learned that too many years ago, Joanie; too many hotels, too many days, too many nights, too many planes, too many miles." He sighed wistfully. "My father was probably right."

"About what?"

"About what he told me I would find away from the farm, and what I would find on it." His eyes seemed very far away. "It's too long a story."

He watched her as she carefully closed his office door.

AFTER A SILENT DINNER AT HOME, BARDIA SITTING AT one end of the long dining table and he at the other, both not saying a word, he decided he wanted to go for a walk. He needed some relief from the funereal atmosphere of the house and the accusatory eyes of his wife.

He thought of Karen. God, how he wanted to lose himself in the wild sensuality of that woman. His need and desire for her was almost a physical pain, but he knew it was too soon to see Karen. His mind somehow turned to Joan, and he knew as his emotions developed, warring with his reason and his logic, that he was going to see her as soon as he could.

He heard Bardia's voice as if it were some distant bell, clanging indistinctly, far off in some gray, unforgiving sea.

"Doug, I have a few things I want to discuss with you. I find this situation between us impossible."

Bardy looked even paler, more fragile, than usual. She no longer made any attempt to make herself attractive for him. She seemed to him like some porcelain figurine that had become gray with age, covered with dust.

"I've decided I am going to move to Phoenix to live. We can both see Gay settled into either graduate school or a job, whatever she chooses. She can live with me if she prefers; I'd adore having her. But I want to be ready to move into a suitable house in Phoenix not later than February first."

He listened as she sat looking at him, her large eyes reflecting the light; her voice trembled at times, but she sat erect, her hands folded in her lap.

"Since I am physically unable to go down there and look for a house, I want you to ask someone from your real estate department whose taste you have some regard for to find me a suitable home with three bedrooms. I'll need a good decorator to furnish it for me. I want the house unmortgaged, in my name, and I want a fund set aside for my living and medical expenses and the maintenance of the house for as long as I live. At my death the property will become part of my estate, to be disposed of as I see fit in my will."

Her voice was low, almost a whisper.

He knew better than to mention money to her. This was her divorce settlement, without a divorce. He would have to sell this apartment and get something smaller. He'd have to sell the cottage in Oxford and possibly the plane. He'd hate like hell to lose the plane. He loved that little bird.

"I expect you to have these arrangements made for me not later than January fifteenth. You can, of course, use my home whenever you like, but frankly I would prefer it if you only came down when it was necessary to keep up appearances. You can tell John we're doing this because of my health; that will sound plausible to him. I'll tell Gay when I think it's appropriate.

"One more thing. I'll need a cook, and someone, preferably an RN, who can serve as a companion and nurse.

"Now, if you will excuse me, I want to lie down."

She got up from the table and left.

He hadn't said one word to her. What could he say? She was handling this whole tawdry affair like the pro she was. He thought of Karen, and then Joan. The thought occurred to him that if there ever was a classy lady, it was his pale, sickly wife. She had just made him feel like the lowest form of bastard that crawls on earth.

He put on his hat and coat and went down to get some air.

The weather had changed from the warm Indian summer they had been having to an unusually cold September night.

As he walked north on Park Avenue, the lights of the buildings, the shopwindows, the moving taxis, the red and green signals blinking their alternate colors, all appeared to him as a blurred, silent montage.

He pulled his coat collar up and lowered his head into the wind, his thoughts drawn inward, an isolated mind hearing nothing but the inner voices of his own pain.

Joan, he thought. He kept seeing her, her vital, intelligent beauty. He desperately needed someone he could talk to, and with Doug that was always a woman; on this night, that woman was Joan.

The phone rang the next morning in the one-bedroom apartment at Seventy-ninth and York Avenue that had a view of the East River and of the new cluster of apartments on Roosevelt Island, which looked from a distance like children's building blocks.

"Do you work on weekends?"

"Who's this?"

"It's Doug Dowding."

Joan Hopkins had been cleaning up after a late breakfast. She had been looking forward to a lazy morning and afternoon. She was meeting Henry for dinner.

"It's nice of you to call, Mr. Dowding. Yes, as a matter of fact, I do work on weekends if I have to."

There was a slight pause. "Are you interested in continuing our talk?"

"Yes, sir, I certainly am."

"Suppose I suggest a place in the country. Maybe a late lunch along the Connecticut shore."

She hesitated. She wanted to be back in plenty of time for

dinner with Henry, but this was business. Did Doug understand that? she wondered.

"I do have to be back in the city by, say, six—or seven at
the latest."

"That's fine. That'll give us plenty of time. Dress warmly.
It's a beautiful day out, but cold, and the place I'm thinking
of is part of an old estate. It's marvelous for walking. Wear
some comfortable shoes."

"What time will you come by?"

"Pick you up in, say, forty-five minutes. Does that give you
enough time?"

"That will be fine, Mr. Dowding."

Doug hung up and wondered what the hell he was doing.

When he walked out of his library, he looked at Bardia,
who was reading. She was sitting in a large wing chair by
the window, the midmorning light behind her, placing her face
in shadow. She was still in her dressing gown.

"Bardy, for Christ's sake, isn't there anything we can do
to make this easier for both of us until January? This is
agonizing, having you sitting there silently like some wax
doll, while I come in and out of the house for meals."

She looked up at him, her eyes not devoid of compassion.
She wasn't malignant in her attitude toward Doug but, rather,
resigned. She was resigned too about her life, and very possibly
her death.

"Doug, I'm sorry I seem so remote to you, but I've had to
develop a life within myself these past few years, and I'm
afraid I've developed the habits of someone who has become
used to being alone.

"I'm not trying to play Camille, and I'm not trying to hurt
you by burdening you with any more guilt than I know you
feel. I realize I've become withdrawn. I know I'm not a wife,
perhaps not even a woman any more. That's why I don't really
blame you for what you've done. I've had a great deal of time

to think about us, Doug, and I know you so well." She put down her book and looked at him, her eyes seeming like two wide pools of soft shadows, her hair backlighted by the window.

"I know the horrible, grinding pressures you're under, Doug. I've watched them accumulate over the years with each increase in your responsibilities. I know the releases you have to have, and I can't give them to you."

He stood there looking at her, listening to her soft voice, watching her eyes that seemed to look through him and past him, back into their lives and forward into their futures.

"You've hurt me terribly, Doug, and a part of me will never forgive you for that. You've betrayed the years we had together, and many of them were good years.

"At first I felt so bitter toward you because I felt you had also betrayed our love, and I must admit that at times that bitterness comes back to me, but then I reasoned, after what seemed like a very long time, sitting in this house day after day, just thinking, that in my own way, beyond my control, I have also let you down. Perhaps it was a kind of betrayal on my part, I don't know. I can't forgive you, but I don't blame you. Is that too strange a paradox?"

As he watched her, listened to her, he felt the ambivalent emotions and the strong bonds of affection that the years had forged between them. He felt a kind of love, perhaps the most enduring kind. But the focus of his emotions was his empathy and envy for this stoic woman who was handling her life, or, more accurately, what was left of it, with so much more dignity and grace than he was handling his.

"Bardy, isn't there some way we can work this out together? There's got to be."

She looked at him for a long time, her eyes regarding him the way a mother looks at a loved and penitent child. When she spoke, it was with a wisdom that he lacked, and a candor that was beyond him.

"Doug, I'm not going anywhere, except Phoenix, and you're welcome to see me there, any time. But I don't have the strength"—she looked at him directly, her eyes going right through him—"and neither do you, unfortunately, to put the pieces back together." Her voice was very quiet, very controlled. The occasional sounds of traffic, the horns, the ticking of the old standing clock, were the only background sounds in the large room.

"We're both facing a turning point in our lives, Doug. Mine is different; maybe it's more ominous than yours, but that depends on your point of view. All I'm trying to do now is to face whatever future I have, with whatever grace and dignity God will permit me. For you, Doug, you'll have to find your own way, without any more help from me."

He listened to her with a lump in his throat that seemed to choke him. He knew, in that part of his mind that wouldn't let him equivocate, that her strength was greater than his. He understood that of the women in his life she could give him more of what he really needed than Karen or Joan, but he had dropped that. It had fallen and broken, and it was irreparable. It had been a small treasure, irreplaceable, and now it was gone. Parts of it were there reminding him of what he had lost, and those pieces cut at his remorse and tormented him more than all the other burdens of his existence.

SHE SAT BESIDE HIM IN THE GRAY MERCEDES AS HE DROVE up the Hutchinson River Parkway. She saw he was preoccupied, and she was sensitive to his mood.

She had dressed carefully for him, choosing an emerald-green cashmere sweater underneath a tweed jacket, which occasionally opened to reveal the outline of her full breasts.

He bore left onto Route 684, going north at the intersection of the Cross Westchester Expressway.

"May I have a hint of where we're headed?"

"Let's just say that it's a surprise."

She felt the car accelerate on the concrete expressway.

They were soon at the eastern edge of Rye Lake Reservoir, where he picked up the cutoff to Westchester County airport. She was puzzled by this, but didn't say anything.

He drove quickly down the country road, past several large estates, and then turned onto the road that sloped down to the several buildings that were hangars, maintenance shops, waiting-room and eating facilities, and the broad black runways that were crowded with weekend air traffic.

She turned to him, smiling. "I believe you said a drive?"

He smiled back at her. "I did. We've had a part of our drive;

the rest of it will be by air. I hope you like to fly."

"I love it."

"Great!" His voice expressed the first enthusiasm he had shown since he had picked her up.

The white Bonanza was waiting for him on the ramp. He preflighted it quickly, checking the oil and gas and draining the tanks of any water that might have accumulated. He removed the chocks from the wheels. He was a careful pilot. It had kept him alive during the war. She watched him with interest as he moved. She studied the big frame, the seemingly large, awkward hands that were surprisingly quick and skilled.

"That should do it." He looked at her, as if seeing her for the first time. She was beautiful. Her face had the straight, clean lines that he liked. She was very tall, with the full figure that he found so physically attractive, but she had so much more: a spark, a vivacity that lit up her large green eyes that seemed to offer him the tonic he needed so badly. She seemed bright, with a perceptiveness he found both intimidating and attractive. There was an air of integrity about her, a directness and honesty that he instinctively trusted. As Henry Cannon had also discovered, Joan Hopkins was a hell of a girl.

She felt a tinge of excitement as he began to taxi toward the active runway, getting into position behind the other traffic waiting to take off.

The sky was a bright blue, almost cloudless. There was a relatively brisk surface wind, so he decided to avoid the turbulence that he might find at low altitude, and fly over the Sound.

She was enjoying every minute of it.

When he had the course and altitude he wanted, he set the Bonanza on autopilot, offered her a cigarette, and lit one himself. She was busy trying to figure out where they were.

"That's Norwalk behind us. Bridgeport will be coming up next."

She leaned toward him to look out of the left side of the aircraft. Her hair brushed his shoulder; he could smell her perfume. They were physically close in the cockpit of the small plane, and they each sensed the somewhat forced intimacy.

"After Bridgeport will be New Haven."

He adjusted the power setting and pressed the DME, which told him how fast they were going over the ground, and how far they were from their destination.

"We're doing two hundred and ten miles an hour over the ground. We've got about a thirty-mile-an-hour tail wind. At this speed we'll be there in less than twenty minutes."

She looked at him teasingly. "You still haven't told me where we're going. If you didn't have such good credentials, I might feel you were trying to abduct me."

He laughed for the first time that day.

They flew on, passing the small coastal towns and villages of Connecticut.

"See that lighthouse on that tip of land up ahead?"

She leaned forward in her seat looking in the direction to which he was pointing.

"See it on that point of land over there?"

She shielded her eyes from the glare of the sun.

"Yes, I've got it."

"Well, that's very near where we'll have lunch."

She really was caught up in the excitement of this brief flight, and in the awareness of the incredible mobility the aircraft gave them.

"That's Goshen Point. New London's up the river about fifteen miles."

He flew closer to the point so that she could see the lighthouse and the area in which they would spend the afternoon. He banked inland and started losing altitude for his approach to the Groton airport.

When they landed and he had chocked the aircraft, they

walked to the terminal building, where Doug had reserved a rental car. They drove out of the airport heading for the Lighthouse Inn.

After Joan had gone to the powder room to comb her hair and touch up her lipstick, they entered the dimly lit cocktail lounge. The walls were hung with thoughtful portraits of attractive women, and a surrealistic painting of the artist's fantasies of women hung over the bar.

It was nearly two-forty-five, and the kitchen was closed for lunch, but they were able to get some chicken sandwiches, which tasted good to Joan; she was hungry after the excitement of the flight. Sitting opposite Doug, looking at him with eyes that held the low level of reflected light, she felt an awakening curiosity about a married man who was the president of one of the world's largest banks and who spent a Saturday afternoon like this.

He drank only a small dry sherry. He explained that one didn't fly and drink. It wasn't a combination that led to a long life.

She sipped a martini slowly. Her mood had become more thoughtful, but she retained that latent effervescence that he found so palliative and which he sensed would rarely be suppressed in her under most circumstances.

"Would you mind if I asked you a few questions, Mr. Dowding?"

"Only if you keep calling me Mr. Dowding. Why not try Doug? Everyone else does."

She smiled. "Fine, Doug. I'd like that." She paused for a moment.

"I realize that all of the coverage your bank has been getting must be very difficult for you, and for Mr. Salisbury. Do you think there is any legitimacy to the questions of incompetence that have appeared in the press?"

He stubbed out his cigarette and thought about her question. It had really cut at him, and the defense and hostility she saw come into his eyes made her regret her directness. She realized that through her inexperience she had been too blunt, that she had touched this man where he lived. She had made a mistake and she knew it.

He toyed with a pencil that he had removed from his pocket; it was one of those swivel pencils in which the lead could be retracted. It made no mark on the tablecloth, and somehow she liked him for that.

"I'm not going to equivocate with you, Joan, and tell you that this is just the result of misplaced trust in one of our officers; it's obviously more than that. It does point up a certain inadequacy in our controls, and perhaps it does reflect on our management. I don't know."

She was impressed with his directness, his willingness to take the blame.

"The problem, as far as I'm concerned at least, is just how do you protect yourself from the breakdown of the moral attitudes and judgment of another human being. What I'm saying is that I don't know how we can guard ourselves against the other Tom Gallaghers of this world. We've got more of them, I'm sure. Maybe our controls can be improved, but all that will do is cut down on the number of Tom Gallaghers. Can we eliminate them—is that your question? If it is, my answer is no, we can't. No business can; no society or government can. And if that's the brush we're being tarred with, I think it's unfair."

He looked at his watch.

"What do you say we walk off this rather skimpy lunch?"

"Good idea."

They bundled up for the cold afternoon breeze that was blowing moist air in from the Sound, and he guided her out to the car.

"I thought we were going to walk."

"We are, but not here."

"You're still full of surprises."

They drove to Harkness Memorial Park and walked the sweeping grounds that overlooked the Sound, past the tall, aging trees, toward the beach. The wind made it seem colder than it was.

They reached the rocks, and he held out his hand to her. "Are you game?"

"Sure," she said, and took his hand as he guided her over the tumbled, irregular rocks and stones, out toward the firm sand, where the pipers strutted their jerky, stiff-legged walk and flew suddenly into drafts of wind, then skimmed the surface of the shallow breaking seas.

He held her arm through his as they walked along the beach in the graying of the late September afternoon.

She would have preferred that he not do this, but she sensed in him a need to get close to someone, a need to be understood. This was what she had originally felt in this man, and it was what had disturbed her when she related her concerns to Henry.

She stopped walking and stood facing him on the beach. The wind blew her hair that hung down below the scarf she had wrapped around her head. She looked at him with eyes filled with more understanding than his. "Doug, you've got to realize something about me. I mean really recognize it. I think you're very attractive and fun to be with, and I've enjoyed every minute we've spent together today. But, Doug, you're news, and my job is to get the news and present it fairly." She paused. "I don't want to fly under false colors with you. I'm trying to be honest. What I mean is, I can't protect you from what you tell me. I can't keep things off the record. If you don't want to tell me something, then don't. If you do, I'll use it."

He looked at her carefully, at the beauty of her face, the clarity and frankness of her eyes. He still had her arm through his, and with his elbow he could feel, even through her jacket, the full softness of her breast.

"That's fair and it's forthright. I hope it doesn't get me into trouble."

They walked back toward the car in the gathering twilight that would soon be darkness. Both of them sensed that they had started down a difficult and unknown road.

NOEL ARAGON LAY STARING AT THE HIGH CEILING OF his bedroom at 6 Belgrave Place, London. His eyes moved over the carved molding that bordered the ceiling to the shadows in the empty grate of the white-manteled fireplace, whose outline he could barely discern in the darkness of the room.

His dinner at the Dorchester with Ali had put him in a mood of great concern. He had a foreboding about this scheme of Ali's to bribe Dowding. In true Middle Eastern style Ali had, of course, stepped carefully aside, while thrusting Noel into the mainstream of trouble.

Ali paid Noel enough to do this if he chose, and he had other reasons equally logical. Ali recognized that with American bankers he, with his dark image of a son of the desert, would be far less palatable than Noel, who was a product of one of the premier Anglo-Saxon London merchant banking families with an excellent worldwide reputation. That was why Ali was willing to overpay Noel so outrageously and why Noel continued the liaison.

But now the spiders in Noel's mind were scurrying their warnings. He knew how vulnerable he was, both with the Americans and Ali. He was well aware of the fragile goodwill that masked a primitive passion for revenge, if Ali's position was jeopardized through all this.

He was the one who had everything to lose, he thought. If something went wrong with Ali's plan, it was he, the Honorable Noel Aragon, whom they would crucify in London and New York. Ali would deny everything. He had the loyalty of a hungry python.

So why was he doing this? Why, in the shadows of the night while he could still withdraw, didn't he call Ali and refuse?

He knew the answer lay within a bleak and lonely mind that fed itself on greed.

Noel shuddered in the semidarkness of the room. He thought of the white teeth and flashing dark eyes of his employer. They were from different worlds, centuries apart, and yet the serpents of their souls were warmed by the same sun. Only their venom was different; Ali's was lethal, Noel's was not.

Noel sighed and set the alarm for six o'clock to call Dowding in New York.

Doug was sitting in his office winding up a meeting with his two senior credit officers when his secretary announced that a Mr. Noel Aragon was calling from London. He remembered John's telling him that Aragon would call in connection with Peter Tennant's project in the Gulf.

The meeting had ended, and its participants were eager to get back to their offices and try to make some progress through their own crowded calendars. Doug waved them out as he picked up the phone.

"Mr. Dowding?"

"Yes."

"Awkward having to be introduced over the phone. I'm Noel Aragon. I hope Mr. Salisbury has had a moment to brief you on my call."

"He mentioned something to me about your group and Peter Tennant."

"Splendid."

"I'm afraid, Mr. Aragon, that Mr. Salisbury was not very informative. He simply said that Tennant was working on a contract in the Gulf."

"Quite so, Mr. Dowding. It's a fourteen-billion-dollar contract, sir, the largest ever put up for bid by any country in that area."

Fourteen billion dollars is an enormous figure even to the president of a bank the size of FMB.

"That certainly sounds like an impressive project."

"It is, sir." The slightly deferential telephone manner of Noel Aragon was balm to Doug's ego. He had almost forgotten what it felt like to be the president of FMB.

"If I may take one more minute of your time, sir. We have been working with Peter's group for over three years on this proposal, and we're ready to make our presentation to the king. I might add that so are our competitors. They are a German and Japanese consortium. Our timing is rather tight. I am going to be in New York tomorrow, and I wonder if I might make an appointment, if you can manage it with what I know must be a very crowded schedule."

"Hold on a minute."

Doug looked at his desk calendar. The whole day tomorrow was jammed with meetings, but he noticed that his secretary had canceled a dinner he was to attend, a reception at the United Nations for the head of the World Monetary Fund. He and John were supposed to attend together; something must have come up.

He buzzed his secretary. "Is that shindig still on at the UN for tomorrow night?"

"No, sir. Mr. Salisbury said that he would handle it, that there was no reason for you both to attend."

Doug thought that odd, but dismissed it.

"Sorry to keep you waiting, Mr. Aragon."

"Not at all."

"I'm absolutely jammed all day tomorrow, but I see here I've just had a cancellation for dinner. If that suits your schedule, we might be able to work it out that way."

"That would be splendid. Would you be good enough to meet me at the Carlyle? I'll be staying there."

"That's fine."

"Say about eight?"

"I'd prefer to make it earlier, perhaps seven if that suits you."

"Splendid. I'll be looking forward to it."

"See you then." Doug hung up, and buzzed his secretary. "Remind me that I'm having dinner with Mr. Aragon tomorrow night at seven."

"Yes, sir."

He sat back in his chair thinking about the importance of the call. What would this guy Aragon be like? he wondered, and would he be a way out for him, possibly even for John? Doug didn't believe it. He put little faith in long shots, especially when they stretched as far as the Middle East.

"What the hell," he said aloud. In his position he didn't exactly have a great deal of room for maneuver. He pushed angrily at the button that would summon his harried secretary.

It had begun to rain. Heavy, petulant drops hit the black streets and sidewalks that shimmered in the darkness. Umbrellas were being blown like round dark sails. People hurried, bent over like shadowed marionettes blown before a harrying wind. Thick gray-black clouds hid the stars. This brooding night that had come to Manhattan was unwelcome.

Doug's limousine, wet black and shining in the lights of the hotel, edged its way toward the curb, fighting the other limousines that were seeking to get their passengers as close to the protected entrance of the Carlyle as possible.

Doug entered the lobby and was given Noel Aragon's suite number by the reception clerk. When he reached the eighteenth floor, he found the number and pressed the buzzer. Noel Aragon opened the door.

Doug towered over the man. Noel was of medium height, about five feet eight, and inclined to put on weight. By dint of great self-discipline, Noel managed to keep his waistline from expanding, but his round, waxen face, with its flesh full and jowly about his cheeks and neck, indicated Noel's constant battle with his metabolism. His skin glistened in the light of the small chandelier that hung in the foyer.

His eyes were the first thing Doug noticed; they were large, dark brown, furtive.

"So nice of you to come on such a beastly night, Mr. Dowding. Let me take your coat."

Doug walked into the living room and sat on the sofa. A small bar stocked with liquor and an ice chest stood on one side of the doorway leading to the bedroom.

"So good of you to see me, Mr. Dowding, really." Noel Aragon leaned over, almost in a bow, his hands at his sides, somewhat in the position of a headwaiter saying "Come this way."

"I've taken the liberty of chilling some champagne. May I?"

Doug for some reason was preoccupied with the thinning strands of dark hair that gave poor cover to the white, glistening scalp of Mr. Aragon.

"That would be fine."

Noel poured two glasses of champagne.

"Do you get over frequently, Mr. Aragon?"

"Not often, actually."

Doug had a practiced ear for the accents of Europeans, and he knew that Noel's reflected good schools, and probably a good family.

"This champagne is excellent, Mr. Aragon."

Noel beamed. "Why, thank you, sir, you must be a connoisseur."

Doug thought that one didn't have to be a connoisseur to

recognize a bottle of Dom Perignon 1952 chilling in an ice bucket.

"Do you like caviar, Mr. Dowding?"

"Yes, I do."

"Splendid. Some people can't stand the stuff." He handed Doug a small tray of caviar hors d'oeuvres.

Doug's first reaction to Noel Aragon was wary. There was a certain unctuousness about Noel. He had a practiced, ingratiatory manner that Doug felt could be converted into shrewd purpose as quickly as a heartbeat.

"I feel a little out of the game with you, Mr. Aragon. The only thing I know is that you're somehow connected with Peter Tennant, and you seem to know John Salisbury."

Doug's tone lacked the warmth Noel was doing his best to elicit.

"Not quite, Mr. Dowding. I do know Peter Tennant, but not well, and I don't know Mr. Salisbury at all."

Doug sipped his champagne quietly.

"Mr. Ageel is well known to Mr. Tennant, and I believe Mr. Salisbury knows of Mr. Ageel. Our company, Mr. Dowding, East-West Trading, Limited, is the largest and most influential of its kind in the Gulf. We successfully represent more American, German, Japanese, French, English, and Italian companies in the Gulf than anyone else." Aragon looked pointedly at Doug. "Mr. Ageel is very close to our king."

That was impressive. If Ageel was close to the king, and Aragon was his number-one man, then he was important, and Doug could enjoy the rest of his champagne. These issues of status mattered to men whose yardsticks of achievement were divided into thirds: money, power, and position. They were particularly important to Doug, who had been brought up to believe they were all that really mattered, or almost all.

"I was planning to take us to Caravelle, Mr. Dowding, but the weather is so beastly I thought perhaps we would simply dine here."

"Perfectly fine with me."

The dinner proceeded slowly. They had switched from champagne to a bottle of Château Haut Brion 1955, and finished with a twenty-year-old French cognac.

With a fine, cool Havana giving off a thin ribbon of light blue-gray smoke, Doug's mood had softened considerably. He was surprised at the contacts Noel had with the senior officers of a wide range of American companies who were customers of the bank.

With British style and skill, Noel had succeeded in completely skirting the real reason why he wanted to talk with Doug. That would come later.

"What do you think your chances are of landing this contract for Peter Tennant?" Doug asked.

Noel paused reflectively. "We have some very difficult competition from the German and Japanese consortium. They're going to be the ones to beat. I don't think the Italians are really in the game on this one. It's too big, and they simply don't have the organization or the financial stability for a project of this size. I do think we have the best chance, but it will be close, very close. We're talking about fourteen billion dollars. Even the initial phase of the contract is worth about nine billion. That's a prize I doubt if we will have an opportunity of shooting for again in our lifetime."

It was getting late, and Noel had more to accomplish this evening, and he could tell by the several glances Doug had given his watch that he had better get on with it.

"Mr. Dowding, if I may make a suggestion. I realize this is not giving you much notice, but Ali has asked me to suggest something to you which really takes more time than we have this evening. You and I have been getting to know one another, and I would like to continue, if you are willing, in a slightly more congenial environment than New York." Noel smiled at Doug, who was listening, waiting patiently for him to get to the point.

"We have a lovely place on St. John, in the Caribbean. What I'd like to suggest, if you have nothing else on, would be that you come down as my guest for the weekend. I can have our jet drop you off and bring you back.

"We have a large sailing yacht at our disposal, and instead of spending the weekend in New York, why not get a little sun, do some sailing, some swimming—fish, if you like—and discuss the rest of our business down there? Bring a guest if you care to. It's just the servants and my secretary when I'm there, so you won't be troubled by spending the weekend with a lot of people."

As he had hoped, Noel had hit upon the ideal way of enticing Douglas Dowding. Doug wanted to get away. He couldn't stand the thought of looking at Bardy, of bearing her silence and fortitude. And Noel had mentioned a guest; the face of Joan Hopkins flashed through his mind.

It was tempting. He thought about it for a moment, and then stood up, a smile on his face for the first time that evening. He extended his hand to the Englishman, who rose when he did.

"Noel, my boy, you're on. Let me get back to you when I can firm things up."

They shook hands, both smiling.

Noel Aragon sighed inwardly. So far, so good, he said to himself, and only hoped his luck would continue.

Joan's attitude toward Henry was a mixture of annoyance and confusion. She found it difficult to understand how he could continue to assign her to cover Doug Dowding when Henry knew of Doug's attraction to her.

"You're telling me I should go down there with him? Anything to get the story, eh, Henry." She looked at him, her eyes now mischievous, probing.

"I hear it gets very romantic down there, Henry; those soft nights and bright stars. You know Doug isn't unattractive.

With a few drinks, who knows what might happen to a girl?"

Henry was not amused. Somewhat old-fashioned, he still carried around a lot of Lancaster, Pennsylvania. He wasn't jealous, at least he didn't think he was, but it wasn't helping his peace of mind to ask Joan to take this trip with Doug.

"I expect you to be a reporter. You're going down there to follow through on the FMB story, not to look at the stars." There was an edge to his voice.

"I'm only teasing, Henry. But I am disturbed. It's very difficult for me to have to use someone, especially when he's troubled and confused. I really feel deeply about that, Henry."

His voice was solemn and far away. "I know you do. How do you think I feel, having to put you, especially you, in such a position?" His mind flicked to all the madness he had witnessed around the world; the unthinkable cruelties, the suffering, the gross stupidities and inequities, and sometimes, thank God, the few warm, compassionate moments when men and women behaved toward one another without the appetites of carnivores. He had seen too much, he thought. He was too jaded, too cynical, too professionally objective.

Joan relented. "I'm a big girl, and I can handle whatever comes up down there, you know that. Harry Truman was right when he said, 'If you can't stand the heat, get out of the kitchen.' "

Henry looked at her with a growing love, and a feeling of regret at the cynicism he was forcing upon her so soon, so terribly soon, he felt. He crushed out his cigarette with slow deliberation. Henry Cannon had truly seen too much.

"IT'S MR. GILES TO SEE YOU, SIR."

"Show him in."

Michael Giles walked into John Salisbury's office and shook hands with the man whom he had only heard about as a legend, as a part of the fabric of a family who had helped to develop the industrial and philanthropic growth of the United States.

John looked somewhat shorter and less robust than his pictures. He seemed pale, almost harried, but his eyes were kind, though appraising, and his manner, though somewhat formal, even courtly, was sincere in welcome.

"So you're the young fellow Dutch thinks so highly of."

Mike remained standing. He was considerably taller than John, slim, and very self-possessed. He smiled easily, but the light-blue eyes were shrewd and analytical. Michael Giles was a charmer, a diplomat, but he was also intuitive and tough. He knew how to get things done without breaking too much glass.

"I don't know about that, sir."

John walked over to his intercom and told his secretary to have Doug come in at eleven-forty-five. The three of them would have lunch together in his private dining room. She was to hold all his calls.

Mike was still standing. John motioned to a chair.

"No, I'm afraid I can't let you off that easily, Mr. Giles."

"Mike, please."

"All right, Michael. But I must insist; Dutch has sung your praises to me so fully that I've been wondering what kind of magician to expect."

Mike Giles leaned back in his chair, crossed his long legs, and laughed.

"I'm afraid, sir, that Dutch overestimates me." He spoke with a slight British accent.

"Are you English?"

"No, sir, American. I was educated in Switzerland and in England. I've lived so long in London that perhaps I've acquired something of an accent." He began to laugh. "But now Dutch has me spending so much time in Houston that I'm surprised I haven't developed a southern drawl."

They talked, becoming friendlier, easing the strain of Mike's presence. Both could not help being aware of the embarrassment one caused the other. Mike was shrewd and intuitive enough to know that his presence in the bank was a hardship for John, a visible indictment of John's tenure.

There was no way for Mike to know the insecurity that swept through the whole fabric of the bank, especially the the sixty-seventh floor. Even these men who had clawed up the slippery cliffs of promotion to arrive at the bank's senior executive suites did not feel secure. The winds of subterfuge and maneuver, the continual shuffling for better positions on the edge of the aerie were terribly enervating, sapping energy for more productive effort. Hiding behind bland smiles, these men were witness to insidious intrigues that had ruined many a career, and made life at the highest levels of FMB murderously political, and for the most part malignant, pernicious, and unhappy.

"Have you spent most of your time in the oil business?"

"Except for a brief tour at Schraders."

"The merchant bank?"

"That's right, Mr. Salisbury. That's where I ran into Dutch. I had an engineering degree from Cambridge, and was working on some petroleum financings at Schraders. Dutch's company had a large piece of a consortium, and we saw a lot of each other during the negotiations. Dutch and I became good friends and he made me an offer. I liked the idea of being a part of a large privately held multinational company, and especially a company where the lines of authority are so short." Mike smiled and reached for a thin Dutch cigar. "Do you mind if I smoke?"

"Not at all. Please do."

John thought of Mike's remark about short lines of authority. He understood clearly what Giles was referring to. At PTM Pacific, Dutch made the big decisions, no one else. He reflected for a moment upon the labyrinthian decision-making processes at FMB, and wondered whether or not they could be made more effective.

They had been skirting around the edges of why Mike Giles was sitting in the office of the chairman of FMB instead of in his own office in Houston running Dutch's oil group.

Finally, John broke the ice. His manner was hesitant, as if he were approaching something he didn't want to touch, something that would be unpleasant and cause him pain.

He was faced with the possible resignation of the chairman of his executive committee and the other two outside directors who served with Dutch if he didn't replace Doug. The resignation of three of FMB's most important outside directors was unthinkable.

He hadn't mentioned it to Dutch or to anyone else, but he was giving some thought to moving Doug into the position of vice-chairman, kicking him upstairs, as they would say on the Street.

He was still not convinced that FMB was drifting because of Doug. He was beginning to acknowledge, but only to himself, and only during those nights when he lay awake, unable to sleep, that perhaps he was responsible for the negative progress of the bank. These disquieting inquisitions hurt his pride and his self-esteem, but they were becoming an idea that wouldn't leave him alone. And now, looking at this young man with the carefully cut reddish-brown hair, the charming, urbane manner, seeing in Michael Giles the hammer of Dutch's anvil, John viewed Michael as a very mixed blessing.

"How do you see yourself operating within the bank? We're not exactly unfamiliar around here with consultants or study groups."

Mike's expression changed. The light blue eyes became intent; the lean lines of his face seemed to harden slightly. John could see the jaw muscles contract as he watched Michael frame his thoughts carefully in reply.

"This is something I've spent a good deal of time thinking about, Mr. Salisbury. I'm certainly not going to approach this as a consultant; that's not my area, and, quite frankly, I simply can't afford to give this project that much time. I don't mean in any way to denigrate the importance of what I'm being asked to do, but I do have a rather significant responsibility at PTM. I'm sure you understand."

John nodded.

"But to answer your question more completely, Dutch has given me his version of what he conceives to be some of your problems here."

John was annoyed by this; he felt imposed upon by Dutch.

"It seems to me," Mike went on, "that it would be useful to talk with Mr. Dowding and with some other key members of your management committee, especially Mr. Bernays, and then with the heads of your international and corporate banks. I would appreciate your setting up these appointments as soon as possible, Mr. Salisbury."

John's impressions of Michael Giles were beginning to solidify. There was steel and know-how beneath the charm. That he was able and bright seemed obvious; that he could penetrate the defenses of the men he wanted to see was a more difficult conjecture. That he could do this effectively, without raising too much dust, was even more unlikely. But John knew that Dutch would expect Michael Giles to get the cooperation he needed. John felt he could accomplish this for Giles as he expected to get most things done, by fiat. But John was not a part of the Old Boy group, the network with its fluid alliances, its tenuous social relationships, its cruel intrigues. He was above all that—apart from it, removed. That was one of the principal reasons he couldn't control this bank. It was his lack of understanding and acknowledgment of that pernicious malignancy that so seriously affected FMB.

The bulletproof clear plastic doors opened. A reluctant and hostile Douglas Dowding walked into the room.

Mike knew by instinct and experience that after his luncheon with John and Doug his mission would be all over the bank within days.

He didn't have time to waste hanging around New York waiting to indulge the sensibilities of FMB's officers, because of his own pressing responsibilities to PTM. He didn't want this job, God knows, but Dutch had stuck him with it. There was nothing to do but go in there and get his hands dirty. John's secretary had left a message at the Pierre that he had a morning appointment with Dan Bernays tomorrow, and a luncheon with Walston Cooper. John had been surprisingly quick to respond to the demands of Mike's schedule. On his own initative Mike had made a date with Clifford Rayburn to get the viewpoint of a junior officer of the bank.

Mike knew Cliff from Houston. Cliff had solicited his business as a lending officer in the bank's petroleum group, but PTM's money management was so sophisticated they rarely

needed a commercial bank for their normal business requirements; their only need for assistance from FMB or any bank
was to finance special projects that their own internal cash
flow might not be able to handle on a current basis.

This was an old story to Cliff and to banks in general.
The companies they most desired to lend money to usually
were banks within themselves, and rarely used anywhere near
their full credit potential with the commercial banks. The
ingenuity of men like Cliff Rayburn was severely taxed in
trying to dream up reasons for the best credits to borrow
money. It wasn't easy.

Now Mike Giles wanted something from Cliff—information. Cliff's attitude was one of surface cordiality and guarded
conversation.

"So they've got you poking around this bank instead of running Dutch's oil group. That's a switch."

Mike laughed easily, but there was no warmth in the light
blue eyes. "I must admit I find it rather strange myself. My
only apology is a direct order from my boss, who just happens to be chairman of the executive committee of your
board."

Cliff lit a pipe. Mike watched the square-shaped face, the
rather set mouth, the thinning dark hair that was combed
from right to left over the pink skull of Clifford Rayburn.
But most of all Mike watched the brown eyes that kept looking away from him.

Mike, backlighted by the morning light from the tall windows in Cliff's office, took out a slim metal box of Dutch
cigars and lit one. The smoke drifted between them.

"Does Coop know you're seeing me?"

"You mean Walston Cooper?" Mike asked.

"The head of our corporate bank."

"I don't know if he's aware of this meeting with you or
not. Why? Should he be?"

Cliff Rayburn laughed. It wasn't a humorous laugh; it was

a statement of sarcasm. He turned to Mike. "You know, Mike, I find all this very strange."

"So do I."

"It's not like this bank to let an outsider prowl around in here, especially a non-banker."

"I would think a non-banker might have a different point of view. Perhaps that's what the board wants."

"I'm sure that's not what Salisbury or Dowding wants. Somebody must have sure twisted their arms to get you in here."

Mike tried to keep his tone light, but he felt the defenses of Cliff Rayburn like a physical presence in the room.

"If I were to ask you what you felt was wrong with this bank, what would you say?"

Cliff looked at Mike in surprise. "You really mean that? Right out in the open, just like that?"

"That's right."

"You've got to be kidding. You think you can come in here and learn the politics of this place in a few meetings. You've got to be out of your skull, sport. This place would make Washington look like summer camp."

Cliff looked at Mike carefully. "You know, Mike," he said, his tone becoming serious. "I've spent seven years in this bank. I came to it right out of Wharton. I've been exposed to more study groups, more task forces working on problems, more consultants, more bosses than I can count. Do you know that in the last seven years I've had five bosses? And no matter how many reorganizations we have around here, it's still the same chilly valley. People get moved around like a shell game. As soon as someone gets enough management background in a job to begin to know a little bit about what he's supposed to do, they'll transfer him to another job, supposedly a better one in the so-called upward mobility thrusting that goes on here. And the poor bastard will have to spend another two years finding out how to do his new job.

"Mike, this is a place of continual change, and yet we seem to keep making the same old mistakes. And you think you're going to get the answers by talking to a few guys like me. You're kidding yourself, Mike. We're not going to open up to you; we can't afford to." He hesitated. "You think that I should be cooperative and spill my guts out to you because you come in here representing the board. Well, this may come as a shock to you, my friend, but I don't work for the board. I work for Walston Cooper. And in the corporate bank, if you want to stay employed, you do things Cooper's way. And Coop's way is to talk only to him if you have any problems; then he decides if and when you should talk to anyone else.

"I'm sorry, Mike, but after you go, there will be some other guy coming in here asking essentially the same questions, and not getting any better answers than you're getting from me." He watched the blue eyes for a clue; they seemed cold and penetrating to Clifford Rayburn.

"It's protect thine ass around here, Mike, or you can get it kicked, and Coop kicks like a mule."

Mike smoked leisurely for a few moments.

"So what you're telling me in essence is to mind my own business because your Mr. Walston Cooper doesn't like anyone making waves in his ocean."

"You got it."

"That's an interesting point of view. Do you think it's relatively common in the corporate bank?"

"Pretty much so."

"Are you aware of how FMB stacks up against the other major New York banks?"

"Of course."

"Are you particularly satisfied with the performance of this bank?"

"Certainly not."

"Are you saying that if others give their time and effort,

such as your directors, who happen to represent the stockholders who own this bank, you're not willing to assist them?"

"I didn't say that."

Mike's posture in his chair was his usual relaxed semi-lounge, but there was nothing relaxed about the edge that had come into his voice.

"That's the only possible inference I can draw. Your attitude, which seems predicated on the rather restrictive philosophy of protecting your own ass, seems to me to make it somewhat difficult to see where you're going." He put out the small cigar, which had burned close to his fingers.

"I of course can leave here, Cliff, without learning any more from you than I already have, but I'd like to suggest that might not be in the best interest of protecting your ass."

Cliff's eyes were now fixed on Mike. He was searching his mind trying to decide who had the clout; was it Giles or Walston Cooper? He knew that if he told Giles anything that would negatively affect Coop, it could get back to Coop, and there would be hell to pay. On the other hand, this guy Giles sounded like he didn't kid around. He'd have to have had Salisbury's O.K. to come in here as well as Dowding's. He represented the most powerful committee of the board. Jesus Christ, Cliff Rayburn thought, don't these bastards ever leave you alone?

Mike was watching carefully. He thought he saw just the slightest change in Cliff's attitude. He looked at his watch. "What are you doing for lunch?"

"I've got a date."

"Is it very important?"

"Relatively."

"Could you break it without too much inconvenience?"

"I suppose so."

"Why don't you cancel it. We'll eat outside the bank. What time would be convenient for you?"

This son of a bitch was really banging his balls, Cliff

thought, but something in Mike's manner told him he'd better cancel his lunch.

"How about in an hour?"

Mike got up slowly. The blue eyes were far from friendly.

"Why don't we make it at the Petroleum Club?" he said. "That should be far enough from the bank to suit you."

Mike left.

Cliff kept looking at his open door.

That prick is a real ball breaker, Cliff thought, and he inwardly groaned at this no-win luncheon he was about to have with Michael Giles. In the paranoid environment of FMB, Cliff Rayburn felt his ass was exposed. The chill drafts were not solely in his imagination.

Mike was having a drink in the bar of the Pierre, after a grim day of walking the long beige corridors of FMB, when Dutch's call came from Seattle.

"We've got to resolve this FMB thing, Mike. I know you've got to raise some hackles to do any good there, but that can't be helped. I don't have time for you to waste. I need that job done at FMB and I need you back in Houston. So get your ass into high gear, boy, and keep moving."

As a result of Dutch's colorful admonitions, Mike altered his intention of talking to more of the bank's junior officers. He had made an appointment with two of the bank's key men. He knew he was entering a mine field, but with Dutch breathing down his neck he had no choice.

The office of Daniel Bernays was like the other executive suites in size, on the sixty-seventh floor of the FMB building. The offices differed from one another in color and choice of furnishings, and in the art selected by their present occupants.

The bank had a large investment in paintings and pieces of sculpture, and the bank's senior executives could choose from a wide variety of oils and artifacts as long as the overall decorative effect met with the approval of the art department. This precaution was an attempt on the part of the bank to keep its executives (or their wives) who might be lacking in good taste, or any taste, from creating eyesores that would offend John's sense of the aesthetic.

Michael Giles had an appointment to talk to Bernays, who was a member of the bank management committee, and to whom the heads of the international and corporate banks reported. He was Walston Cooper's boss.

It was ten-thirty, and Mike was waiting in the office of Dan Bernays, who was tied up in a management committee meeting.

Mike had a chance to look around Dan's office. The walls were hung with two large Japanese paintings, and on the circular conference table stood a plastic cube with the Japanese symbol of harmonizing differences. From what Mike had heard about Bernays, this seemed to describe a part of his character. He was a conciliator, as were many of the FMB executives who had reached the sixty-seventh floor.

"I'm terribly sorry to have kept you waiting."

Mike got up to take the hand Bernays extended to him, and noted the broad smile, the prominent teeth, the dark brown eyes that smiled less, behind horn-rimmed glasses.

"No trouble at all. I'm sorry to interrupt what I'm sure is a busy schedule."

Dan motioned to the couch. Mike selected a chair. He took out one of his thin, dry Dutch cigars from the slim metal box that he carried in his side pocket. "May I offer you one?"

"I don't smoke, thank you. I'm sorry I couldn't have lunch with you, but I have a date I just can't break."

Dan settled back and looked at Mike, who was still smiling. He reminded Mike of two things: the Cheshire Cat and a piranha. Dan Bernays had an easy charm that could be very deceptive. Mike knew his background and his accomplishments in the bank, and they were impressive.

"I hear you're having lunch with Cooper."

"That's right." The grapevine was very effective, Mike thought.

"Well," said Dan Bernays, spreading his fingers across his knees, "we've heard a lot about you and your unusual mission."

Mike laughed. "I hope at least some of it was complimentary."

Dan measured the light blue eyes that were measuring him. He found little warmth there. He quickly decided that Michael Giles smiled easily, but that his surface cordiality was not reflected from within.

"Yes. Your reputation as an emissary of Dutch's is rather impressive."

"I'm afraid Dutch is prejudiced. We've been together a long time."

Dan was not one for prolonged chitchat, and he had the conversational habit of waiting until whoever he was talking to began speaking first. It was an irritating but useful ploy that didn't escape Mike's notice.

"Dan, I keep apologizing to all of your people that I've talked to that my being here is an embarrassment for me. If it weren't for Dutch's insistence, I'd be back in Houston minding my own business."

The Cheshire Cat smiled and nodded his head.

"But since I have been asked to gain an impression of how this bank is functioning, I'd like to be somewhat direct, if I may. It will save us both some time, and hopefully help me to accomplish what I believe the board has directed me to do."

At the mention of the board, the Cheshire Cat's smile disappeared, and his face became intent.

"An impression I got from talking to one of your officers, Dan, is that this bank functions on a collective decision-making basis, much more so than would be the case, say, in my company, or, for that matter, in several of the banks I'm familiar with. Would you say that's a fair statement, and, if so, how do you think it affects this bank?"

Dan thought about that for a while. "I would have to agree that the bank does lean toward a collective decision-making apparatus, but Doug still makes most of the operating decisions around here. John, of course, is very influential in establishing the broad policies of the bank."

Mike tipped his cigar and put it out in the ashtray on the low glass table in front of the couch.

He thought for a moment. "I read a report last night which showed that this bank has spent a good deal of time and money studying and reorganizing its merchant banking effort. The operation you started in London, Dan, has been quite successful, and I gather that a considerable amount of effort had been expended on your domestic merchant banking program. Yet, that has been discontinued, in spite of the fact that general loan demand is off and the services an American merchant banking group could offer would generate fees that don't use the bank's capital. Why was that allowed to disintegrate?"

Dan thought about the implications of Mike's question. All of the major New York banks offered extensive services to their clients that helped generate business and that didn't require the use of the bank's capital; these services included arranging long-term loans with insurance companies, leasing big-ticket items, such as airplanes, railroad cars, and other capital equipment, and helping with corporate mergers and acquisitions. In Europe this merchant banking effort extended as well to underwriting syndicated loans, which meant that the banks involved would guarantee, or underwrite, to lend the necessary funds to a borrower.

A merchant banking activity was of increasing importance to major American banks, and FMB, after having successfully created such an effort in Europe, headquartered in

London, attempted to do the same thing in the United States,
within the restrictions of United States law. But when Arthur
Perry, who had headed the corporate bank, left FMB, his
successor, Walston Cooper, dissolved the domestic merchant
banking group. Mike knew that the real reasons behind this
were one of the malignancies that infected FMB. It was a
very touchy subject around the bank.

"The merchant banking effort in the United States reports
to Cooper. He decided to parcel most of it out to London,
which has done the best job. I didn't want to interfere with
his decision."

Mike remained thoughtful for a minute. "Wouldn't it have
made sense to put the two efforts together under a single
head and have that person report directly to you? Why
should such a decision be left to the corporate bank when
they have very little knowledge of merchant banking?"

It was a damn good question, and Dan had a faraway look
in his eyes as he thought about the real reasons for the de-
mise of the American merchant banking activity. They were
principally two: a political decision on his own part not to
rock Cooper's boat, and Cooper's suspicion that the head of
American merchant banking posed a personal threat to him.

Mike had suspected, after his conversations with others on
a lower level, that the breakup of merchant banking had
been effected with little regard for what was best for FMB or
its stockholders. It was just this kind of mismanagement that
Mike had been sent to uncover.

"My suggestion, Mike," said Dan, "is to take this up with
Cooper at lunch. It was his decision, and he should tell you
about it."

Walston Cooper's private dining room looked north, over
the sprawling vertical towers of Manhattan and the weathered
gray waterfront areas of New Jersey, whose aging piers pro-
truded into the Hudson River. The river wound north past

the twin towers of the World Trade Center, past the new as well as the ancient docks of Manhattan that berthed ships from all over the world.

The light from the midday sun came from a cloudless azure sky to reflect off the thousands of windows of Manhattan's towers.

Mike Giles had talked carefully with Cooper. The latter was not communicative. He was wary, protective, secretive, and obviously not enjoying his lunch. Hostile, suspicious gray eyes stared out from a fleshy, perspiring face. More often than not, they were averted from the penetrating gaze of Michael Giles.

"Would it be a fair statement, Mr. Cooper, that the corporate bank is somewhat lacking in what I might choose to call vertical communication?"

"I don't think that's an accurate statement at all. I think communications within the corporate bank are excellent."

Mike waited a long minute.

"If I told you, Mr. Cooper, that some of your junior officers feel it's not in their interest to discuss any of the corporate bank's problems without your permission, would you think that's good communication?"

"I think it's damn good policy. We can't have the officers of this bank washing the bank's linen in public. What purpose does that serve?"

"I wasn't aware, sir, that I was considered a member of the public. I was under the distinct impression that I was authorized by the chairman of the executive committee of the board, and through it by your chairman and president, to gather information about this bank that might be helpful to the board." Cooper started to speak, but the blue eyes were coldly fixed upon him, and a slim hand was held up, which indicated to Walston Cooper that its owner had not quite finished.

"Do you consider your stockholders to be outsiders?"

Cooper folded his napkin, looking for the hook in that question.

"In a way I do. They have their money invested in the bank, but for the most part they are almost totally ignorant about how a multinational bank is run."

"And the directors who represent their interests—how much better informed are most of them?" asked Mike.

Cooper's eyes were down; his mouth was compressed into a hard line. "Not a great deal more. Oh, our directors know from the borrower's side how a bank like ours functions, but their knowledge of the actual workings of this bank is not very substantial."

"Then I assume, Mr. Cooper, that anything that would help to inform or educate the directors would be useful?"

Walston Cooper shrugged. "I suppose so."

Mike smoked quietly, but was relentless. He was making an enemy, but there was no way to avoid that with a man like Walston Cooper. Cooper could only be obsequious to his superiors, tolerant toward those who agreed with him, and devastating to those who fed his paranoia. Walston Cooper was the incarnate manifestation of the Peter Principle; he had no flair, no style, and very little talent.

"What might have been your reasons for disbanding the American merchant banking operation? As I understand it, a great deal of time, effort, and money went into that, and if I'm not mistaken, it was one of the few truly innovative services this bank has come up with."

Cooper's face flushed red. "I didn't disband the thing. I put it where it belonged, with the London group. And I don't know what the hell was so innovative about it. It had a bunch of fancy guys who were paid a lot of money and weren't doing much. The merchant banking group wasn't just pulled apart; it was a carefully thought out reallocation of resources."

Mike didn't press further. He had gotten what he came for. He stood up; there was no smile on his face. He did not extend his hand to Walston Cooper. He hadn't even waited until the customary two o'clock, when these luncheons normally broke up.

Mike had met too many Walston Coopers. When he spotted them in his own business, he tried to weed them out. They were sick people who ruled by fear, and their influence was usually corrosive.

Not once had Mike called Walston Cooper by his first name.

"It's been a very informative luncheon, Mr. Cooper."

Mike excused himself and left the rather short, corpulent man wondering what in hell that lanky bastard was going to tell Dutch Dernberg.

THE MIDMORNING WAS GRAY WITH A BITTER WIND AND occasional sprinkles of showers. It was a marvelous day to be leaving New York for the Caribbean.

The thought of getting out of the bank was like a tonic to Doug. With Mike Giles prowling around, it was an embarrassment to be in the goddamn place.

Doug had called Noel Aragon in London and told him that if his invitation was still open, he could make it for this weekend. Noel had lunged at the opportunity like a hungry barracuda.

He and Joan were to meet Noel Aragon at Butler Aviation at LaGuardia. His jet would take them on the approximately eighteen-hundred-mile flight to St. Thomas, and then they would go by boat to St. John.

Doug had discussed this meeting with John, who had urged him to go. They both felt that if the deal were solid and the bank could participate in the financing, it was worth Doug's time to pursue it. This contract that Peter was attempting to close might be the answer to both their problems. If Doug was successful in getting the bank involved, no one on the board, including Dutch, would seek his resignation.

The project was too big. It would be too important to the bank.

His limousine pulled to the curb, and he saw Joan standing just inside the entrance of NBT. His chauffeur got out with an umbrella and struggled with the gusts of wind as he took Joan's suitcase and guided her to the warmth of the car.

"Well, Doug, once again you're full of surprises. I must admit this is a marvelous one; to get out of New York for some sun does wonders for my morale."

He laughed. "It doesn't hurt mine, either."

They had worked their way to the East Side in the late-morning traffic. If they were lucky, they would make La-Guardia in half an hour.

"Is this going to become a habit, your taking me to faraway places?"

"Do you mind it?"

She laughed. "I certainly have no objection. It's a novel way to cover the president of a bank."

Noel was standing near the entrance of the terminal, reading the *Journal*, when they arrived. He saw Joan, her coat over her arm, and made a quick, detailed examination of her face and figure. He smiled inwardly. Mr. Dowding had brought along quite a guest.

"You're early, Doug. Splendid." Noel advanced, his soft hand extended, a practiced smile of welcome on his face.

"Joan Hopkins, our host, Noel Aragon."

Joan, who in heels was considerably taller than Mr. Aragon, shook his hand and gave him her most attractive smile. She found his manner unctuous. His stooped aspect with those averted dark eyes alerted her.

God almighty, Noel thought, she's magnificent.

"It's kind of you to allow me to tag along, Mr. Aragon."

"I can assure you it is my pleasure. You will brighten the whole island."

Doug noticed a man in uniform with two gold stripes on

his arm waiting discreetly behind Noel. As Noel turned toward him, he advanced quickly.

"This is our flight engineer, Mr. Dan Riley. Dan, will you take their cases out to the courtesy car?"

Mr. Riley smiled at Doug and Joan, and touched his cap in a brief salute. "Yes, sir."

Flight engineer, Doug thought. What kind of plane do these birds have? Even the bank only operated their jet with a pilot and copilot.

"Is everybody ready? We might as well start."

"All set, Noel." Doug took Joan's arm and then followed Noel to the courtesy car.

Doug was used to the business jets and small general aviation aircraft that were usually parked on the ramp of the Butler facility, but he noticed a Boeing 737, a medium-range commercial airliner, and realized that they were driving toward it. The plane looked enormous beside the smaller ones.

When they entered the aircraft, Doug couldn't help being impressed. An entire commercial airliner capable of carrying a hundred and twenty-five people had been outfitted to form nothing less than a flying executive headquarters, only this one was complete with bedrooms. These were not just sleeping facilities; they were actual bedrooms.

There were long couches and conference tables on both sides of the aircraft, as well as individual chairs. Forward were latticed partitions which formed separate conference areas with large high-backed swivel chairs.

There was a complete bar, galley facilities, and an elaborate air-to-ground communications system.

The whole interior was done in varying shades of blue, which, with the carefully concealed lighting, gave a cool, tranquil impression.

Doug had spent a lot of time on corporate aircraft, but he had never seen anything like this.

A very attractive uniformed flight attendant with a slim but arresting figure came toward them.

"Where would you like to sit?" asked Noel.

Doug looked around. Joan was completely astonished. She had never seen anything even vaguely approaching the ostentation of this airplane. It was a twentieth-century version of the Arabian Nights.

"Do you think we have enough room, Noel?"

Noel laughed. "I agree it looks a bit much with only three passengers, but Mr. Ageel often has this plane filled to capacity on business trips. He's always on the go, and he uses this as an alternate executive headquarters."

Doug motioned toward the forward end of the aircraft, where he saw high-backed swivel chairs grouped around a circular table. "Perhaps that might be a little cozier, Noel."

They walked forward and sat down; the flight attendant, with a surprising, immaculate British accent, asked them if they would like some champagne.

"Joanie?"

She looked at Doug. "Will you have some?"

"I sure will. Let's start this trip off right."

"I'll join you."

It began to dawn on Doug, who knew a good deal about the cost of operating an aircraft, that Ali Ageel had not parted with his flying office casually. He realized that the plane had probably been flown over from London for the express purpose of taking them to St. John.

This would turn out to be quite an expensive trip for Ageel, and Doug had been around too long to know that there was no such thing as a free lunch.

They were drinking champagne as the plane taxied to the runway for takeoff. Joan was still in a state of shock.

"How long will it take us to get to St. John, Mr. Aragon?" Joan asked.

Noel was sitting opposite Doug and Joan, his mind occupied with wondering what role Joan played in the life of Douglas Dowding. Ali had briefed him thoroughly on Doug, and Noel knew there was a Mrs. Dowding, who was seriously ill. This full-bodied, magnificent woman in front of him— could she be the "woman trouble" Ali had referred to?

"About four and a half hours, Miss Hopkins. We can't fly to St. John. We have to land at St. Thomas and go over by boat."

Doug had never met Ali, but he knew him by reputation. He had heard about this flying palace, but being in it was something else again. What Doug knew about Ageel was not necessarily uncomplimentary, but bankers are usually uneasy with obvious ostentation; they are skillful, but less theatrical, at contriving the same effects.

The hell with it, Doug thought. He would enjoy the flight.

They were flying over the Atlantic with the east coast of the United States passing rapidly below them. They would come close to the Carolinas and Florida, then fly in an east-southeasterly direction over the Bahamas, Haiti and the Dominican Republic, Puerto Rico, and finally St. Thomas.

They had switched from champagne to the best malt Scotch whisky Doug had drunk in a long time. Joan had never drunk Scotch of this quality before, and never like this— with just spring water, no ice. It was very special.

Conversation was stilted because Doug and Joan knew Noel too superficially to overcome their reticence until the effects of the alcohol had bridged their separation.

Doug excused himself to go up to the cockpit and talk to the flight crew. He wanted to see what type of electronic gear kept this bird moving in the right direction.

Noel was waiting for just such an opportunity.

"So, Miss Hopkins. Might I ask what you do?"

"I'm an assistant producer with NBT."

"That sounds very interesting."

"It is."

"I assume you meet a good many people."

"That's one of the attractions of my job, Mr. Aragon."

She had pointedly refrained from telling Noel that she was associated with the news department at NBT.

"Do you get to travel?"

"My fair share. But hardly like this."

Noel smiled. She was captivating. He liked tall women, and this one seemed to have the social graces to go along with a stunning face and figure.

Noel's instincts told him not to pry. She was far too bright, and would immediately discern any attempts on his part to learn more about her relationship with Doug.

"I dislike leaving such an attractive lady alone, Miss Hopkins, but I do have several calls to put through. I wonder if you would be good enough to excuse me for a while."

"You go right ahead, Mr. Aragon. I'll just sit here and enjoy this incredible experience."

"So kind of you." Noel walked toward the rear of the plane and the communications console.

Doug came back from the cockpit. "They've got everything up there but NASA," he said.

"My God, Doug. What does this man do?"

"If you mean Noel, he's the number-one boy for Ali Ageel. Ageel is a kind of broker who represents several companies in the United States, Japan, the United Kingdom, West Germany, France, Italy, and so on. He's close to his king and is able to make the communications and technical bridges between his own feudal society and the advanced countries of the West. He is handsomely rewarded, I might add, for these skills and connections."

They had a succulent filet mignon for lunch, with a bottle of Château Margaux 1953. They continued to drink as the Boeing flew toward the string of islands that wind through the Caribbean and the Atlantic to curve like a lazy diagonally slanted S, and nearly touch the northeastern edge of Venezuela.

* * *

As they lost altitude on their approach to St. Thomas, Joan noticed the clusters of cumulus clouds that cast purple shadows on the surface of the sea. She saw an occasional whitecap and realized that the surface winds must be brisk.

She felt the shudder of the big plane as it raised its spoilers and lowered its gear and flaps on approach for landing. The turbulence below the cloud level was giving them some moderate bumps.

She saw the emerald green of the island's foliage and the scattered white houses that seemed a part of the dark hills. The island had been vigorously developed, with clusters of houses and hotels bordering its largest port, Charlotte Amalie.

Suddenly they were low over the blue water, which became aqua, then green near the white beaches.

She could see a part of the runway and the mountain that seemed to be at its opposite end. She didn't know anything about flying, but she had enough common sense to know this was a dangerous approach.

When they had reached the general aviation area and the plane had cut its engines, Doug looked at his watch. It was three-forty-five exactly.

Noel waited for the flight attendant to open the door and the ground crew to secure the movable stairway.

Their coats had been taken by the flight attendant, and as they descended the stairs, Joan was struck with the humid, eighty-degree temperature and the strong warm breeze that blew at her hair.

They walked through the airport to a large air-conditioned limousine that was waiting to take them to Charlotte Amalie.

They had been a careful trio on the flight down. Joan was cautious lest Aragon discover her true role at NBT. Doug was not facile at small talk and, though pleasant, remained somewhat distant toward Noel, more so than Aragon would have liked. Doug had not had enough time to separate himself from the vines that entangled his life.

Noel's intuition told him it was not judicious to discuss his business with Doug as yet; it was far too soon. He had designed this whole weekend to dissolve the suspicions, if any, of Douglas Dowding and to arrive at a level of relationship with the president of FMB that might create in him some sense of obligation. If Noel Aragon could effect this, he could broach to Doug the real purpose of this elaborate seduction.

The limousine moved smoothly into the congested traffic of Charlotte Amalie. A large white cruise ship was anchored in the harbor, and its eight hundred passengers added to the noise and congestion that reminded Doug of New York.

The car proceeded to the quay, where it stopped. The chauffeur took their luggage, walking awkwardly under his heavy load behind Noel.

"Would you follow me, please?"

"We're with you, Noel."

Doug had acquired the habit, which Joan found annoying, of holding her arm when they walked together. She kept her dislike for this disconcerting behavior to herself.

They walked along the cement quay with its noise, its marine traffic, its brown pelicans and skimming gulls, and its view of the crescent-shaped harbor that faced the pink and white hotels and stores that crowded the edge of the waterfront.

As they approached the ketch, Doug saw that the yacht must be nearly seventy-five feet in length. Her brightwork glistened like an operating room, and at the sight of Noel a uniformed member of the crew dressed in a white short-sleeved shirt, shorts, knee socks, and deck shoes moved quickly down the gangway to greet them and take their luggage on board.

Doug was again surprised. He had expected a small launch to take them across Pillsbury Sound to St. John, not this deepwater vessel that was built to cruise the oceans of the world.

A sun awning had been rigged over the aft portion of the deck, and a table and chairs were set for three.

The crewman smiled at Noel and his guests. "Nice to have you aboard again, sir."

"Thank you, Harold."

Noel stepped aside to allow Joan to board first.

"It's a short run, Joan, so we can have some tea if you like."

He turned to Doug.

"Welcome aboard the *Ka'ba*, Doug."

Doug had been aboard John's yacht many times, and it was almost the size of the *Ka'ba*, but the luxury of this vessel made John's seem almost spartan by comparison.

"I must say, Noel, that your Mr. Ageel certainly knows how to live."

Noel smiled again. "We put the *Ka'ba*, just like the plane, to very good use, Doug."

"I'll bet you do."

They seated themselves around a table in the shade of the deck awning.

From below came the uniformed captain, who was dressed in white like the crewman but who wore an unmistakable air of authority. He was in his early forties, deeply tanned, tall, with full dark hair and light blue eyes. He was a very handsome man.

"Hello, sir. Good to have you with us again." His accent, too, was British.

Noel turned to Doug and Joan.

"Captain Roger Morgan. Miss Joan Hopkins, Mr. Douglas Dowding."

A muscled, tanned hand reached for Doug's in a firm, strong handshake.

"Pleasure to have you aboard, sir." He turned to Joan and

bowed slightly. "We're pleased to have you with us, Miss Hopkins. We'll try to make your brief stay as pleasant as we can."

The engines had already started. Ali had a passion for redundance in case of emergencies, and had twin diesels fitted in the *Ka'ba*. She could cruise under power at eight knots for over sixteen hundred miles if she had to. The crew moved expertly and silently, casting off mooring lines as first the stern and then the bow of the *Ka'ba* began to swing slowly away from the quay.

From below came a tall blond woman dressed in a horizontally striped blue and white long-sleeved shirt and white flared sailor's trousers that were tailored to fit the rounded contours of her hips and derriere. Her long blond hair was tied behind her head with a piece of blue ribbon. She too was deeply tanned. Her breasts were full and heavy, and she wore no bra. Her nipples pressed visibly against the thin cotton pullover, and as she walked toward them her breasts moved unencumbered.

She obviously had the attention of Doug and Noel; Joan viewed her with instant covert hostility.

"May I present my wife, Katherine, gentlemen?"

They both stood up; Joan remained seated. Katherine Morgan, in an accent slightly North German, greeted Doug and Noel with firm handshakes, and smiled pleasantly at Joan.

"We're very pleased to have you with us."

They had moved out of the harbor, and the yacht began to roll slightly. The sea had turned a dark blue. St. Thomas was on their port side as they headed toward Long Point and Pillsbury Sound. Water Island was to starboard. Doug watched a crewman swing the yacht toward St. John.

"It's only a short haul and a beat at that, Mr. Dowding, so we're not going to raise sail," said Captain Morgan. "Might I suggest some iced tea, or something a little more exciting?"

"I'd like some tea, Captain, but make mine hot," said Noel.

Joan was cool under the deck awning with an eighteen-knot breeze blowing.

"I'll second that, Captain," she said.

Captain Roger Morgan saw that Joan was shivering in the stiffening breeze. The yacht was pitching slightly as it picked up speed, heading into a quartering sea.

"Captain, if you can come up with a daiquiri, I'd love one," said Doug.

Captain Morgan disappeared briefly below, and came back with one of his wife's sweaters for Joan.

"Thank you so much, Captain. It's a little chilly out here."

"Yes, it can be when it breezes up and you're out of the sun." He turned to Doug and Noel. "Are you gentlemen comfortable?"

"Tip-top."

"Just great, Captain, thanks."

"Would you like to see where you're going?" He reached into a port locker and drew out a pair of binoculars. He handed them to Joan, who looked at the purple bulge off the starboard bow and brought it into focus through the eight-power lenses.

The heavy yacht took the seas gracefully, lifting her bow in easy thrusts while she settled back again, spreading white foam behind her in a wake of deep blue green frothed with white.

They entered Cruz Bay on St. John slowly, Captain Morgan now at the helm, conning the large vessel into the anchorage he wanted.

Doug heard the engines go into a slow reverse and the chain rattle up forward as the anchor plunged for the bottom.

Joan watched the crew swing out an eighteen-foot Boston Whaler with a big outboard motor. The anchorage was calm. A crew member rigged an elaborate ladder complete with handrail and suggested that Joan take her shoes off before attempting to get into the launch.

At the quay in Cruz Bay, Joan noticed the squat steeple of the pink church in the square, the languid pace of the blacks as they moved or talked in their incomprehensible patois, and the Land Rover with a khaki-uniformed driver in British walking shorts.

Joan and Doug followed Noel to the Land Rover.

"Hello, George."

"Hello, sir."

"This is Miss Hopkins, and Mr. Douglas Dowding."

George shook hands with Doug, looking very much like the Guards sergeant he used to be before he was recruited out of the service by Noel.

"George is the only one of us down here who is indispensable, Doug. He runs the place, keeps everyone in line. Even Captain Morgan reports to him."

George seemed to blush through his ruddy tan. He had sandy graying hair and kind eyes, but the six-foot-two ramrod-straight ex-Guardsman was flat-bellied and extremely fit for a middle-aged man, and there was an air of quiet competence and authority about George that impressed Doug.

"You're too kind, sir."

George hefted the luggage into the back of the Land Rover, and they all got in.

The drive along the main road of the island took them over volcanic hills, winding under green overhanging trees and wild vines that made Joan feel remote from the benign civilization of Cruz Bay.

When they reached what appeared to be the top of the island, George turned left onto a dirt road rutted from the daily sporadic rain showers that kept these islands so verdant.

They came to a large iron gate that had been left open, and drove onto a well-kept private drive that was bordered with high bushes of pink, yellow, and red hibiscus.

The house was built from local stone. As they approached, Doug saw its flat, sprawling roof, which had been designed to take winds of up to a hundred and fifty miles an hour. It was a great comfort during the hurricane season.

On their left was what could only be described as a field of poinsettias; their brilliant red contrasted with the azure of the sky and the mist blue of the whitecapped sea far below.

The house had been built on a slope of land that was part of the highest peak of one of the two mountains that made up the inner land mass of St. John.

As they got out of the Land Rover, Joan was overwhelmed by the beauty of the view.

The house looked out toward Sir Francis Drake's Channel and the British Virgin Islands. Joan could see Jost Van Dyke in front of her and Tortola off to her right, like purple landfalls that seemed to rise from the sea. She was captivated by the scenery, the high clouds, the soaring frigate birds, the soft yet gusty breezes that blew at her hair. She was enchanted.

She turned to Doug. "Oh, Doug! It's the most beautiful spot I've ever seen!"

He felt the same way.

"Do you ever tire of this, George?" he asked.

"Well, sir, even paradise can become a little commonplace when you live in it year round. I do enjoy getting back to England now and then."

His remark caused both of them to think about what he had just said as he took their luggage into the house. Joan wondered if she could ever tire of this scenery, this climate. She thought about it for a while and grudgingly conceded that perhaps one could become bored with anything after a while, even paradise.

The house was a lovely hilltop hideaway. They entered a hallway that gave entrance to a large dining and living room whose windows were panels of special glass needed to withstand the heavy winds; they brought the magnificence of the view to the comfort of the house.

The servants' quarters were in a separate wing to the right; George's room was off the central hall on the right adjacent to the kitchen. To the left of the hall was a large office that Doug assumed was used by Noel.

Noel guided Joan to what was obviously Ali's bedroom, which overlooked the sea, and Doug to a connecting room just behind it; it was a smaller room but with the same view. A separate outbuilding served as an office for Ali.

"Why don't you both take your time? Get into some comfortable clothes, and we can have some drinks before dinner."

"Sounds good to me," Doug said.

Joan stopped. "Are we dressing for dinner, Noel?"

"Oh, nothing so formal. We usually manage a jacket and tie for the men, but that's as far as we go."

Doug thought that was far enough.

Joan took the hint and opened her bags.

Before she began to unpack, she reached into her handbag for her miniature tape recorder. She began to record her impressions of the trip; the plane, Doug, Noel, the house, Ali and his business. She dictated for approximately ten minutes, and then put the recorder back in her handbag.

It was getting late, and Joan felt that Noel's idea of "informal" would be somewhat different from that of her friends in East Hampton.

She put on one of the two long summer print dresses that she had brought for the evening, both of which were cut just low enough to awaken the most somnolent dinner partner.

Doug, too, had decided that Noel's idea of informal might be somewhat different than his own. Doug knew the British. He settled for the white linen jacket he had brought.

When Doug and Joan came back into the living room, the broad sweep of sky was going rapidly from rose to orange yellow, then gray, then darkness. Night comes swiftly in these latitudes, but the short bursts of color of the sunsets are made up for by the more enduring brilliance of the stars.

"I'd like you to meet my secretary, Mrs. Bonham Channon."

They saw a rather tall, robust-looking middle-aged woman who was dressed as Joan had suspected, rather formally. She had a classic English face, with a thin, straight nose, chiseled, well-molded chin, and bright, mischievous hazel eyes.

"So pleased you could come, Miss Hopkins, Mr. Dowding."

Dinner was an attempt by Mrs. Channon to guide Joan away from interrupting any conversation the two men were having. It was only partly successful.

It was obvious to Mrs. Channon that her wit and charm could not isolate Joan Hopkins from the frequent glances of quiet admiration from Mr. Dowding. He was going to be difficult, if not impossible, to separate from Miss Hopkins, Mrs. Channon thought. She couldn't blame him; this American girl in a country known the world over for the beauty of its women was the most smashing thing she had seen anywhere. Both Mrs. Channon and Noel could see that Doug wanted to be alone with Joan.

"Excellent dinner, Noel, Mrs. Channon; really delicious." Doug turned to Joan. "How about a short walk through the gardens, Joanie?"

"I'd love to. I've been admiring them since we arrived."

Joan was referring to the gardens that were ablaze with flowers, inclining away from the house toward the edge of the mountain that overlooked the sea. They were terraced with stone ledges and steps, and lighted at night for dramatic contrast between their brilliant splashes of color and the velvet of darkness.

Noel watched them go outside. Joan had wrapped a silk *étole* around her shoulders; she felt cool in the steady trade winds.

* * *

"Have you had any luck?" asked Mrs. Channon

"Have to move slowly with this chap. He's very cool, almost distant; very preoccupied. For an American, he seems to be a most reticent chap. I really haven't had the glimmer of an opportunity."

"You will. If anyone can do it, you can."

"It isn't a case of 'can'; I have to. He'll be back in New York Sunday night."

"Do you think he has the foggiest as to what you want to talk to him about?"

"Don't be ridiculous. How could he?"

"Well, Noel, if I've ever seen a man with a girl on his mind, it's Mr. Douglas Dowding, and separating them won't be easy."

"For fourteen billion dollars, Bonham, I'd attempt to separate the baby Jesus from Mary."

The *Ka'ba* was under full sail tacking toward Virgin Gorda.

The seas in Drake's Channel were moderately rough, but the big yacht beat them off with little effort, throwing clouds of salt spray as her white bow clove the dark blue water.

"Have you ever been to the caves, Miss Hopkins?" It was Captain Morgan who spoke.

"I've never been down here before, Captain."

"Then it will be exciting for you. Do you swim well?"

"Yes. I swam competitively in college."

"Have you ever snorkeled before?"

"Some. I never found it very difficult."

He turned to Doug. "Down here some refer to the caves as Neptune's Chapel. They're the work of thousands of years of sea and wind erosion. If you've never been through them, it's truly an unforgettable experience."

Noel's enthusiasm for underwater exploration was reserved for offshore oil drilling rigs. He was content to stay aboard the yacht with a gin and tonic.

* * *

They swam among the grottoes and the twisting tunnels of underwater rock and coral. They explored the caves, always with a member of the crew who watched them, for their own safety, from the launch that was pulled up on the beach.

Doug followed Joan as she dove through an underwater arch of rock and came out on the other side to a small strip of sand that was bathed in very shallow water.

She was in a tiny bikini. She stood with her face mask pushed back, her snorkel tube secured by her rubber headband. She was listening to the incredible acoustics of the caves as the sound of the movements of the sea reverberated through the grottoed rock. She was captivated.

He walked toward her slowly. She stood there, her breasts heaving from the stress of the long underwater swim, her wet hair hanging to her shoulders.

She looked like a sea goddess. Doug was aware only of his desire. He moved toward her as relentlessly as the sea. He turned her toward him, holding her tightly. He kissed her passionately, longingly. He wanted her, right there, right now.

Her mood was shattered, and as he held her she felt anger at the impertinence of his interruption. But as she felt him hold her hard against him, a part of her mind, that empirical part that in this instant she disliked, assured her that if she denied him this, she would lose what she came down here for.

"Wait, Doug. Please."

"Joanie, I want you so damn much. I want you now." He drew her to him again, not realizing in the fullness of his own emotion her reluctance toward him.

"Doug, stop. Please. You're embarrassing me. That crewman can see us."

"I don't give a damn."

She tried to keep her tone light, but it wasn't easy. What Doug didn't know was that Joan Hopkins held a brown belt in karate and she could have dumped him on his presidential ass any time she felt like it, and unfortunately she was feeling like it right now.

"Doug. You've got to behave, really. I thought we were getting to be good friends, now let's not spoil it."

"But I don't want to be just good friends, Joanie, I want you."

She smiled at him. "Sometimes, Mr. President, we can't always have everything we want."

When she called him "Mr. President," it caught him and diffused the recklessness with which he had tried to take her. He thought of Karen and then Bardia. His mood changed as quickly as a passing shadow. She saw his eyes become morose and far away.

She put her arm around him, and laughed lightly.

"Come on, Doug. Let's not spoil this extravagant day that God and Noel seemed to have planned for us." She gave him a hard hug. "Come on, Doug, buck up. I love being with you, but you have your own attachments and so do I."

She raised his chin and looked into the somber eyes that were beginning to brighten and come back.

"It's very easy for a girl to be carried away by the likes of you, Mr. Dowding." She was smiling at him, using the same gesture to divert him that Karen used. He shook off the thought.

"Come on, let's get back to the launch. I'm hungry and I'm getting cold," she said.

They spent the rest of the day swimming, sunning themselves aboard the *Ka'ba*. They enjoyed a magnificent lunch of broiled crayfish, salad, wine, luxuriating in paradise.

Joan lay on the foredeck sunning herself while Noel used the opportunity to be alone with Doug, aft.

"I hope you two are enjoying yourselves."

"It's been really marvelous, Noel. I am truly indebted to you."

"Not at all, old boy. It's been my pleasure to have you, I can assure you."

Doug had come to like Noel Aragon, a little. The patient old-world British manner was paying off, and that mixed with the sun and sea, the incredible scenery of the Caribbean, all deftly blended with superb food and drink, was conquering some of the reserve and hesitations of Douglas Dowding.

Noel had provided him with the relief he so badly needed and he was grateful; but Doug was too experienced not to realize that Noel and Ali had not gone to all of this trouble without purpose.

"How does that contract look for Peter?"

Noel had been waiting for an opportunity to start talking some business, and he was happy to see Joan asleep on the starboard side as they ran under full sail on their way back to Cruz Bay.

"Do you have any idea of the scope of the project, Doug?"

"Some, but not in any detail."

The wind had picked up, and the *Ka'ba* ran before a twenty-knot breeze; she flew through the sea, her tall sails like great white triangular wings against the sky.

"Ali's king has called for nothing less than the development of the southern portion of his country within fourteen years. This means the development of an entire infrastructure—ports, roads, plants, airports, schools, hospitals, military bases, communication systems. In other words, he wants to build a modern industrialized country where today only the sun burns empty sand in heat that gets to be a hundred and twenty degrees in the shade in summer."

"Is it possible to do that in so short a time?"

"It's possible provided we get the necessary cooperation.

"Our biggest problem is the lack of a trained or even literate manpower. We'll have to import thousands of workers—technicians, teachers, doctors, engineers, all sorts of specialists—and they have to be housed. They need transport and the necessary services and living amenities to keep them on the job. It's one hell of a big undertaking, I can tell you that. One advantage we do have is that the project is so vast that those who can handle such a venture are very few indeed."

"And Peter believes his company is capable of heading up such a project?"

Noel paused thoughtfully for a moment. "I don't know, Doug, how familiar you are with the Tennant Corporation, but I sincerely believe—and not just because we represent Peter in the Gulf—that his company is the most qualified in the world to do this job, if anyone can do it."

Doug thought about this for a moment and then happened to glance forward. Joan was still asleep, and he knew if she didn't get back under cover she would be badly burned.

"Excuse me, Noel, but I want to get Joan out of the sun."

Noel wasn't annoyed. He had broken the ice, and he wanted to finish this talk back at the house. He had plenty of time now. The weekend was turning out just as he had planned.

* * *

After dinner they were sitting around the table discussing the day's sail, and planning for tomorrow's last trip on the *Ka'ba* before returning to New York.

Mrs. Channon caught the very discreet signal from Noel and folded her napkin. She turned to Joan.

"I expect these men would like to bore each other a little with business, my dear. Why don't you let me show you George's orchid collection? It's famous all over these islands."

"I'd love to see it, Mrs. Channon. Flowers are a special passion of mine."

Noel and Doug got up from the table and went into the living room. Doug did not notice that the servants hadn't cleared the table. He started to sit on the couch, when Noel interrupted.

"Would you mind, old boy, if we sat here?" He pointed to a circular table by the windows on which was arranged a large bowl containing several varieties of small orchids in individual clay pots.

"I don't get down here nearly often enough, and I like to get as close to these sunsets as I can."

To Doug that sounded surprisingly aesthetic for Noel Aragon, but he too enjoyed the painting of the sun's artistry upon the clouds, especially with the magnificence of this view.

Noel brought a humidor of cigars and handed one to Doug. He cut the end off one for himself, and they both smoked quietly for a while.

"You were asking me on the *Ka'ba* about Peter's company, and his chances for landing the contract. Did you know that the initial phase is worth nine billion?"

"No. I had no idea."

"Yes. The whole business is almost too much to comprehend."

"And you feel Peter can do it."

"Yes, we do. Ali is convinced of it, or he wouldn't have suggested Peter's company to the king."

"Even for fourteen billion dollars?"

Noel looked directly at Doug. "Even for fourteen billion dollars."

Doug smoked thoughtfully. He wasn't sure he believed that, but something in Noel's manner convinced him that Noel believed it.

"Can we be helpful to you in any way?"

It had come at last, Noel thought. He didn't reply immediately; he seemed lost in thought.

"There is something you can do, Doug, that could put it over for all of us."

Doug felt on firmer ground now. This is what he understood: getting it on the table and finding out what the hell this bird had on his mind. Doug waited.

"I'd like to tell you a brief story, Doug, as Ali told it to me. May I?"

"Shoot."

"I won't bore you with a history lesson, but in 1929 the father of the present king made war on some fractious tribes over a matter of political insubordination; it was purely an internal affair. The king's father looked to the British to finance him, but the negotiations were laborious and he needed the money quickly. His lands were being opened for oil exploration and recovery, and the British for historical reasons held the most desirable leases. That was why he sought the help of our Foreign Office. His need was desperate, and we did not act in time." Noel looked carefully at Doug. "Have you any idea who financed the king's father when he could not obtain money anywhere else?"

Doug shook his head.

Noel paused to let it really hit home.

"The grandfather of your present chairman."

Doug was floored.

"You mean John's grandfather?"

"Precisely."

"My God, that's unbelievable!"

"It may be unbelievable, Doug, but it happens to be historical fact."

"Jesus Christ, that's amazing!"

"I thought you would find it so. The family of the king have never forgotten what the Salisburys did for them, and consider themselves, even apart from the favorable oil leases and contracts made to Salisbury interests in the past, to be under a kind of obligation, though that's a strong word; let's say they have a very warm and affectionate feeling for the Salisburys." Noel looked sharply at Doug. "If John Salisbury acted as an ambassador, so to speak, representing our interests in this situation, there is no doubt in Ali's mind that the king would look favorably upon our group."

"I don't see any problem in that. That's just the kind of thing John likes to do. He's the best there is at greeting kings."

Noel looked away from Doug briefly. "Ali's sources—" He hesitated. "We hear, Doug, that John is having major problems at the bank." He saw Doug's jaw set, his eyes become hard.

"Forgive me, Doug. I know this is your affair, not mine, but it has a great bearing on what I wish to say to you." Noel was in this far, and he had to carry on.

"Whether Ali's information is correct or not about FMB is immaterial. What is important—to you, I might add—is what Ali is willing to do, to ensure John's participation as an envoy, if you will, to the king."

Doug's eyes had not softened as he looked steadily at Noel. Noel in grim determination went on.

"Doug, Ali has authorized me to open a Swiss numbered account for you, upon your ability to secure John's participation, and to deposit in it eleven million nine hundred thousand Swiss francs."

If Noel had hit Doug in the mouth with a saber, he couldn't have been more startled. "What the hell did you say?"

Noel repeated the offer.

"Jesus Christ, that's about five million dollars."

"That's correct."

"To get John to do something he'd do anyway? That doesn't make any sense at all."

"It does to Ali."

Doug blew cigar smoke slowly into the room.

"Well, I'll be a son of a bitch." He paused thoughtfully. "Do you mean you're offering me a five-million-dollar bribe?"

"Not at all, Doug. As you said, John would probably do this anyway. What we are paying for is insurance." Noel smiled. "We'll make you a director of East-West Trading, Limited. You can call it a director's fee if you like."

"That's a hell of a director's fee."

Doug's mind was slowly taking hold of this, and he began to analyze it. He thought of his own not considerable net worth, of the new expenses Bardy was making him undertake. He thought of the board and his tenuous position at the bank. He thought of the independence this money would give him. He also considered the consequences, if it should ever get out.

"Are you telling me, Noel, that you're offering me a five-million-dollar bribe?"

"That's a subjective reaction, Doug. I'd rather say that the enormity of this project, and its rewards to us, are of such magnitude that a fee of five million dollars to you for services rendered is in relative proportion. Simply put, old man, we think it's worth it."

Doug had never been placed in this position before. He didn't know whether to be flattered or offended. Five million dollars was very satisfying to the ego, but this Limey son of a bitch was offering him a bribe, no matter what the amount.

"When would these monies be placed in an account for me?"

Noel smiled inwardly.

"When John Salisbury makes a personal visit to the king in behalf of our project."

Doug thought for a moment. "Regardless of whether Peter gets the contract or not?"

"Regardless. You will have fulfilled your end of our bargain."

"I'll be damned."

Noel watched him carefully. "Can we shake hands on it, then?"

Doug eyed him coolly.

"I'd rather think about that, Noel." He got up. "If you don't mind, I'd like to find Joan and get a breath of air." Doug felt tired after the day's sail, and wanted to spend some time with Joan before going to bed. They were all tired, and would have to be up early for tomorrow's last trip on the *Ka'ba*.

Joan awakened from a disturbing dream about herself and Doug in the caves. She sat up in bed. She was fully awake. She looked at the dial of her luminous traveling clock. It was three-fifteen.

Her room had a door which opened into the adjoining living room. She thought she heard the sounds of a low, unin-

telligible conversation. The voices sounded thin and artificial.
She got up and put on her dressing gown and silently opened
the door a crack.

She saw Noel Aragon sitting at the table near the windows.
His back was toward her. He was in pajamas and a dressing
gown and was illuminated by the soft glow of the single lamp
on the table at which he was sitting. She could see a dull re-
flection of him in the living-room windows. The rest of the
room was in shadow.

Joan listened, recognizing Doug's voice, then Noel's, but she
couldn't understand what they were saying. She instantly
recognized that Noel had taped a conversation between himself and Doug, and thought it important enough to play back
at three-fifteen in the morning.

She had not turned on the light in her own room and was
able to watch Noel undetected.

She saw him reach into what looked like a hidden compartment in the side of the table and disconnect a wire and close
the compartment. She saw him rise, his face hidden in shadow,
and walk silently toward his office, holding a cassette recorder
in his right hand.

Suddenly Joan knew what she was down there for.

This British fink had bugged a conversation with Doug, and
she realized that her job was to find out what was on that tape.
She could almost feel Henry breathing down her neck.

Her heart began to pound. She sat on her bed trying to
think. She had to give Noel enough time to go to sleep, and
she had to guess how long that would take. She decided to
wait an hour.

At four-thirty she took her own miniature dictating machine out of her handbag, and her cigarette lighter, and with
a pulse that was beating so loudly she was sure it was audible,
she crossed the living room toward Noel's office. She stopped
after each few steps straining to hear the least sound. She saw
only the descending moon's light on the water, the dark shapes

of drifting night clouds. The only sound was the wind rustling the fronds of the tall palms near the house.

She prayed that no one would discover her. What could she say if that happened? The simple explanation that she couldn't sleep would be plausible until she got to Noel's office. And if someone saw her there? She'd have to think of something. Perhaps only the truth would suffice under those circumstances. She'd simply have to take her chances. When she got to Noel's office, she stopped again. Still there was no sound; only the music of an occasional night bird, and the wind.

She didn't dare to turn on a light. She flicked her lighter, and in its feeble light she looked around quickly but didn't see the recorder. She was about to open the desk's center drawer when she noticed Noel's briefcase near a pile of neatly stacked manila folders.

Her heart almost stopped beating. She moved toward the case and prayed it wouldn't be locked. It wasn't. She opened it. There was the recorder.

She removed it silently. She examined the controls with her cigarette lighter. They were fairly standard, and she took special care to adjust the volume to *low*. She switched on the tape and put her ear to the speaker. She heard Doug's voice.

DOUG: "To get John to do something he'd do anyway? That doesn't make any sense at all."

NOEL: "It does to Ali."

DOUG: "Well, I'll be a son of a bitch. Do you mean you're offering me a five-million-dollar bribe?"

NOEL: "Not at all, Doug. As you said, John would probably do this anyway. What we are paying for is insurance."

She advanced the tape, her heart pounding. She felt as if she were choking.

NOEL: "That's a subjective reaction, Doug. I'd rather say that the enormity of this project, and its rewards to us, are of such magnitude that a fee of five million dollars to you for services rendered—"

She advanced the tape again. She was shaking all over with excitement and fear. Please God, don't let them find me, she breathed.

DOUG: "When would these monies be placed in an account for me?"

She clicked off the tape, looking hurriedly around the room. She had noted where she had started it on the cassette and was trying to find out where it ended. She clicked it on again.

NOEL: "When John Salisbury makes a personal visit to the king in behalf of our project."

DOUG: "Regardless of whether Peter gets the contract—"

She moved the tape forward again.

NOEL: "Can we shake hands on it, then?"

DOUG: "I'd rather think about that, Noel."

She noted the spot on the cassette and rewound the tape. It rewound rapidly. Her lighter was hot in her fingers and its flame wouldn't last much longer. She had been lighting it intermittently to conserve the butane.

She took her own recorder and put the microphone next to the speaker on Noel's machine. She turned her control up to high. She knew the sensitivity of her own machine, and she knew it would catch every word. She recorded the section of Noel's tape that she wanted, waiting what seemed like an eternity. She was shivering with an awful dread for what she now knew was on that tape.

When she had finished, she tried to make sure of leaving Noel's tape in the same position she had found it. She had to guess at this, but if her luck held she would soon be done.

She slipped silently back to her own room, trembling, her mind now burning to hear the tape all the way through.

She put her small recorder by her ear as she pulled the covers tightly around her. Her teeth were chattering from the ordeal she had just been through, and she shivered convulsively from anxiety and fear.

As she listened to the tape in the violet graying dawn, she

began to cry. She sobbed softly to herself, tasting her tears.

"Oh, Doug, what have they done to you? My God, what am I doing to you? Oh, Doug, Doug, I knew I could only hurt you. I knew it."

Her body was racked with sobs as she thought of what she had to do.

Joan tried to conceal the shock of her discovery of last night, but the portents for Doug recorded on the small cassette in her handbag were too enormous for her to disguise completely. She had to tell Doug and Noel that she wasn't feeling well and wanted to rest.

She lay on the foredeck in the sun, her mind numbed by her responsibilities. She was stunned by the moral dilemma she saw herself facing.

She felt a hand on her back and turned to see Doug looking at her, his eyes showing concern.

"Is there anything I can do, Joanie?"

She looked up at him, then looked away. She had to fight to hold back the tears that she knew would come if he didn't leave. Why was his vulnerability so damned appealing?

"Doug, please. I just don't feel well. It's nothing, really, but I would prefer to rest."

"Be careful of the sun."

"I will."

"You'd be better off below if you want to sleep, Joan. This sun is really murderous, and you've got a lot of color already."

She got up slowly. It would be better below, she thought, away from the solicitude of that bastard Aragon, and Captain Morgan, and Doug.

She touched his arm briefly, not really daring to look at him. "I think you're right. I'll go below and try and get some sleep."

He watched her walk aft and go below. He didn't know what her problem was, but then consoled himself that with women you never knew what the hell was bothering them. He shook his head resignedly and walked back to the cockpit, where Noel was seated.

Noel's idea of sailing was to sit in the sun in a weathered yachting cap, drinking gin and tonics and waiting for the next meal. On this occasion, as Doug approached him, he seemed particularly satisfied with life.

The sun streamed off the white sails and sparkled the sea with infinite reflections of light. The *Ka'ba* was running before the trade winds, lifting her stern under the rolling seas and racing before the following wind like a great white seabird.

Doug caught the eye of the helmsman. "Could you have Mrs. Morgan or someone send me up a Scotch and water?"

"Yes, sir."

The crewman put the ship on autopilot and went to the main companionway and yelled below for Doug's drink. He came back to the helm.

"Noel, I've been thinking about our talk last night. I must say, more than I thought I would."

Noel looked at him, smiling. "I hoped you would, Doug. I wish I was on your end of the conversation."

Doug looked at the dark eyes under the faded blue Swedish yachting cap. His own eyes were cool. Noel saw hostility in them.

"I'm going to suggest to John that he assist you in Peter's project, but only because I feel it will be good for the bank."

Noel sat up more erectly in his chair and looked at Doug. His expression moved from doubt to incredulity.

"As for the rest of it, Noel, I hardly find it flattering. I have no idea what Ali's sources have told him about the bank, or about me, but your proposal is, quite frankly, insulting."

Noel had no idea how badly Doug wanted this money. But, oddly, it was the thought of Bardia's loss of faith in his integrity, and the loss of Gay's respect, that really stopped him. The thought of John's contempt for such a breach of trust didn't mean as much to him.

Noel nearly dropped his drink. This unflappable Britisher had just had his guts turned inside out.

"I say, old boy, don't take it that way. Really, the last thing we wished to do was offend."

"Well, I found it offensive, Noel. Let's leave it at that."

I<small>T WAS A CHILLY RIDE BACK TO</small> N<small>EW</small> Y<small>ORK ON THE</small> 737.
They occupied their time reading and drinking in compara-
tive silence. It was very difficult. Joan resisted Doug's dem-
onstrations of concern, and Noel occupied himself with trying
to analyze what kind of man would turn down five million
dollars in cash.

Doug insisted on taking a cab back with Joan. Noel Aragon was left to ride back to the Carlyle in his limousine,
wondering what had gone wrong.

It had been Ali's plan. Ali was the devil himself in knowing
who could be approached and who couldn't, and Noel had
found damned few people who couldn't. What made this big,
awkward American so virtuous, when their sources had reported he was so vulnerable?

Both Ali and Noel had spent their lives living Thackeray's
philosophy that "virtue was a deficiency of temptation." God
knows, thought Noel, as the limousine drove quickly through
the light traffic of the East River Drive, that they had given
Mr. Dowding sufficient temptation.

Could Thackeray have been wrong? Had Diogenes finally
found an honest man? Noel shook his head in disbelief as the

driver braked hard to avoid the stalled car in front of them.

It had never happened before, he said to himself, and suddenly, in the warmth of the limousine, Noel Aragon felt cold.

Joan was only partly aware of the gray morning with flat, heavy clouds that hung like a pall outside the windows of Henry's office. She was only vaguely alert to the abrupt change from the aquas and reds of the Caribbean to the monochromes of New York. She wished to God she had never heard of the Caribbean.

Henry had had to rearrange his whole morning to work her into his schedule, but when she called him last night, she sounded so strange on the phone that he knew something was very wrong.

He saw immediately that she was troubled. Her face glowed from the sun. Physically, she looked marvelous, but Henry saw the shadows in the green eyes, and the taut, nervous line of her mouth.

"It seems as if you'd been away a long time, Joan. I never realized a weekend could pass so slowly. I missed you terribly." He said this quietly, earnestly, and he watched a quick, fleeting smile come to her face.

"It seemed very long to me, too, Henry." She had been sitting in one of the black molded chairs in a corner of Henry's office. She got up, but did not move toward him to touch him or kiss him, which he found strange. He could see that she was terribly preoccupied. It was almost as if he weren't in the room.

She had begun to pace his office, head down, not looking at him. Henry seated himself in a chair by the circular conference table.

Something had come between them. She had taken her bright spark, and cupping it in her hand was holding it away from him. Its light was so vital to him that without it he felt dark and cold.

His voice was cautious, exploratory. He didn't want to come upon her too soon.

"What's up, Joan? For a girl who's just come back from the islands, you don't look as if you'd enjoyed yourself very much."

She stopped pacing, turned and looked at him very directly. She had been walking with her head down, biting gently on the nail of her right thumb.

"Henry, I've got two weeks' vacation coming, and I want to take it starting today, starting right now."

He looked at her carefully, sensing the seriousness of her mood.

"Is something wrong?" He paused. "I've got you set up to go to Washington for an important interview. It could mean a lot to you." He waited for her reaction.

"You'll have to get someone else. I'm not feeling very well, Henry, and I need some time to get myself together."

Henry knew something was very wrong; something had happened down there.

"Can you tell me about what's bothering you?" he asked gently.

"Nothing's bothering me, Henry." She shook her head without a great deal of conviction. "I've got some time coming to me and I want to take it."

He waited before replying.

"It's an inconvenient time to have you away, Joan," he said softly, "but if you feel strongly that you have to get away, I'm sure we can work things out."

She looked at him, her face tense, her eyes telling him that she was desperately confused and worried.

"Joan, something happened this weekend," he said quietly. "There's no use telling me it didn't, because it's written all over your face. Now, why don't you tell me what's going on?"

He saw the quick, passing annoyance in her eyes.

"Henry, I'm telling you nothing's happened. I'm going to take some time off, that's all."

He was annoyed that he had had to rearrange his morning to have this nonconference with Joan, but his natural awareness and tact told him not to push. He felt her withdrawal. It was a symptom his father had taught him quite early to recognize. It had made him melancholy.

She walked to him quickly and bent down and kissed him. She raised his chin and looked at him for a long time.

"I love you, Henry," she said, and walked out of the room.

J OHN HESITATED BEFORE PLACING THIS CALL TO DUTCH. If Dutch bolted, if he carried out his threat to resign and took the other outside directors on the executive committee with him, John was through. An open breach on the board of that magnitude would not be sustainable. John and Doug would have to resign.

"I'm sorry I've taken so long to get back to you, Dutch, but Doug has just returned from the Caribbean with Aragon. They seem to have hit it off."

He heard Dutch grunt his acknowledgment over the three thousand miles from Seattle.

John's distaste for this phone call required all his discipline. He inhaled deeply. Here goes, he said to himself.

"I told you I'd give you my decision about Doug in a week, Dutch. I've run over that time a little, and I apologize." He paused. "I've decided to move Doug further away from operations and get closer to that role myself. I'm going to use him on this Middle East thing, and I would appreciate your withholding any personal decision until after we find out how successful we are in supporting Peter Tennant."

He could hear Dutch's reluctant growl. "John, what the

hell do you need Dowding for? He can't help with the king. You're the only one who can do that."

John was ready for this.

"Dutch, Doug has a good deal of experience in these kinds of complex negotiations; he's very effective in that type of role. If I'm going to 'get closer to the store,' as you put it, I'm going to need someone at the highest level to follow through for Tennant. The king will expect that kind of representation and would be offended by anything less." John paused. "Dutch, I know that part of the world. My role has to be as an intermediary with the king. I can't get involved with the day-to-day wrangling; that will destroy my influence and whatever prestige I may be able to lend to this project."

Dutch knew he was being backed into a corner, and he didn't like it. It didn't solve the bank's management problem, which, as far as Dutch was concerned, could only be resolved by replacing Dowding. But if John was willing to take on more of an operating responsibility, and if he would "pitch" for the bank in this Tennant deal, then what the hell? Dutch would ride for a little while longer, and pray that something else didn't blow up in that fucking bank.

"It's not the answer, John, but I'll go with it for a while."

John sighed inwardly in relief. "I appreciate that, Dutch." They both hung up, each far from being satisfied.

It was a wet, dark day in London. Everything dripped. Cold wind blew at the trees in Hyde Park. The colors were gray and black: automobiles, taxis, raincoats, umbrellas. The streets glistened with rain.

Ali wiped his mouth with his napkin, his face reflecting his concern and confusion.

They were finishing up a late luncheon at the Savoy. The cold Scottish salmon had been particularly delicious that day.

Ali had been watching Noel intently. Ali's normal spirited luncheon banter had a decided edge to it. His manner, always potentially volcanic, was usually covered by a nervous foot-tapping attempt at appearing calm.

But Ali was never calm: the nomadic movement of his schedule prevented it. His constant travel, the endless negotiations carried on late into the night, the incredible number of details concerning each of the deals he was currently negotiating and that he kept in his head to be recalled at will, the lightning capacity of his Western-educated brain that no one could keep up with—all of this made it seem that Ali had some unknown race with time, perhaps with death. It was as if he had to get all of this accomplished before his clock ran out. His only relief was in the pleasures of women.

This intense force of Ali's always made Noel nervous. It was a constant presence, like boiling lava that bubbled and glowed and could erupt with incredible suddenness.

Ali's black hawk's eyes fixed themselves coldly on Noel.

"If I didn't know you better, my friend, I would suspect you of bungling. But I know how skilled you are in placing the hook." He paused, talking principally to himself. "The Caribbean exercise has never failed us before, Noel."

"Never."

"And God knows we gave him a significant incentive."

Noel smiled wryly. "I would certainly think so."

"Then is it possible, my dear Noel, that we have to wake up Diogenes and tell him we've found an honest man? I don't believe it."

Noel sighed. "I'm afraid you may have to, Ali."

Ali shook his head incredulously.

The most interesting part of this late luncheon at the Savoy was what was omitted from the conversation. For as the two of them stepped into Ali's Rolls, to be driven back through the bleak September afternoon to 41 Brook Street, the headquarters of East-West Trading, Ltd., Noel had made no mention of the tape, which had not been part of plan. It had been strictly Noel's idea.

Far back in the dark, suspicious places in Noel's mind he wanted something tangible with which to face Ali, should circumstances in the Dowding affair get out of hand, should Ali be tempted to jettison him. For in the dead of night, when each man is alone, stripped to his fears and fantasies, Noel Aragon would admit that he trusted no one. Especially not the Bedouin Ali, who called him "brother." Noel was no man's brother, no woman's man. He was truly alone.

IT WAS THE FIRST TALK THEY HAD HAD IN WHAT SEEMED like weeks.

It was unusual for Bardy to join him at breakfast. Usually she got up later than Doug. This morning she was dressed, which was also not her habit at this hour.

They were unfailingly polite to each other, both skirmishing around a center that was coming apart.

It was evident to him that she had somehow gotten hold of things, pulled herself together. Even though her life was fragile, there was a strength at its core that sustained the crumbling at its edges. She was hanging on.

He, on the other hand, seemed awkward, as if he were searching for something in a closet and had forgotten what he was looking for.

"You going somewhere?"

"Yes, I have an appointment at the doctor's."

He didn't want to ask her if she was still seeing Dr. Harding, but she volunteered the information.

"I have an appointment with Dr. Patterson. He's been highly recommended to me." She paused over her tea. She sat erect, thin and very pale; the morning light from the dining-room windows touched her eyes and her hair. "I hope he's a little less morose than Harding."

She looked at Doug with a touch of humor. "You certainly seem the picture of health."

He smiled. There was cynicism in his eyes, which were tired despite the bronzed skin.

"I should. I've just been offered five million dollars in cash."

She saw by his manner that he was serious.

"You mean you personally, not the bank?"

"That's what I mean." He folded his napkin and got up from the table, standing near the draped dining-room windows that looked out on Park Avenue.

He turned and looked directly at her.

"How would you like to be the wife of a really wealthy man?"

She paused, her voice low, almost as if she were talking to herself. "I think I'd settle for just being a wife."

She saw the anger come into his eyes. Her voice softened. "I'm sorry, Doug. We won't go through all that again."

He seemed so big to her, standing there backlighted by the window, and yet his eyes seemed confused, almost lost, like those of a small boy. He looked frightened. He was at the same time angry, almost threatening; and yet there was that sad vulnerability she had known for so long.

"You didn't answer my question."

She looked at him with new purpose. She was really listening, for the first time in a long while.

"It's a little difficult to answer. I've never thought of us as being wealthy, but I certainly don't consider us any charity case."

"We're not, but even as president of the bank, on an after-tax basis, our net worth is probably less than fifteen percent of that."

"But what on earth is someone willing to give you that kind of money for? It seems obvious they don't need a loan."

He told her what had happened on St. John.

She listened carefully. There was a touch of fear at the edges of her eyes.

"My God, Doug, that's incredible."

"It is. What's more, I turned them down, like a damn fool."

"I should have thought you would."

He looked at her with an expression very close to real anger, his voice coming at her like some great bronze gong.

"Why the hell should I? What's ahead for me in the damn bank? I expect any day to have John ask me to resign. I've lived in that paper jungle ever since I got out of college. I've given every damn thing I've had to that bank, and now I am going to be the fall guy.

"John isn't going to resign, I can tell you that. That would tarnish the family image. He would be the dynast who couldn't cut it. So who does that leave, Bardy?" He walked over to her, looming over her, his face close to hers.

"Who does that leave? It leaves me, that's who. Tell me, Bardy, what do I owe that goddamn bank? Loyalty? Integrity? I've given that to FMB for twenty-five years, and to John as well."

He pulled a chair aside and sat down beside her, looking at her in her dark blue Chanel suit with the red and blue scarf that she had tied about her neck. She looked so frail to him, with her thin legs and her slender feet in their dark pumps.

"Bardy, I told you I turned them down, but what I've been asking myself is, why the hell did I do it? Bardy, it boils down to this. Any day now I'm going to get screwed by that bank, by John, by the board. I'm going to be the fall guy! And God damn it—" He banged the table, his hand hitting the edge of her saucer, sending it and the cup crashing to the floor. He was on his feet instantly.

"Bardy, I'm terribly sorry. Did I get anything on your suit?"

"No. Don't bother about it. It's only a teacup."

He was bending down picking up the pieces.

"Just leave it there. Stella will get it."

He picked up the several pieces and held them in his hand. He looked at her, touched by her graciousness, his face reflecting his concern.

"Bardy, this is from your mother's set. She gave us these when we were married."

She didn't say anything.

He walked into his library to find an envelope.

"I'll see if I can have this repaired," he called to her from the other room.

"Don't bother, Doug, it's not that important. You can't put back the pieces."

She had gotten up to get her handbag as he came back.

"I'm late now, Doug, I've really got to be going."

They looked at each other, coming together only for an instant, then found their eyes looking away.

"I'm not sure you want my advice, but if it's worth anything to you, I'd say your initial reaction was the right one." She was getting ready to go out, with quick little jerking movements.

"It seems to me that not only would you be damaging your reputation, which has taken you all these years to build, but you would be putting yourself in a very compromising position with this Ali whatever his name is. I'm not at all sure you'd find that a very comforting prospect in the long run."

She had walked to the closet and handed him his coat; he stood looking at her. "As far as the bank is concerned, Doug, my suggestion to you, if you are forced to resign, is to do it with as much grace and dignity as you can. FMB isn't the only bank." She looked at him with steady, understanding eyes. "You might even rediscover what it's like to live again, outside that 'paper jungle,' as you call it—without the pressures, without the intrigues."

She opened the hall door which led to their elevator. "Can you drop me at Sixty-eighth and York Avenue?"

He stood with her in the elevator, towering over her. He very much wanted to put his arm around her, but he wasn't sure how she would react. He looked down at the slim, frail figure that was Bardia Colefax Morrison Dowding, the woman to whom he had been married for twenty-six years, and who had given him two children.

It occurred to him that this woman with whom he had spent a quarter of a century, and from whom he had allowed himself to become estranged, was perhaps the most important influence in his life.

As he held the door of the car for her, waving the chauffeur away, and got in to sit beside her, he felt the width of the gulf between them, that he had created, and that her pride had maintained. More frightening than the possibility of his forced resignation from the presidency of FMB was the revelation of how much he had really lost.

"HELLO, DAD?"

"Yes, Joanie. I see you got there all right. Pete met you at the ferry and had the heat turned on?"

"Yes, Dad. He's been a jewel. He's split wood for me and stocked the place with food, and insists on coming over each morning and night just to check up on me."

"That sounds like Pete. He's a brick."

"He sure is. He doesn't look much different than when I was a girl; a little thinner on top and grayer, but he doesn't seem to change." She was aware of her father's concern on the other end of the line.

"Joanie, I don't want to pry, and I'm not going to, but you know if you need any help or someone to talk to—"

"You're sweet, Dad. You always have been. But I'm afraid this is something I have to work out for myself. I've got an important decision to make affecting the life, perhaps the lives, of other people. I'm afraid I'm on the hook for this one."

"It sounds portentous."

"I'm afraid it is, Dad." She hesitated. "Please don't worry about me."

"Would you give me a call now and then so I'll know how

you're coming along?" Her father's concern was evident. "I'd appreciate it, Joan. Your mother will too."

"I'll do that, Dad. Give my love to Mom. I'm sorry if I'm worrying you two, but believe me I'll be O.K. Send you a big kiss."

"You too, sweetheart."

Chip Hopkins hung up. His next call was his biggest surprise of this day of surprises. It was from Henry Cannon.

When Joan hung up after speaking to her father, she went to the fireplace in the living room, where Pete had left the split pinewood and paper in the grate, ready to light.

She lit a fire and went back to the kitchen to boil water for tea. She could hear the crackle of the pitch as the fire grew in intensity.

After she had washed her breakfast dishes, she went into the living room to look out across the small harbor, whose surface was a cold blue gray. The sun was gaining height in the east and lighting the undulating shadowed land masses of the Camden Hills. At the mouth of the harbor was Pulpit Rock, on which was the vacant nest of an osprey, that magnificent fish hawk whose rapid disappearance in North America was hastened in this instance by an ignoble human who had shot the bird. The vacant nest made Joan want to weep.

She recalled how horrified they all were when news of the shooting of the osprey was reported. Everyone on the island felt as if he had lost a member of the family.

She looked out at Pulpit Rock, which was shaped like a church pulpit, and saw the lonely, vacant nest. It depressed her. Only man, she thought, the ultimate predator, killed for pleasure. She watched the small, cold waves flutter in the shelter of the protected harbor.

She lit a cigarette and wandered about the living room, looking at the familiar summer furniture that had been covered by sheets before Pete had removed them, at the shells that she had found as a child, at the pictures of her father and mother, and of herself as a girl and as a young woman at Wellesley. There was also a photograph of their sailboat, the thirty-seven-foot auxiliary sloop *Discovery*. She thought of the yacht, of the cruises to those dark green islands, the mussels for dinner, handpicked from some sea-washed ledge and boiled in salt water from the icy Atlantic. She could almost taste them, dipped in butter; they were better than anything in the best New York restaurant. This place held so many wonderful memories for her.

She started to concentrate on why she was here. As she walked back and forth, biting lightly on the nail of her right thumb, she began to talk to herself.

"It's a problem of ethics; that's what the damn tape represents. I have a duty to Henry, and to NBT. But I also have an obligation as a human being not to destroy the life of another human being, and maybe more than one." The thought made her look out at the osprey's nest.

"Are they worth saving or caring for," she wondered aloud, "when they can be as bestial as that?"

The sun grew higher. Outside it was clear and cold. She decided to walk. She bundled herself in the hooded parka and fleece-lined boots she had brought with her, and took her search for an ethical solution to the dilemma she faced out into the world of icy sea and sky.

That night, she listened to the moan of the wind in the fir trees. She had walked out to the front porch earlier to take one more look at the sweep of stars over the waters lit by a pale moon, and the shape of the dark hills silhouetted subtly against the sky. She fell asleep to the occasional squawking of a searching gull.

The next day she roamed the coves of the island, looking for the odd piece of driftwood, the occasional interesting rock or shell, the flotsam washed up by the storms of approaching winter.

She exulted in the cold, clean air with its scent of salt and pine. This was what she really knew and loved. Not the ephemeral paradise of the Caribbean, but the hard granite, the dark trees, the ice-cold waters of this northeastern island. There was a reality here that she understood. The façade of ease and languor were stripped here in Penobscot Bay by laconic self-reliant people, whose bone-spare humor was as wry and as sharp as a winter wind.

What a tonic this was for her, away from New York. What an opportunity to regain some perspective; to be a part of elemental forces that seemed eternal. She began to feel renewed, and waited to gain the insight that would tell her what to do.

She had started to walk back along the beach, more of which was exposed than when she had left by the ebbing tide. She looked up and saw two men standing on the lawn of her house, waving to her.

It was late afternoon and the sun was in her eyes, so she had difficulty seeing who it was. She walked along the rough, granular sand, which was mostly pieces of eroded broken shells, over the rocks covered with dark olive-colored seaweed, past pieces of charred driftwood, until she got to a part of the beach where a tall stand of fir trees hid the westering sun. She looked again. It was Pete and— "Oh, my God!" she said, clapping her hand to her mouth. "It's Henry!"

ALI MADE IT A HABIT NOT TO ALLOW HIS INTEREST IN women to be publicly displayed. In a casino, a restaurant, or at a dinner party, he was always witty and charming, but with a hidden edge. There was a furtive twist of cruelty in this Arab who always insisted on being the host. He paid for everything, everywhere. His friends and associates accepted this. They had consistently tried to entertain him, but without success. Ali carried the traditional hospitality of the Bedouin tent wherever he went, but it was more than that; somewhere in that dark, lightning-quick mind was a hostility toward those whose skin was white. He didn't want to be indebted. The new oil wealth had broken the old colonial yoke, but the recollection of the past humiliations flowed deep within Ali and his people.

His largess was frequently bestowed upon the flight attendants of the world's international airlines. Ali showed a preference for the American girls, if they were not too tall. He preferred them dark of hair and eye, which undoubtedly reminded him of the women of his own country.

Tonight in his suite at the Dorchester he had made love to the charming brunette who was asleep beside him, whom he tried to see each time they were both in London or New York. This was not easy with their mutually hectic schedules. Whenever Nancy Keating was in London, she would call Ali, and if he too was in town, they would arrange their early-morning rendezvous, which was the only time Ali could be with her without the attendance of the constant circle of so-called friends and business associates who kept him up until the small hours of the morning. Ali usually got no more than three or four hours' sleep, but Nancy Keating had long ago adjusted to the strange ways of this son of the desert.

She was fascinated by him, in awe of his erudition, which was considerable, as was his charm and skill with women.

Nancy Keating, whose own appetites were as intense as Ali's, was his special favorite. She combined an Anglo-Saxon independence—which he tolerated, even found amusing—with an almost Asian desire to extend her sexual skills to their exquisite infinity.

During the long flights between New York and London, she sometimes wondered what it would be like being married to Ali. She didn't allow herself to dwell on this, as she was aware of the absent, submissive wife and children in Jidda, and well aware of the Islamic conservatism regarding irresponsible divorce. She didn't mind being his mistress, at least for a time. He was generous. She had cultured pearl necklaces, an enormous ruby ring worth a small fortune, and a continual flow of flowers, perfume, and designer clothes that Ali sent her from Paris and Rome.

As he watched her in sleep, still alive to the skills of her lovemaking, he saw in the shadows the softness of her shoulders, caught the scent of her perfume. He smiled to himself, acknowledging that she was the best he had ever had. He loved those long, distended nipples. Twin sensors that set her on fire. They're wonderful, he almost said aloud. God how I love women!

But even after the exquisite lovemaking, something worried Ali, nagged at him.

He didn't like loose ends, and with Doug's refusal of his very generous offer, Ali was definitely left with an important loose end.

He reached for a cigarette. Nancy sighed in her sleep and moved closer to him.

Suppose Dowding were to report this to Salisbury? If it got back to the king, Ali had a very big problem. Maybe a fourteen-billion-dollar problem.

He sat up in bed, having piled the pillows behind him, and smoked and thought about his predicament.

How could he have misjudged Dowding so badly? All the information he had on him and on FMB led to the unassailable conclusion that Dowding could be had. What streak of contentiousness (Ali could not believe in integrity; the word had no real meaning for him) could this embattled American have?

Never before, in his whole adult experience, had he ever found the human animal able to withstand an offer at some price. Sooner or later every man everywhere had a price. To Ali this was not figurative, but a literal assessment of life as he had experienced it. It didn't make any difference what culture, what environment, as long as you understood how to play the game, and played it knowledgeably, with a certain deference to style. You had to succeed. Then why had he failed? It wasn't logical. He had once said to Noel that Dowding was "a man walking unprotected in the blast-furnace heat of the desert." He, Sayed Saif Ibn Abdul Ageel, had furnished the water. It was unthinkable that anyone had the fortitude or the stupidity to refuse to drink.

Ali had chain-smoked half a dozen cigarettes. Nancy hadn't stirred. A soft light from the living room kept the shadows muted. Outside a blustery wind rattled the edge of a loose window.

The problem was to contain Dowding, and, with luck, Salisbury. Suddenly it came to him. He got out of bed and put on his slippers and dressing gown. He went into the living room, his mind alive with the ramifications of the chess game he had begun to play in his head.

He sat down in the gentle darkness relieved only by the glow of a single lamp, and dialed the number of the house on Belgrave Place. A sleepy, irritated voice answered the telephone.

"Noel, dear chap. Good morning."

"Ali. For God's sake, do you know what time it is?"

"I should, old man. While you're embraced in the arms of Morpheus, I am working for us. Now, is that not democratic of me? You must admit a certain egalitarianism of spirit about your employer—eh, my friend?"

"Ali, for heaven's sake, couldn't this have waited until morning?"

"It is morning, my friend. It's your British penchant for starting the day at ten that is the difference between us.

"Now, my friend, if you are wide-awake enough to listen to me, I have a plan to protect our interest in our little transaction in the Gulf. Are you with me?"

The exasperated sigh of Noel Aragon was loud and clear. "I'm with you, Ali, for God's sake. I'm with you."

Ali laughed and looked up to see a naked Nancy Keating standing in the doorway to the bedroom, smoking quietly, waiting for her Arabian stallion to come home.

THEY HAD WALKED A GOOD PART OF THE DAY—DOWN HARD wintered dirt roads, along rocky beaches where they could smell the frigid sea. They heard the gulls, felt the timeless immobility of the hard granite, and now they were seated on the couch in the living room listening to the roar of the wind from a squall that was blowing hard at the island, and drawing comfort from the crackle and warmth of the fire.

"Don't you think it's carrying things a little far to refuse to tell me what this is all about? I came nearly five hundred miles to see you in Maine, which I can assure you, Miss Hopkins, is not a location I would normally choose at this time of year."

She was dressed in heavy woolen pants and fleece-lined boots. She had on a woolen shirt and two sweaters. Her face glowed from the sun of the Caribbean and Penobscot Bay. She was everything he had ever wanted in a woman. He had come to love her quietly, completely. When she was troubled, it troubled him.

They kept staring at the fire. She spoke without looking at him. "Our problem, Henry, is that something very important is standing between us. I mean, it's very important to me."

"If it's important to you, darling, it's important to me."

She took a long time before replying. There was a great foreboding within her, warning her of what this would do to them. She sighed audibly as she turned to look at him; her voice was low and hesitant.

"Henry, the only way we can possibly handle this is if you will agree to play by my rules. I know that isn't exactly fair, and in most instances I would never ask you to do such a thing, but there is a great deal more at stake here than either you or me. I'm faced with an ethical problem, Henry, and if I tell you about it, you're going to be faced with one too."

He waited a moment before replying. "Joan, if we are going to share a life together, I think we'd better get started. If something has driven you all the way up here, then it must be extremely important to you. I want to know what it is, not out of curiosity, but so I can help you."

She had got up and was sitting on the rug in front of the fire. He moved to sit beside her. She turned to look at him, really look. At the shadowed dark beard that he had to shave twice a day, at the full dark hair which was beginning to streak lightly with gray, the heavy eyebrows, the quiet, thoughtful eyes. She touched his face with her fingers as if she were blind. She closed her eyes and with her fingers gently went over the contours of his face, as if her eyes were not enough. It was as though she were trying to etch what he looked like indelibly in her mind.

She got up and went into her bedroom and came out with her handbag.

"Henry, do you give me your word that I'll be the one to make the decision on the information I'm going to give you?"

He thought about that. "I'm not sure I can make you that promise, Joan. If it has to do with your trip to the Caribbean, that's a story I sent you to cover. They pay me to decide what's news and what isn't, and if one of my staff runs across something, where that kind of judgment has to be made, I'm afraid, Joanie, that I'm the one who has to make it. I can't in good conscience abdicate that role to you or anyone else."

She lit a cigarette, her mind exploring the ramifications of what he had just said. Her intuition told her they were approaching dangerous ground. She understood this because she knew what the problem was, but she understood more than he would have had he known. She was convinced of that because women sensed more about the forebodings of human relationships than men.

"This may put a terrible strain on us, Henry. It could hurt or destroy what we've got together."

He didn't say anything; he just watched her, waiting for her to tell him when she was ready.

She got up and began pacing the floor, biting gently on her thumbnail as she did when she was concentrating or upset.

"When you sent me down with Doug, I couldn't figure out at first what I was supposed to do. I couldn't understand what that little son of a bitch Aragon was doing either, flying us down in a private 737—the thing looked like the Lincoln Tunnel. Then all that sun and sea, the incredible beauty of the place, and all despoiled by a bastard like that." She thought of the osprey's nest sitting unoccupied in the bitter wind, and he watched her face harden. He saw the fear in her eyes as she looked at him.

"Henry, this is so important to me. It's not just a story, it's human beings—their lives and their futures. I can destroy that, and I don't want to. Not for the sake of a ten-minute spot on the evening news so that a bunch of damn morons with no taste can sit around the country gawking at one more broken life, one more shattered family." She looked at him.

"Henry, is this what you want me to do? I'm not sure I can, even for you."

She went into the kitchen to pour herself a drink. She called into him, "Do you want one?"

"What have we got left?"

"Bourbon. We're all out of Scotch."

"Some bourbon and water."

She came in with the drinks. As she handed Henry his glass, she looked at him intently. She knew this thing was going to hurt them.

"Henry, I haven't had your experience, either covering the news or with life. I don't have your objectivity or your professionalism. I doubt if I'll ever have it. Maybe I'm just a lucky girl who's led a happy and probably sheltered life. I adore my parents, I'm happy with my friends, I love my life" —she looked at him with fear touching her eyes—"and I love you. Now all of a sudden this thing comes along, instigated by you, I might add, and my whole life has changed. It's not fun and games any more, Henry, it's the crunch. This is really it for me; this is finding out what kind of person I am, and just how much character I've got. I'm discovering what my values are and what I'm willing to sacrifice for them." She looked at him with heartbreaking honesty and a lack of compromise made stronger by her youth. "Henry, this is for all the marbles."

He watched her as she spoke, thinking of the young shavetails he had seen in the Army, in the Marine Corps, and how quickly the savagery of war blew away their illusions. He had watched them change from fresh-faced kids who didn't know what it was all about to hollow-eyed men who sent other kids on their order to die, or worse, to be permanently mutilated.

She seemed like that to him now. She was growing up fast the way they did, and it hurt him to watch it, to see her move into such a painful phase of her life, where he couldn't help her. His pain was in having to watch hers.

"Joanie. Let me hear it, and then let's take it one step at a time. If what you and I have together means anything, it will survive this. If what's between us isn't strong enough to take it, then you can be damn sure we won't make it together over the long haul. Not when the wind really begins to blow. Listen to me, Joan. There's nothing easy about life, and that's all the news really is. We're paid to watch people parade their victories and defeats, their joys and their sorrows, their incredible stupidities and ignorance and cruelties. Our job is to chronicle life; edit it perhaps so we don't all get sick reading the papers or looking at television. And every once in a while, through a free press, which somebody, somewhere, is always trying to subjugate, we can uncover a Watergate or prevent an injustice, or help push a bill through Congress that will take care of the elderly, feed some more kids, or do something constructive. There are worse ways to earn a living, Joanie. But when we take on an assignment to cover a story, we are taking on the obligation to bring it back to our bureaus with the facts straight, and let those whose job it is to select, edit, or editorialize do what they're paid to do. Perhaps this business isn't for you, but you're still in it and you have a responsibility to fulfill."

She listened to him, knowing what he would say and knowing far better than he did what all this was going to do to them.

Slowly she began to tell him what happened on St. John, and then she played the tape for him. She never let the recorder out of her hand, but she let him hear everything.

Henry Cannon had heard a lot in his day, but this was dynamite. A wealthy Arab trying to close a fourteen-billion-dollar contract offers to bribe the president of one of the largest United States banks. And the tape ending with that gentleman saying, "I'd rather think about that, Noel." My God, it's incredible, Henry thought, and it was. He also understood, now, Joan's reluctance to part with that tape. This could ruin Dowding, seriously affect Salisbury, and would probably blow a fourteen-billion-dollar contract for somebody. The repercussions of this thing were enormous.

She got up to throw some more wood on the fire. She

turned to him. "Well, Mr. News Director, where do we go from here?"

"Joan, it's an incredible story. Absolutely incredible."

"I've known that for some time." Her voice had an edge to it. "Now, just what do you propose we do, Henry?"

He thought for a while before answering. "Well, let's see what we've got. We have an attempted bribe. I say 'attempted' because we don't know how Dowding responded. But we do know how Washington feels about that kind of thing. We also have one of the richest nations in the Gulf, with their enormous leverage through their oil exports to our allies—France, Italy, and especially Japan—and even ourselves, if things should really get rough. If we tell this story, our relations with the Gulf will be less than cordial—to say nothing of our own government, which probably won't be thrilled to have us create a breach in relations with the king. In addition, this thing will probably tear the roof off FMB and blow up Dowding and Salisbury with it. Joan, I would say that for a cub reporter you've got very sharp teeth and claws."

"Henry, everything you've said reinforces my belief that not one positive contribution can be made by releasing this story. Oh, perhaps we can tell ourselves that we're exposing corruption. That's bullshit, Henry. They've been bribing each other in the Middle East since time began. It comes with their mother's milk. Exposing one Arab who is giving or receiving is about as meaningful as trying to kill all the flies in Africa."

"And do I infer, Joan, that your idea is to suppress this story?"

"I don't see what is accomplished by telling it. Who wins besides us, Henry? Oh, maybe I'll wind up with an award for best investigative reporter, or you with another silver cup to add to your collection. And maybe the ratings will go up for a while, and we'll sell more advertising or increase the cost of our spots. Maybe you'll get a bonus, maybe Lionel will let you take over the whole news department. But outside of those very fragile benefits, Henry, who wins? Nobody, that's who. Everybody loses in this thing. The guy who's drinking his beer in front of the tube won't miss a beat if we broadcast this, or if we don't. The whole thing is so commonplace it won't surprise anyone. The only thing that's newsworthy are the players, and the size of the numbers."

He was beginning to glimpse the dark underside of what she feared would come between them.

"Joan, let me ask you where this country would be if every reporter made the subjective decision to be his own censor, his own editor. Suppose the initial Watergate break-in had never been reported because it was thought unimportant, not newsworthy. After all, what's so special in a city with a crime rate as high as Washington's about the break-in of a political headquarters? What are they going to steal—posters?

"But think what would have happened if an alert press, for whatever motives, had not dug into that story. And what did they have to begin with? Not a hell of a lot. And who were they taking on? Not an Arab middleman, not a dynast; those guys took on the President of the United States. And initially they had very little support, even from their own paper. Suppose those fellows had stopped. Is it unreasonable to assume that this country could have been permanently injured by a neurotic, amoral President?"

He saw the expression on her face, in her eyes. He hadn't moved her.

"Henry. The press always has a rationale for whatever they want to print. And you're comparing apples and oranges. You're equating Watergate to a tawdry little affair between unscrupulous men."

"Do you mean Dowding?"

She hesitated. "No, I don't. I don't think Doug is that kind of man."

"But we don't know that."

"No, we don't."

"Do you think that's important to find out?"

"For whom?"

"For everyone."

"That's not very specific, Henry."

"I don't want to sound corny, by saying in pursuit of the truth."

"Pursuit of the truth, my foot. When this hits the street, no one will give a damn about the truth. All they'll smell is blood, and they'll hound Doug and John Salisbury until they've ruined both of them."

"It'll be quite a job to ruin John Salisbury."

"Well, you know what I mean, Henry. In any case, it will destroy Doug, and I don't want to be a part of that."

"But you didn't create those circumstances. You're a reporter, or at least where Dowding is concerned you are, because I assigned that role to you and you undertook to oblige me, for which I am grateful.

"Are you going to make me tell you what you already know? You can't be the judge of what's right and wrong, what's newsworthy and what isn't. I'm afraid the fourth estate isn't ready for someone wise enough to decide for all of us what we are going to see, read, and hear. I believe that's why we have a free press, and if my historical perspective is accurate, it's served a pretty vital role in preserving our institutions against crooks, incompetents, con men, and just generally some of the insidious characters who would ruin this country."

"Henry, that, in my book, is part poetry and part bullshit. Every time a member of the press wants to do a story, especially if it's controversial, he raises the sacred flag of 'freedom of the press.' Never mind who gets hurt or what the personal ramifications are.

"Oh, I'm sick of all this, Henry." She put the tape back in her handbag and went to the kitchen to get another drink.

The wind had risen to gale force, and the tops of the trees were moaning in its blast. The gulls huddled in protected shelters, their cries obliterated by the sounds of the storm. Occasionally a wave would crash against the rocks and ledges of the harbor entrance, sounding like a dull, far-off explosion. The initial tracers of wind-driven rain began to strike with their first scattered tappings against the windows.

"You want another drink, Henry?"

He had got up again to put more wood on the fire. The split pine filled with pitch didn't last as long as the beech and ash that were burned on his father's farm when he was growing up in Pennsylvania. His mind went back to that strange, terse man who still lived there holding tightly to his beliefs and principles.

Henry wondered what it would have been like if he had stayed, if he had played out the old man's dream of the last male Cannon holding on to the land.

There was a time when Henry was very tempted to do that. It was in the warm spring, when the ground was soft underfoot, when everything came to life, and that life was in front of him to see and smell and touch. Sometimes he was tempted, even in winter, when the long, blue shadows fell across the snow and the world was silent and white, occasionally touched with the black silhouettes of birds. But Henry had a restlessness that the land couldn't contain, an inquisitiveness that had to be satisfied. And was he satisfied? A failed marriage, scrapbooks full of faded clippings, memories of a disordered world, of lonely hotels, and cities filled with strange, hurrying, closed faces. And now there was Joan. Was he going to lose her too, to this insatiable profession that seemed to devour everything in his life that was important? He didn't think he could handle that.

They grew silent as they sat, each lost in thought, hearing with only a part of their minds the increasing fury of the storm. The rain was hard now, slashing against the sides of the house.

They could feel the tension that had begun to separate them, and they were depressed by it.

"The long and short of it, Henry, is that, regardless of

who's hurt, you want me to give you that tape so that you can go ahead with the story."

She looked at him challengingly.

He nodded his head affirmatively, sadly. His voice was melancholy. "I do, Joan. I think that as my assistant and as an employee of NBT you have that obligation."

Her green eyes flashed at him. "So you're going to pull the loyalty to dear old NBT, eh, Henry?"

Henry felt the force of what this was doing to them, but his professionalism, the beliefs he had given his adult life to, persisted.

"No, Joan, although I'm old-fashioned enough to think that you have a responsibility to those who employ you."

She looked at him in exasperation. "Henry, for God's sake. Am I supposed to help you destroy a man's life because of a supposed obligation to an insidious predator like Lionel Emden? Henry, what's come over you? Is this really the way you think? I don't believe it."

"Joan, whether or not the president of NBT elicits any great feelings of warmth for you, whether or not he inspires you to loyalty is immaterial. It's your own character we're talking about."

"That's the problem, Henry. If I didn't have any character, we wouldn't have a problem. I'd just give you the tape, and you'd become the darling of Lionel, of the whole damn company, and we'd simply walk away from the anguish we'd cause and go on to the next story. Isn't that what you'd like, Henry? Joan and Henry—or would you prefer top billing?"

This angered him. "I want you to cut this out. Stop playing St. Joan long enough to really listen to me." His tone was very strained. "I have no idea what all this is going to do to us. It seems to have already driven a wedge between us. But I believe you know that I love you, and I know that you love me. Do you think I would jeopardize that for NBT or Lionel Emden or any financial consideration or self-aggrandizement? If you have no more regard for me than that, Joan, I should think you'd want very little to do with me."

She was still seated in a chair next to his looking into the fire. He got up and knelt beside her, turning her face toward his. He could see her torment and her desire for some equitable resolution to all this. He kissed her gently, and pressed her head against his chest. "Joanie, this is a horrible thing for the two of us to have to go through. I don't want anything to happen to us over something like this. You said it in the beginning—we have a problem in ethics, and each of us sees it from his own point of view.

"You're so young, Joan, and there's so much you haven't seen. I've seen too much, and maybe I've been around too long, and maybe I'm just too old-fashioned for this game any more; but, Joan, I have some ethical standards of my own; certainly as to how I perform my job. And I'm afraid that as far as you're concerned I haven't done it very well."

"What do you mean by that?"

He looked at her for a long while. He kissed her again and got up to find his cigarettes. He stood near the fireplace looking at her, and smoking quietly. She was becoming apprehensive because of his manner, which seemed so constrained to her.

"Joan, you are my direct responsibility at NBT. No matter what your own feelings may be regarding this hole we find ourselves in, I gave you an assignment which has become an important piece of news, one that as a professional I have no right to withhold. If I can't manage my own people, Joan, so that I can do my job properly, then the only honorable course I have open to me, at least from my point of view, is to resign."

She sat up, half out of her chair. "Henry, you wouldn't do that!"

"I'm afraid I'd have no alternative. Doing my job means being able to handle my own staff properly, and at least as far as you're concerned, I haven't been very successful."

She got up and started pacing the room, occasionally whirling around to look at him, her eyes now bright with anger and despair.

"Well, that's just great, Henry. You really know how to work on somebody, don't you? So now you're going to lay this on me—your resignation. I'm going to be the cause of your leaving NBT. Jesus, Henry, if that isn't a beaut." She stopped pacing and turned to look at him angrily. "How long have you been saving up that one? Have you been trying to soften me up so that you could hit me with that?"

Henry had lost his patience. "Damn it, Joan, stop acting like a sixteen-year-old and have the grace to believe a simple statement of fact. No one in my position who has a shred of personal esteem could do anything else. When the time comes that Henry Cannon can't do his job properly, he isn't going to wait for a Lionel Emden to tell him. You've put me in this position, Joan, and I don't happen to like the feeling any more than you do. Now, you can take the tape and do anything you damn please with it, but if you don't give it to me, I'm resigning. That's all I can do, and that's what I'm going to do, with the single exception of going to bed. I've had enough of this."

He started to go into the bedroom.

"Wait, Henry. I'm sorry. This whole thing has been a nightmare for me too. I want you to promise me one thing. If I give you the tape, will you meet with Dowding and Salisbury in my presence before releasing the story?"

"Certainly. I have no objection to that."

The house shuddered under the impact of the wind. The rain struck the windows with such force that it seemed they must break.

The two of them lay in each other's arms, alert to the shadows and the sounds of the storm.

She reached for him, feeling him harden in her hand.

She put him inside her and rolled on top of him, beginning the slow, rhythmic pulsations of her hips that began to move faster and faster.

"Henry, suck on my tits. Suck hard, Henry." She licked him, buried her tongue deep in his mouth. She raked him with her nails.

"Henry, now! Hard, Henry! For Christ's sake, hard! Oh, Henry, what a magnificent prick you have. I want all of it. All of it. Every inch. Henry, now. Now! Jesus, Henry! Oh, my God!"

She lay on top of him, panting, spent. He held her, feeling the rapid beating of her heart. She was a lot of woman.

But as they lay in each other's arms, they knew that something important had come between them, and silently wondered if they had enough together to keep it from tearing them apart.

JOHN HAD BEEN CHANGING FOR A FORMAL DINNER TO be held at the Council of Latin American Affairs. There was a knock on the door of his dressing room, and Margret came in.

He took one look at her and knew that something was very wrong. Her eyes seemed far away, and there was a look of hurt in them that made him stop fixing his tie and look at her with concern.

"What's the matter?"

Margret was still his tall, straight, controlled New England patrician, but she was getting older. The winds that blew affected her more visibly. Deep in the light blue eyes was a sadness that he hadn't seen before. Her voice was hushed. "Jane would like to see you, alone."

He looked confused. "Well, send her in." Without another word, Margret turned and left.

He waited for Jane, wondering what this was all about.

When she stood at the doorframe, at that threshold of formality that had always seemed to separate them, she reminded him so much of Margret. But as she stood there, he saw his sharp, somewhat pointed nose, and his brown eyes and the color of his hair when he was younger.

He looked at her in her flared slacks, which seemed to emphasize the grace of her long legs. Her hair was neatly brushed.

They looked at each other, each sensing that this was an end, and possibly a beginning.

"May I come in?"

"Of course." He hesitated. "You look very attractive, Jane."

"Thank you." Her voice was subdued; her eyes occasionally found his, but more often they avoided looking directly at him.

He sat on the edge of a table looking at her, still standing in front of him, so young, so much a part of him, and yet so removed. Each of them was isolated from the other, but saw and cared far more than either could express.

"Do you want to sit down?"

"No, Father, I prefer to stand. I just came to say good-bye."

The words cut through him, deep into where he lived. A place so far down that he kept it hidden even from himself. Not because he wanted to, but because that was the way he was.

"Good-bye. That's a word I've always disliked, Jane. Good-bye is very cold and final. Why are you saying good-bye?"

"Because my plane leaves in three hours, Father."

"Your plane? But where are you going?"

"I'll be traveling, for at least a year. I'm leaving for India tonight."

"India!"

She didn't answer. Just looked at him with a slight tightening of her mouth. Her eyes caught, then lost his.

"Why India, for heaven's sake?"

"That's too long and too personal to discuss now, Father,

but I can tell you that there are places I want to see, philosophies I want to hear firsthand, and I want time to be by myself and think."

He was stunned by all this and hurt, deeply hurt. His only child walks into his dressing room and announces three hours before departure that she's leaving for India.

"When will you be back?"

"I don't know."

"Do you have an itinerary?"

"No."

"How will we know where you are?"

She lowered her eyes slightly; she could sense his fear, and his anger.

"I guess you won't until I write to you."

His mind raced with the practical implications of all this; one of the richest young women in the world was going off by herself, prey to every nut and brigand who might want to kidnap her, marry her, get her money. The family would do anything to protect her, rescue her if necessary. She wasn't just some ordinary headstrong young woman who had decided to see the world.

"Have you provided yourself with funds?"

He saw her lips tighten. "I've budgeted a very small amount to see me through. When I run out of that, I'll support myself."

He knew it was useless to argue; she would do what she wanted.

He stood up, his dinner shirt still unbuttoned, his black tie hanging untied about his neck, his jacket on a hanger next to the full-length mirror.

So this is what it had come to, he thought; this is what she had meant when she said that she had had no father. All the commitments, all the time spent away; each day and night had separated them further, and now there was a gulf between them like a deep ocean trench, a dark abyss where there was no light.

"Jane, must you do this?" He felt the loneliness of his own

childhood well up inside him, and he understood hers. But it was too late.

"Jane."

"I'm afraid I'd better finish the rest of my packing, Father."

She stood there, looking at him. They both stood there. He wanted to take her in his arms and tell her how much he loved her, how sorry he was for all the years he hadn't been there.

She came toward him, just a few steps. She had paled visibly. She stood straight and slim and tall, like her mother, only she looked at him with *his* eyes. There was sorrow in them, and anxiety, and confusion and some hostility; but there was determination.

She extended her thin hand. He took it, hurt, filled with guilt, and held it. He was so overcome with emotion that he could hardly speak. He wanted to clasp her to him, to wrap her in the love he felt for her, but that might embarrass both of them. Formality, convention, something puritanical and destructive, kept them apart.

They remained standing there as he held her outstretched hand. She, too, wanted to rush to him, to throw her arms about him, and tell him how much she loved him, needed him; how she longed to be with him, close to him, if only for an hour, a day.

But they remained standing, looking at each other, their hearts breaking, separated by all those years that had created the gulf. Both their hearts were pounding because it was one blood, and the love was there.

His eyes misted as he looked at her. "Jane. Promise me you'll come back; that you'll write and let us know where you are, how you are." The lump in his throat was choking him.

She looked at him for a moment, quickly brushed his cheek with her lips, and then hurried out of the room.

She had taken the most important part of his life with her.

DOUG WAS GOING THROUGH HIS MAIL WHEN HE NOTICED a piece of white bond paper on his desk. It said, "Gneist Bank, Zurich, 4961325."

Doug turned the paper over in his hand. There was nothing else on it.

As a banker, Doug didn't have to be told what it was. It represented a numbered Swiss account in a private bank, the Gneist Bank in Zurich. What he didn't understand was how it came to be on his desk.

Doug called his secretary and asked her to find the envelope it had come in. When she had searched her wastebasket and had brought it to him, he was surprised to see it had a Cayman Island postmark.

This was not exactly a routine piece of correspondence.

He sat and thought about this for a while. He was about to put in a call to the Gneist Bank when his secretary buzzed and told him that Mr. Salisbury wanted to see him immediately.

Doug groaned. What the hell's up now, he wondered as he started for John's office.

* * *

John had just received a devastating phone call.

The memory of that call would be etched in his mind for the rest of his life.

John Salisbury had picked up the phone. "Good morning, Mr. Cannon."

Henry Cannon wasted no time.

"Mr. Salisbury," he said, "I have in my possession a taped conversation between your president, Mr. Dowding, and a gentleman I will name in your presence, offering Mr. Dowding a five-million-dollar bribe."

John nearly dropped the phone. His face went dead white. For a moment he felt as if his heart had stopped beating.

"Would you mind repeating that, Mr. Cannon?"

Henry repeated what he had just said.

John's voice was almost a whisper. "How soon can you come down here?"

"I can be there in half an hour, Mr. Salisbury."

"I'll be waiting for you."

John leaned back in his chair, the life almost drained out of him. This was the end, he thought—a shattering, ignominious end. He had hoped to leave this bank with some credit for all his years of hard work, but now any chance of that was gone. This Cannon fellow would never have made such a statement on the telephone if he didn't have what he said he did. It was all over. In the worst possible way. John Salisbury thought of the family, of Jane—his heart wrenched at that. My God, all the years, the movement, the worry, the continual criticism—for this? Is this what his life had come to? He shuddered.

When Henry Cannon and Joan were shown into John's office, Doug stood facing them, glaring hostilely at both of them. His real enmity was reserved for Joan. She had difficulty even looking at him.

"Mr. Salisbury, this is my assistant, Miss Hopkins."

Henry nodded to Doug. "Mr. Dowding."

The atmosphere in the room was as cozy as an Arctic night.

"Now would you mind enlightening Mr. Dowding and myself as to what you told me over the phone."

Henry sighed. "It's not particularly pleasant to bring this to you, gentlemen, and yet I felt it only fair to advise you of these circumstances before I released this story."

"May I ask how you came by this information, Mr. Cannon?"

"I'm afraid I'm not at liberty to tell you that, Mr. Salisbury."

John paused. "I see."

Henry took the recorder from his inside breast pocket and put it on the conference table.

"Would you like to hear this now, Mr. Salisbury?"

Henry looked at John, whose eyes were riveted on the small black machine as if it were a poisonous snake.

Doug's face was dead white.

Joan's heart beat so heavily that she felt it would burst.

Henry played the tape.

When it was over, John turned toward Doug. His face was ashen, incredulous.

"What did you mean when you said, 'I'd rather think about that'?"

Doug was so floored by the existence of the tape that he was literally unable to speak.

John was able to control himself at least to the point where he realized that it would be inadvisable to discuss this in front of Cannon and Miss Hopkins.

They had been standing when the tape was played, and now each found a seat in John's office, where the light blue sky seemed inappropriate for the general gloom they all felt.

"Well, Mr. Cannon, it looks as if NBT has quite a story."

"So it would appear, Mr. Salisbury." Henry turned to Doug. "Mr. Dowding, I'm afraid I have to ask you if that is your voice, and if indeed such an offer was made to you."

Doug nodded incredulously.

"Then, Mr. Dowding, would you care to elaborate as to whether or not you accepted this offer?"

Henry's last question seemed to shake Doug out of his trance. He rose quickly from the couch, his face flushed. He began to walk back and forth.

"Of course I refused the damn thing."

John's voice was very strained.

"That's not quite clear from the transcript, Doug. More to the point, Mr. Cannon, do you plan to release this story?"

"Yes, sir, I do."

"And if I call Lionel Emden?"

"He'll leave that decision to me, Mr. Salisbury. It's my area of responsibility."

"What do you hope to accomplish by the release of such a story, Mr. Cannon?"

"It's news, sir. That's the business we're in."

"I see." And it's as simple as that, is it? thought John. You ruin a career, a family, perhaps two families, and your only rationale is that it's news. It seems a shoddy business. "Have you given any thought to the repercussions of such a disclosure to Mr. Dowding and, I might add, to myself as well?"

"A good deal, sir."

"And yet for a momentary cheap piece of sensationalism, you would inflict on the two of us the ignominy of such a disclosure, Mr. Cannon?"

"Mr. Salisbury, if I withhold this story, you can be assured that sooner or later it's going to leak."

"I'd be very willing to take that chance."

"I'm sorry, sir."

"I see."

John got up and walked to the windows, looking out into the void of sea and sky. He did not turn around as he spoke to them. His voice sounded very old and very tired. But with it all, in the most difficult period of his life, John maintained a certain degree of dignity that was mighty impressive as far as Henry Cannon was concerned.

"I wonder, Doug, if you and Miss Hopkins would wait for me in my outer office. I'd like to speak to Mr. Cannon alone."

Doug got up silently and Joan followed.

They went into John's outer office. When he had closed the door, Doug turned to her; there was a look of cold fury on his face.

"Just where the hell did that tape come from, Joan, and how did it happen to turn up in your Mr. Cannon's pocket?"

Joan told him the whole story of the tape.

"And you didn't even have the decency to tell me about it. What kind of a woman are you?"

Her eyes flashed. "Now hold it, Sir Lancelot. Before you go stomping off in search of the Holy Grail, just tell me how I'm supposed to know you didn't take that money?"

His eyes blazed. "For Christ's sake, Joan, just what kind of a man do you think I am?"

She looked at him, coolly. "The kind who says 'I'd rather think about that.'" If she had slashed him with a razor, he couldn't have been cut more deeply.

"But, Joan, I'm telling you I turned that bastard down." He towered over her, glaring at her, his eyes burning with the fever of his frustration.

She had not taken her eyes off him. "I know, that's what you've told us."

"And you don't believe me?"

"I didn't say that."

"Well, then, why in hell would you have put me in such a position?"

She was furious. "Now, get this straight, Doug. The only reason that you're getting any forewarning of this at all is because I twisted Henry's arm to come here. As for putting you in this position, I think that's slightly inaccurate. You put yourself in that position when you didn't immediately turn Aragon down."

He looked at her inquiringly. "Joan, has anyone ever offered you five million dollars in cash?"

"Not since at least yesterday." She saw the anguish in his eyes, and for the first time since they had left St. John, she began to believe in him.

John had been cut adrift. He had no moorings. This cataclysm had struck him from the mists where there were hidden rocks that could tear his life apart.

"Mr. Cannon, I certainly appreciate your giving me the opportunity of hearing this before I saw it in the papers or on television."

Henry was morose. He was twisted by his distaste for all this.

"I'm not particularly pleased about this, Mr. Salisbury."

John looked at Henry for a long time. He was beyond antagonism. His voice came from somewhere in the past.

"Mr. Cannon, when you release this news Mr. Dowding and I will be forced to resign. That situation is degrading enough, but Mr. Dowding may be subject to possible criminal prosecution on a charge that could be very difficult to prove. After all, we still don't know whether he took the bribe or not."

"That's true, sir."

"And, of course, if he didn't take it, he would be crucified in the press on an unwarranted charge. He'd be ruined unjustly."

Henry was silent. This was worse than covering the damn war, he thought. This quiet patrician under the most excruciating pressure was defending an associate, not referring to his own disgrace in having been responsible for creating such an association. John Salisbury had a lot of moxie, Henry thought, and a lot of class.

"Would you consider it against any ethical or practical

considerations, Mr. Cannon, if I asked you to delay the release of this story for five business days? That would be until noon next Friday. Would that be asking too much of you, sir?"

Henry watched him closely.

"For what purpose, Mr. Salisbury?"

"Well, for one thing, to plan for the succession of my stewardship of this bank. For another, to find out whether or not Mr. Dowding accepted that offer, and finally, to prevent this kind of thing from happening again if I can."

Henry lit a cigarette and smoked thoughtfully for a while. "If I agree to this, Mr. Salisbury, have I your word that our exclusivity to this story won't be jeopardized?"

"You have my word, sir."

"And can you speak for Mr. Dowding on this?"

"I'm sure I can."

Henry tried to figure out why he shouldn't accede to this request. Salisbury and Dowding certainly had every motive for keeping this quiet, and if NBT's exclusivity was protected, what did he have to lose?

"I think we might work that out, sir."

John rose wearily. "I'm indebted to you, Mr. Cannon. We have our bargain then."

"Yes, sir. Until noon next Friday."

John paused, seeing but not seeing, drained of his capacity to feel. "That's a very short lifetime, Mr. Cannon," he said, hearing his own voice as if it came from someone else, out of a fog.

Henry did not reply. He felt lower than he ever had in his entire career.

Doug sat with John in his office after Henry and Joan had left, both of them stunned.

A part of John's mind believed in Doug's betrayal, yet he couldn't wholly accept that; not after all the years, and the trust that had grown up between them.

Doug was seated on the sofa, shattered. He was a gigantic marionette whose strings had been cut, a punctured balloon.

John stood looking out the window. This was characteristic of him when he was troubled. He seemed to want to reach out for the elements of nature that were permanent, for earth, sky, and water. He needed to escape the trials of the human condition whose only constancy lay in its change.

He turned slowly toward Doug, his eyes not seeing, his voice detached from the rest of him.

"Why did you say 'I'd rather think about that'? Why didn't you simply then and there refuse him?"

Doug's voice came from the part of him that was dying. He said softly, in that deep bass voice, "John, I was so taken by surprise I was lucky to say anything at all."

John turned it all over slowly in his mind, as if the whole thing was separate from him, a dream, something he could awaken from.

He had known Doug and Bardy for almost twenty years. He had always had the highest regard for both of them. John was convinced that a woman like Bardy could never have spent a quarter of a century married to a man who was dishonest; not Bardy.

John's mind, the part that could still function, prayed for an affirmation.

"Doug, for both our sakes, tell me the truth. We're in this together. We'll have to resign a week from today. That's my pact with Mr. Cannon. He's willing to give me until then before he releases the story. But I simply have to know, for the preservation of my own sanity, that the man I personally selected to be president of this bank, whom I have known for twenty years and trusted, has not soured on me." John looked at Doug imploringly; the guard between them was down. They were now naked before a capricious fate.

"Did you take that money, Doug?"

Doug's face was crimson. His body snapped taut with the

whip of John's mistrust. "For Christ's sake, John. I didn't take it. I turned Aragon down cold." He stood up looking battered, bewildered. "John, you've got to believe that."

John wanted to believe it—if for nothing else, to vindicate all the years.

Doug reached into his pocket for a cigarette, and his fingers touched the piece of paper he had put there from the Gneist Bank. He took it out and looked at it, not really seeing it, not reacting with his usual instinct for self-preservation. Henry's disclosure of the tape had blanked out a part of his mind. It was as if he were shell-shocked.

John watched him holding the paper. "What's that?"

"What's what?"

"That paper you're holding."

"Oh, this. I got this in the mail this morning. I don't know why the hell it was sent to me." He handed the paper to John.

John looked at it carefully, and then at Doug. John knew what it was immediately, and he too was somewhat at a loss to know what the president of FMB was doing with the number of a Swiss bank account in his pocket.

John buzzed his secretary. "I want you to place a call to the Gneist Bank in Zurich. Find the name of their Managing Director in the overseas directory. Tell him, or anyone who answers, that this call is most urgent."

"Yes, sir."

He turned to Doug. "You don't have any idea, Doug, what this Gneist thing is all about?"

"Not the slightest."

John remained thoughtful. "You know, Doug, the only course left open to us is to handle this tape business with whatever grace and courage we've got. And, I might add, with some dignity too, if we can manage it." He paused, half talking to himself. "That's about all that's left to us, Doug."

John was so stunned by the events of the day that he seemed to be sleepwalking. His buzzer interrupted his thoughts.

"I have Mr. Kurt Ahlwardt on the line, sir. He's Managing Director."

John picked up the phone. "Mr. Ahlwardt?"

"*Ja*, Mr. Salisbury. This is an honor, sir."

John caught the heavy Swiss Deutsch accent.

"I'm pleased we found you in, Herr Ahlwardt." John paused to pick up the paper from his desk. "We have a rather unusual message here, Herr Ahlwardt, that concerns your bank."

"*Ja?*"

John could hear the surprise across the North Atlantic.

"I'm holding a piece of paper which was mailed to Mr. Douglas Dowding from the Cayman Islands. Does your bank have a branch there?"

"*Ja*, Herr Salisbury. Ve do."

"Let me read this to you." John read the single typed line. "Does that mean anything to you, Herr Ahlwardt?"

There was a pause at the other end of the line.

"One moment, Herr Salisbury."

John held the phone, looking inquiringly at Doug.

"*Ja*, Herr Salisbury. This is an account number here at our bank."

"Could you tell me whose account, Herr Ahlwardt?"

Another pause. "I'm afraid not, Herr Salisbury. You have the correct number, sir, but this is a two-signature account, and we would need at least one signature before we could release that information, sir."

John remained thoughtful for a moment.

"Do you have facsimile transfer equipment, Herr Ahlwardt?"

"Ja. Ve do."

"I would like to impose on you, sir, if I may. I realize it's getting late there, but I would like to transmit a signature to you. It's very important, Herr Ahlwardt."

"*Ja*, sure, Herr Salisbury. Ve vould be delighted to be of

any assistance, sir. Ve vould be honored."

"Thank you, Herr Ahlwardt. Would you please call me when you get this signature, and if it's the correct one—and since we also have the correct account number—would you be good enough to give me the particulars of the account, sir?"

"*Ja*, Herr Salisbury. If it's the correct name and signature, we can do dat. I call you back, sir."

"*Danke schön*, Herr Ahlwardt."

"*Auf Wiedersehen*, Herr Salisbury."

John hung up. He buzzed his secretary.

"Would you come in, please, and transfer a signature of Mr. Dowding's to Mr. Ahlwardt of the Gneist Bank."

"Yes, sir."

Doug stood up, his face beet red. "John, what the hell is this? I told you I don't know a damn thing about that account."

John looked at Doug carefully. "I'm sure you don't, Doug, but one of two things is happening. Either you're the victim of some Machiavellian mind, or you're a charlatan and a liar."

Doug jumped to his feet, his voice bellowing.

"John, I don't have to take that from you or anyone else."

John looked at him wearily, and waved him to a chair. "Sit down, Doug. It might get to be a very long morning."

They had canceled their schedules for the rest of the morning. As they sat waiting for the facsimile transfer to take place, Doug felt as if he were living in a nightmare, the kind that makes its victim want to awaken, though he can't. He writhes, contorts, groans in fear until the terror finally bursts through his consciousness and he lunges awake, finally freed from the torment of his mind. This was the way Doug felt, but it was worse for him. He *was* awake. All of this damned insidiousness was really happening to him. He had acted honorably, and his only reward was the vilest kind of accusations.

Jesus Christ, Doug said to himself, this whole damn thing is insane.

"I have Mr. Ahlwardt, sir, on sixteen."

John picked up the phone. "Herr Ahlwardt. I appreciate your getting back to me so soon. I'm going to put you on the speaker phone. Mr. Dowding is in my office. There's no one else here."

Kurt Ahlwardt's telephone manner had changed. John could hear the bewilderment in the guttural voice.

"*Ja*, Herr Salisbury. Ve got de signature. I don undershstand it but de signature matches. It's Herr Dowding's signature, sir."

Doug looked at John incredulously. "But it can't be. I've never been in that bank in my life. John, for Christ's sake, what's going on here?"

The speaker phone picked up part of Doug's outburst and transmitted it across 3,800 miles to Zurich.

John didn't look at Doug.

"Can you describe the account to us, Mr. Ahlwardt?"

"*Ja*. It's a two-signature account in de name of Herr Douglas Dowding und allzo a Mr. Ageel."

John paused. "What's in the account, Herr Ahlwardt?"

They could both feel the hesitation on the other end of the line.

"Ah—it's interest-bearing negotiable securities, Herr Salisbury."

"In what amount?"

"Eleven million nine hundred thousand Swiss francs."

John calculated quickly. "That's about five million U.S. dollars."

"*Ja. Das ist richtig*—ah, das ist correct."

Doug almost collapsed on the couch.

"You've been a great help, Herr Ahlwardt. *Danke schön. Auf Wiedersehen.*"

"*Wiedersehen.*"

John hung up. He looked at Doug, who was sprawled in his chair, his face dead white, his eyes glazed, unseeing, as if he were dead.

John was so disturbed by this transatlantic inquiry that he simply couldn't talk. He sat at his desk, his hands trembling, his own face ashen.

Doug's voice seemed to come to him from some great distance. The voice was choked, broken.

"John, I swear by Bardy and the children I don't know anything about this. I didn't take any money. I never heard of this account. For God's sake, John, you have to believe that."

John was sitting with his head held between his hands as if he wanted to shut out the voice of his associate and friend. His reply was more of a mumble than anything else.

"Be at my place for dinner tonight, Doug. We can talk about it then."

He sat alone, wondering if it were possible that he had been betrayed. Of all the things that had happened to him, with the exception of Jane, the thought of a breach of trust from a man he had known for over twenty years, whom he had treated like a son, was the cruelest blow of all.

Doug had left the bank in a trance. His mind wouldn't function.

When he walked into his apartment a little after one o'clock, his manner was so strange, so completely preoccupied, that Bardy put down the *Times* and looked at him, knowing that something was terribly wrong.

She came to him quietly, touching him very gently on the arm. "Doug, what's happened? Tell me. You look simply ghastly."

He stood in the center of the room, noticing her with only a part of his mind; the rest was a total blank. The trauma of the morning had been too much for him.

She guided him toward a chair with great concern. "Doug, for heaven's sake, what is it?"

He looked at her, past her, not really able to acknowledge her presence. He spoke as if he were talking in his sleep, his voice a flat monotone. He told her what had happened this morning.

"My God, that's unbelievable, Doug!"

With the instincts of a woman who had lived intimately with a man for over twenty-five years, she knew that he had not accept that money. How it came to be in his name with this Ageel or whatever his name was, she didn't know, but that her husband was being insidiously crucified, that she did know.

She got up and poured him a drink.

"Here, take this, Doug, then go in and lie down. This thing will get itself straightened out. Someone is giving you a very dirty deal, and I think I know who that someone is. What I can't figure out is why."

He obediently drank the Scotch she had poured him. Then she walked with him into his bedroom, and helped him to undress. He was completely exhausted. His last words to her before he fell asleep were, "I have to be at John's for dinner."

She covered him with a light blanket and went into the living room to think. She had sat alone for more than an hour when an idea struck her. She reached for the telephone and called Margret Salisbury. She was very lucky, for it was one of the few occasions when Margret was at home in the middle of the day.

"Bardy, what a nice surprise! It's been ages. How are you feeling?" Bardy thought Margret sounded tired, a little down; that was unusual for Margret.

Bardy's voice was troubled but controlled. "I'm fine, Margret, but I'd like to come over as soon as possible if I may. It's really quite urgent."

Margret knew Bardia Dowding very well. She knew Bardia

to be sensible and undramatic. For Bardia to use the word "urgent" something had to be very wrong.

"Bardy, are you all right? Is something the matter?" Margret was now alert for trouble and very concerned.

"It's not me, Margret, it's Doug. Something's come up at the bank that's really quite terrible. I have to talk to you about it."

This was the first time in twenty years that she had ever heard Bardia talk like this.

"May I come over there, Bardy?"

"No, Margret, thank you. Doug has just come home. He's asleep, and I think it would be better if I came over to see you."

"When can you be here?"

"In ten minutes."

"I'll see you then. Have you had lunch?"

"Yes, I have. Don't bother with anything, Margret. I'm leaving right away."

The two women sat in Margret's study, crammed with books, paintings, pictures of the family, and the general memorabilia collected by an active and interested woman.

"My God, Bardy, that's the most incredible thing I've ever heard."

"That's the reaction I had. It's almost too cruel. I can't explain how those securities got into that Swiss bank account. All I can tell you is that Doug had nothing to do with it."

Margret looked at the slim figure in the dark blue suit sitting erect and proud, her hands resting quietly in her lap. Bardia Dowding's pale face was grim and determined.

"Margret. I can't let this happen to Doug. Would you speak to John for me? They're going to have dinner here tonight."

Margret looked carefully at Bardia Colfax Morrison Dowding, a valiant woman and a dear friend. She leaned across the space that separated them and touched Bardia's hand. "Don't worry, Bardy. I'll speak to John. I'll make him understand."

And Margret was right. If there was a single human being on this planet who could be persuasive with John under these circumstances, it was Margret. Bardia's intuition had been dead on the mark.

When John returned from the bank around six o'clock, which was early for him, he looked exhausted. He was paler than Margret could remember, and his whole manner seemed so listless and resigned that it nearly broke her heart.

Jane had gone. The two of them, with the exception of the servants, were alone until Doug arrived.

It was unusual for them to have this amount of time together, just the two of them, without some college president, the mayor, or the foreign minister of a developing country sitting as a guest at a small dinner for ten or twelve people.

The firelight in John's library sent scattered shadows flickering about the room; there was no other light. The two of them sat together on the small divan facing the fire, not really speaking; holding each other's hand, and drawing strength from just being together. The absence of Jane weighed heavily upon them.

"Bardy was here this afternoon."

He looked surprised. "Bardy? Was she well enough? I didn't think she went out any more other than to see her doctor."

"She came about Doug. She told me the whole thing."

John turned to her, his face half hidden in shadow.

"That's not like Bardy."

"She's frightened, John. Not for herself, but for Doug. It's absolutely insidious." She touched her husband's face and leaned forward to kiss him. "Oh, John, this whole business is so completely frightful. I'm so sorry for you."

He sighed. His voice was quiet, almost forlorn. "With everything that's gone on around here lately, I'm feeling a little sorry for myself, Marge."

She kissed him again, understanding only too well what he

was saying. "But, John, surely you can't possibly believe Doug had anything to do with this? It's too preposterous."

His voice sounded far away. "I wish I could be certain of that, Marge. I've spent an entire day telling myself the same thing—that I couldn't possibly have spent all these years observing Doug, working with him so closely, and have misjudged him so badly. But I keep coming back to that Swiss account. How did those funds get there? I just can't rationalize that away, Margret."

She thought for a moment. Margret hadn't been a banker's wife for twenty-five years for nothing; she was no novice to the profession.

"Was the account in Doug's name?"

"Doug's and another man's by the name of Ageel."

"Who's he?"

John told her. Margret sat watching the flames throw their harlequin shadows about the room.

"Was that a joint account, John?"

"It was a double-signature account; it amounts to the same thing."

"Meaning you couldn't withdraw the securities without both signatures?"

"Right."

She thought silently for a while, the idea taking form in her mind.

"Then Doug really wouldn't have access to those securities without this Ageel's signature?"

John turned toward her, seeing the trend of her thought. Funny. Neither he nor Doug, reeling from the impact of the morning's revelations, had picked this up.

"Margret. Why would Ageel do such a thing? What possible motive could he have?"

"I don't know, John, but I know one thing. If Doug were going to take a five-million-dollar bribe, he'd be smart enough to arrange things so he wouldn't need a cosigner."

Her tone was sarcastic, and it should have been. John should have caught that himself. It was stupid of both him and Doug to have overlooked something so obvious.

He looked at Margret for a very long time, and then cupped her face in both hands, looking at her with great tenderness; she was all he really had left to hold on to.

"I love you very much," he said.

She put her arms around him and kissed him.

"I love you very much too, John—very much. And no matter how this all turns out, whatever happens, we'll be able to handle it together."

Jane's face suddenly came to him; he almost winced. "It's a shame you two couldn't have spared a little of that for me." His mind heard her say it; he was assaulted by his guilt.

Margret knew him so well. She sensed what he was thinking, and was depressed by it. Jane's leaving had cut a hole in her own life. She was the mother; her child had sprung from her; from inside her in blood and in pain. She felt the silent accusations that seemed to hang in the corners of the house. Had she been wrong—so very wrong—in trying to shield her husband? But from whom? From their child? She knew the answer to that, and it had melted the ice of her eyes. Her hands trembled; only her iron will kept back her tears. Jane had left a long shadow.

Outside, the early evening of approaching winter had come upon the city, supplanting the feeble warmth of a dying sun with a damp, cold, sighing wind that brought comfort to no one.

John had arranged to have dinner with Doug alone in his library.

Doug had slept all afternoon and felt more rested than he had in weeks. Another thing that added to Doug's peace of mind was the very noticeable change in John's attitude. Something had happened between this morning and this evening, and although Doug didn't know what it was, he was grateful.

John was smiling, and under the circumstances Doug thought that strange.

"You seem a lot more cheerful than I expected, John."

"I'm afraid I don't feel exactly cheerful, but I am amused."

"About what?"

"Our wives."

"Our wives?"

"They've got more brains and courage than the two of us put together."

Doug was still confused. John told him about Bardy's visit and her talk with Margret.

Doug was very moved by what Bardy had done. After all the humiliations he had subjected her to, that she'd still have the compassion to be his advocate was very difficult for him to bear.

"At least I don't have to live with the thought that I was wrong about you during all the years we've worked together, Doug. I've got Margret and Bardy to thank for that." John paused. "I apologize for doubting you, Doug. I'm afraid that tape and those securities in that Swiss account threw me off. After what happened this morning, I suppose we both weren't thinking too clearly." Though John spoke cordially, he still remained thoughtful.

"Do you have any idea why Ageel would rig such a scheme?" he asked finally.

"John, I've gone over that in my mind a hundred times. It's a blackmail attempt of some kind, of course, but what or why I'm at a dead loss to understand. I just can't figure it out."

John got up for cigars. He offered one to Doug. He himself rarely smoked.

"Doug. I'm afraid we both have to face our resignations. I've been trying to think of a way to avoid it, but when Cannon releases that story, we won't have a choice. There's no way we could continue in the face of that kind of publicity." He paused.

"I've got a lot of things I want to do before Friday, which will take me out of the country for most of the week. My secretary will know where I am. If you want me for anything important you'll be able to get me.

"I'd like you to talk to Dan Bernays and tell him what's up. I don't want him to talk about this to anyone, including his wife. Tell Dan that I am going to propose him to the board as president."

John looked at Doug and saw a tightening of the line of his jaw and mouth. "The chairmanship will have to remain vacant until the board decides on my own replacement."

Doug was silent for a long while. "There's no way we can persuade Cannon to forget about this?"

John smiled sadly. "I tried that. He says the news is his business. It seems as simple as that."

Doug smoked quietly for a long time, and then raised his glass of cognac to John. "Well, John, it's been a long war."

The fire crackled, and the muted horns of the stalled traffic outside blared like irascible trumpets.

When Doug returned to the apartment after dining with John, he saw that Bardy had gone to bed.

He opened her door softly, listening to the sounds of her labored breathing. He stood over her bed for some time, a giant shadow, and then very gently bent over and kissed her. He remained looking at her for a moment and then silently left the room.

She had not been asleep, and she was deeply touched. They had traveled a long and very arduous road together, and the journey that was yet to come would be even more difficult. She hadn't cried in a long time, but the tears came and she tasted their salt as she wept silently in the darkness.

Margret noticed that a change had come over John. She felt it in the way they had just made love, in the paths of each other's bodies that both knew so well; they knew what to give, what to withhold. But something had slipped between their lives, like a thin knife.

He seemed resolved on some deadly purpose. It was as if he had called up some hidden resource from his heritage, a part of his blood link to the past, to his grandfather; something of that cold, implacable spirit haunted their room. She felt it; she could almost touch it.

The double windows kept out the noise of the street; the quiet hum of the climate-controlled units hidden behind the draped windows was the only sound in the room.

She drew him closer to her; she wanted nothing between them.

"Darling, you're so strange tonight, so far from me."

His voice was almost a whisper. "I'm sorry."

She hesitated. "Can you tell me what you're thinking?"

He was silent for a long time. "I'm afraid it's not very pleasant, Margret."

A slight shudder went through her; he could feel it.

His voice was a whisper from some far-off cave of the winds; it could have been the voice of his grandfather, precise, brittle, cold. "I've never thought of myself as an avenger, Margret. I've spent my whole life trying to be constructive—and failing—"

"Darling, you haven't failed—"

"I've failed where it has meant the most to me, Margret—with Jane. And now, through no fault of my own . . . but perhaps that's not even accurate. Perhaps I have failed at the bank—"

"Darling, you haven't." Her heart was breaking for him.

"But if I have failed at the bank, at least I did what I thought was right, the way I felt it should be done." His voice took on an edge she had never heard before. "But I don't deserve the ignominy these bastards have covered me with, Margret, and neither does Doug." He was quiet for a long while, staring up at the shadowed ceiling. When he finally spoke it was in a voice that came from a place that was unknown to her. "I'm going to destroy them," he said, and her body shivered in the cold beside this temporary stranger.

The bank had recently taken delivery of a new Gulfstream II with tip tanks. The pilots had finished their indoctrination courses on the aircraft, and the magnificent bird was waiting for its lone occupant to lift him across the country to talk with Peter Tennant.

Margret had got up early to cook John a simple breakfast and to say good-bye.

He had hinted to her last night in the darkness of their bedroom what he intended to do.

He'd be away the better part of the week, he had said, with a murderous flight schedule. He had to be back no later than Thursday. He wanted to go over with Doug their joint resignation, which would be announced to the press Friday morning, before the noon deadline agreed to with Henry Cannon.

She walked with him to the door and looked at him with a fear in her eyes that he didn't see. She saw his grim face, the increased pallor, the fatigue, and the gray that streaked his dark brown hair that seemed forever to hang over the right side of his forehead. She brushed it back, saw the dark purpose in those luminous brown eyes. She noticed how his shoulders seemed just a little rounder, more stooped.

The car was waiting.

She didn't want to let him go on this trip. She wanted him to forget the whole thing, to resign and say the hell with it. He had enough interests for five men. They could spend more time together, which was the only thing she really wanted.

She drew him toward her. "Au revoir, darling. Come back to me safely. I love you very much."

He kissed her again in the cold morning air that misted their breath.

"This is probably all for the best, Marge. I've learned a

long time ago that God has strange ways of protecting us from ourselves. Perhaps it's my time to quit. That's what Dutch has been trying to get me to do. Maybe he's right." His face hardened. "But not before I leave a little blood on the floor." She recoiled a little inwardly at this.

They kissed again, and he walked to the car.

His chauffeur had tactfully left them alone, but now he went into the house to get John's baggage. The boss is leaving again, he thought, and on a Saturday. He shook his head. The boss was getting too old for this kind of life.

John would have been the first to agree.

I T WAS HIS FIRST FLIGHT IN THE NEW AIRCRAFT. HE FELT a little guilty being the sole occupant of a plane designed to carry up to nineteen people, and a little lonely too. He would be spending a good deal of time in this expensive magic carpet.

He would leave New York and have lunch with Peter Tennant in San Francisco, and around three o'clock Pacific time, they would take off for London via Greenland. Even John, who almost lived in airplanes, was astounded at the mobility available to him. He shook his head in wonder as he entered the Gulfstream.

The flight to the Coast found John lost in thoughts of his past and future.

The big bird flew over the ripples of the Alleghenies, across the flat, white snow-covered squares of the Midwest, through the arctic temperatures of the azure sky with the deck of high white clouds far below them, across the thin strings of great silver rivers, above the thrusting peaks of the Rockies, and finally, the low flat approach over San Francisco Bay.

The crew had been attentive, but he would smile and shake his head. No one could allay the loneliness he felt, nor the touch of darkness and despair.

* * *

Peter had been waiting for John in the club lobby, and got up quickly as he saw him enter the door.

John didn't appear as tall as he seemed in the newspapers or on television, and he looked thinner and paler. It had been a long time since Peter had seen John in person.

Ever since John had called him, Peter wondered what was so important that John Salisbury would fly nearly three thousand miles to see him on a Saturday for lunch. It didn't matter, for there were very few men anywhere in the world who would not have rearranged their schedule to see John, especially when he had described the meeting as "very important."

"Mr. Salisbury, welcome to San Francisco."

"Thank you very much. I must say the weather is an improvement over New York."

"Yes, I imagine that at this time of year very few places aren't an improvement." They both chuckled.

"Can you tell me what your schedule is, Mr. Salisbury, so that I'll know how much time you'll need?"

"That's thoughtful of you. I'm afraid I have rather a full day planned. I'm flying to London after I see you."

"Well, you certainly chose the long way around."

They both laughed.

"I'm afraid that can't be helped. What I want to talk to you about will have a significant effect on how I handle certain things in London."

"I see." Peter was puzzled. "Well, then, may I suggest we get started. Have you been to this club before?"

"Yes. Several times. It's a delightful club."

"Thank you. Why don't you follow me, and we'll get started on some lunch."

"Fine."

John asked to sit at a corner table where he could observe the entrance. He wanted to be sure he could see who was coming into the room. He didn't want to sit with his back facing the entrance and be surprised by someone coming up to him and greeting him in the middle of a sentence. Not with what he intended to talk about.

They chose the jellied consommé, stone crabs, a salad, and a five-year-old California Chardonnay.

"Now, what can I do for you, Mr. Salisbury?"

John looked at the genial face with the careful eyes. He had a good deal of difficulty reading Peter Tennant.

"Mr. Tennant—"

"I'd be flattered, sir, if you called me Peter."

John smiled. "Peter it is then. It's my understanding that you've employed East-West Trading, Limited, to represent you in the Gulf."

"That's correct."

"And therefore, I assume you're on familiar terms with Mr. Ageel."

"Quite."

"I'd be most appreciative if you told me something about him."

Peter looked at John with growing concern. "There's really not much to tell that I'm sure you don't know already. He represents a wide range of American and European companies, as well as Japanese, in the Gulf. He's probably one of the most effective agents in that area. He knows how to package a proposal and get it sold, which, as I'm sure you're aware, Mr. Salisbury, is no mean trick in the Middle East."

"Yes, I'm aware of that."

"He's representing us on the largest project we've ever bid on. I'm hoping that we'll be successful. We've tied up a great deal of time and money on this proposal, and I'd hate to see us lose out to the Germans and Japanese."

"Is that likely?"

"It's a possibility. They've put together a first-rate team, and they have the financial wherewithal. As you certainly know, they represent two of the strongest currencies in the world. The Arabs put a great deal of emphasis on that. I believe that's the principal reason they turned down the

French and the Italians. But all things being equal, putting aside any political aspects such as this country's policy of aid to Israel, which the Arabs certainly oppose, the king knows that the United States is the home of the most powerful economy in the world, with the broadest and most sophisticated technological base. I would say that normally that would give us the nod, but in this case I don't know. Fourteen billion dollars can turn a lot of governments on. In this country, if we look to Washington for any help in a project like this, the damn liberals start screaming about special privilege. In Europe, the partnership between business and government is inseparable, as I'm sure I don't have to tell you. In Japan, it's hard to tell where the government leaves off and business begins. So if you're asking me what our chances are in winning this contract, I'd say if we were simply competing against other business competitors our chances would be excellent, but we're also competing against Bonn and Tokyo, and when you factor that in, I'm not so sure."

"So your agent, Mr. Ageel, could be the deciding factor?"

"Well, not quite. Our technology and the financial resources of the companies we put together to do the actual work, as well as the practicality of our proposal, are what will really put us over, as far as the technical advisers to the king are concerned."

"But without the proper presentation to the king, or, for that matter, without access to him—and I'm referring to the kind of access that is meaningful in the Middle East—your proposal would undoubtedly fail."

"I think that's a fair statement."

"So that Mr. Ageel's role is quite critical."

"I would have to agree."

John paused. "Do you know a Mr. Aragon? I believe his full name is Noel Aragon."

"Not well. I've met him several times both in this country and in London. My contact with him is purely as Ali's deputy."

"Would you care to tell me what you know about the character of these two men?"

Peter's antennae were up. It was a peculiar question, and he didn't know why it was being asked. He wished Salisbury would say whatever he had on his mind, but then John was a banker and bankers were usually more oblique than frontal.

"It's really difficult to give you an informed answer on that, Mr. Salisbury. I don't know either of those gentlemen well enough for that." Peter started to smile. "I doubt if I'd want either of them as executors of my estate."

John smiled as well, but Peter didn't miss the searching, penetrating inquiry of his eyes.

"Mr. Tennant—" John's formality was habitual, and a coolness in his manner did not prompt Peter to any increasing cordiality of his own. "I'm going to reveal to you some information that unfortunately will be made public, but before I do, I'm going to ask you to hold whatever I say to you in confidence. May I rely on you for that, sir?"

"Of course."

John looked at Peter for a long time, his gaze steady and penetrating.

"Something has come up at the bank that involves Mr. Aragon. I'm afraid it's quite serious, and I'm here to find out what, if anything, you can tell me that might help me to understand this whole affair."

Peter waited.

"Mr. Aragon has attempted to bribe Doug Dowding of our bank by offering him five million dollars."

Peter nearly fell off his chair. His face went dead white at the cold, blunt shock of John's revelation.

It was what John had wanted. It was the only way to tell where this fellow stood. There was no way to fake the way Peter had reacted. It was physiological as well as psychological. The blood had drained from his face. He sat there with his mouth open, his eyes absolutely incredulous.

"You can't be serious!"

"Unfortunately I am. The evidence, I'm afraid, is recorded on tape, and one of the most shattering experiences of my life was to have to listen to that tape being played."

"Jesus H. Christ! I can't believe it. Why the hell would Aragon do something as dumb and as dangerous as that?"

"I'm sure I have no idea."

"It's unbelievable, incredible."

"It's all of that."

"Jesus! I'm dumbfounded."

"So was I when I heard it. More to the point for the moment, Mr. Tennant, are two things: I am now persuaded that you had nothing to do with this—"

"Well, I hope to hell not. I'm not so sure I like the implication in that, either, Mr. Salisbury."

"I apologize. But since you and Mr. Ageel are tied up in this project, I had to be sure. I hope you'll understand that."

Peter was somewhat mollified by John's manner, which was genuinely contrite.

"The only point I'd like to make to you, Mr. Tennant, is that under no circumstances do I want you to contact Ageel or Aragon about our conversation. I might add that it will not be in the interest of your project to do so."

A cold spear of fear cut through Peter.

Those stupid bastards! Noel or Ali, or both, had antagonized Salisbury, the one person in this whole deal they were trying to persuade to help them. Jesus Christ, thought Peter, those two bastards must be insane.

"Can I rely on you, Mr. Tennant, not to discuss this with those two gentlemen? I repeat"—John looked directly at Peter, the dark brown eyes level and cold—"it will not be in your interest to do so, Mr. Tennant."

"I'll honor your confidences, Mr. Salisbury."

John looked at his watch. "Well, sir, I have 'miles to go before I sleep,' as they say, so if you'll excuse me—"

Peter interrupted. "Can I have one of our cars take you to the airport?"

"That's kind of you, but I have a car outside." John looked carefully at Peter. "I'm glad to know you had nothing to do with any of this, Mr. Tennant."

"I'm certainly appreciative of your taking the trouble to find that out, Mr. Salisbury. The last thing I need is to be associated with this kind of insanity."

John nodded. "Thank you for lunch, it was delightful."

They shook hands, and John began the second leg of his journey of retribution.

San Francisco tower cleared them for takeoff at 3:07 P.M. Their flight to London would really stretch the wings of their new bird. With tip tanks the Gulfstream II had a range of slightly more than 3,600 miles. The great-circle route that John's captain had planned was 3,300 miles. They were flying to Söndre Strömfjord, in Greenland, to refuel for their flight to London.

Had Doug been on board, he would have been up forward with the flight crew, checking the route, winds, weather, fuel planning, ground speed; he was a pilot and such things interested him.

On this particular flight Doug would have had little peace of mind. They would be flying over very hostile terrain, stretching their fuel consumption, and would come into Greenland, where the winter weather is notoriously fickle. Doug would have been sweating the letdown on this flight until the approach at Strömfjord. He would have had the pilots checking the weather every ten minutes until they were on final; that's the way he was, but not John.

The aesthetics of flying appealed to John, and he was always amazed at the incredible ability to compress distance and time in a machine like this, but he trusted the flight crew completely and left his fate to them and to God.

Out of courtesy, the copilot always came back to show John the flight plan and give him an approximate ETA (estimated time of arrival) for their next destination. He'd ask

John if there was anything he needed during the course of the flight. If it was a long one, he or the captain would come aft to chat with John briefly, if he wasn't working or sleeping.

Unlike Ali's flying carpet, there was no stewardess aboard, and John was content to take care of himself, often going to the galley and heating up his own frozen meal, which cooked quickly in the microwave oven.

When they had climbed high over northern California and were out of San Francisco's control zone, the copilot came back with the flight plan.

"Here's what it looks like, sir. It's a long one. We'll be crossing Oregon, Idaho, then into Canada, across Saskatchewan and Manitoba, and over the top of Hudson Bay; then we'll head across the southern tip of Baffin Island and Davis Strait into Söndre Strömfjord."

John listened attentively.

"We should have some good following winds according to weather information, so the captain is calling for an ETA of one A.M. local Greenland time. We'll spend about an hour refueling and should be in Heathrow at eight-thirty A.M. London time."

John nodded. "You'll have the car meet me at the usual place?"

"Right, sir. Hugh will pick you up with a customs official at the gate."

"How's the weather look in Greenland?"

"It's good now, sir, but we'll get a detailed fix on it over Manitoba. If there's anything that looks like a problem, I'll let you know." The copilot looked at John, who seemed small and alone in the large, empty cabin.

"May I fix you a drink, sir?"

John shook his head. "No, thanks. I've got some work to do."

The copilot returned to the flight deck, and John opened his briefcase to begin to go through the correspondence, re-

ports, memorandums, studies, and general snow shower of
paper that followed him everywhere. But this time it was
different. His mind was troubled, and more than that, there
was the practical intimation of the futility in bothering with
all this paper. Friday he'd be through. An ignominious end
to what he had hoped would be a career he could look back
on with pride and gratification. But no more. He was on
his way to the Arctic Circle at over six hundred miles an
hour, rushing toward the source of his troubles. His face
hardened at the prospect of the meeting he would hold in
his suite at Claridge's.

John Salisbury was not a vengeful man. Many people disliked him, he knew that. Some actually hated him, or perhaps not him personally, but the symbol of capitalism and
power he represented. But the people in London whom he
was going to see, whom he hardly knew, had wounded him
savagely. He didn't know why, but that wasn't the point.
They had destroyed his career, embarrassed him before the
world. And why? Why was it in their interest to do this? As
far as John could figure out, it was not. Quite the contrary;
for as a result of this trip John would mortally wound them;
he would cut their legs off in the United States and in their
own country. Why would they want that kind of retribution?
He shook his head. The whole thing was exhausting, its
logic beyond him.

The Gulfstream flew over the frozen surface of the Cana-
dian provinces at forty-five thousand feet. Below them the
land was silent, waiting, hostile. Any forced landing in this
territory and they would have had it.

John noticed it was getting dark outside. He was always
fascinated by the way the earth seemed to darken first, reaching up for the sky as if to lower the shades of night slowly,
reluctantly. The sun touched the layers of clouds with orange,
then yellow, then mauve, then the purple-blue grays of night,
which gradually revealed the pinpricks of stars.

He set his watch on Greenland time, which was two hours ahead of Eastern Standard. He went aft to the galley and took out a frozen filet and put it in the oven. He was startled to hear the copilot's voice behind him.

"Here, sir. Let me fix dinner for you."

"That's very kind, thank you."

"How about a drink, sir?"

"That's beginning to sound like a good idea."

"Scotch?"

"Right."

The copilot knew how John liked his Scotch.

He ate leisurely, his mind wandering over the spectrum of his past, present, and future. He wasn't particularly pleased by this introspection. He felt tired. The port side of the aircraft had a long couch with two removable armrests. He walked back to the galley with his now empty tray and returned to make up his bed.

He put two pillows down, lifted the armrests, and set them on the large high-backed swivel chair opposite him, and then remembered he wanted to take a sleeping pill. He was aware that the combination of a sedative and alcohol wasn't advisable, but he wanted to get some sleep during the long flight.

The flight crew was alert to what he was doing; the copilot came back to see if he could help.

"The temperature O.K., sir?"

"Fine."

"Would you like one blanket or two?"

"I think one should do. Would you mind getting me some water? I want to take a pill."

"You want the cabin lights down, sir?"

"Please."

John reached in his briefcase for his earplugs and eyeshade. He took off his jacket and draped it over the chair, and lay down. He was tired, and the thirty milligrams of Dalmane plus the liberal portion of Scotch poured by the copilot soon had him deep in a sedated sleep.

"How's the boss?"

"Sleeping like a baby."

"This is one hell of a schedule he's got."

"You're telling me. He's no kid any longer. I don't know how these guys make it."

"A lot of them don't."

"Can you ever remember the boss traveling alone like this?"

"Never. He usually has at least three or four people with him."

"Wonder where Carter is. He never goes anywhere without Carter."

"Not in the six years I've been flying him."

"Doesn't that seem strange to you?"

"Strange as hell. The boss usually has people falling all over themselves waiting on him. He seems so damn lonely back there. You know, I've noticed in the last several months he's beginning to look old."

"How old do you think he is?"

"I read somewhere he's sixty. Crank up Greenland Weather, will you, and pray the bastards don't have a snowstorm when we get there. We're not exactly going to be loaded with fuel."

They were lucky. They touched down at Söndre Strömfjord at twelve-forty-six, fourteen minutes ahead of schedule.

"Let's get this bird refueled and get the hell out of here while the weather holds."

"Ah men, Captain."

"He still asleep?"

"Out cold."

"I wish to hell I was. And don't say 'Ah men.' "

WHEN THEY ARRIVED IN LONDON IN THE MORNING, John still didn't feel rested. It was almost ten o'clock London time when the manager of Claridge's showed John to his suite.

John was almost as at home at Claridge's as he was in New York. The high-ceilinged rooms with the full-length windows that opened out to a small balcony were all familiar, as was the furniture in the living room. There were the bud roses on the writing desk and the note of welcome from Lund Hansen, Claridge's ubiquitous manager, who had known John for over twenty years.

They should be here in two and a half hours, John thought.

"A pleasure to have you with us again, Mr. Salisbury."

"Thank you, Hansen. Always nice to be back."

"Anything else we can do for you?"

"I don't believe so."

John undressed, hanging his clothes in the enormous closets, which could have easily accommodated a family of five. His two suits hanging in unaccustomed isolation reminded him of how separated he felt from everyone and everything.

He ran a hot bath in the cavernous tub.

He relaxed in the hot water, letting his mind wander to this luncheon meeting he had flown almost eight thousand miles to attend. It was the first time in his life when his sole purpose was to get even.

He dressed leisurely and sat reading the morning *Times,* which an attentive management had placed in his room, and was engrossed in the financial section when he heard a knock at the door. He opened it to see the smiling dark face of Ali Ageel and the hesitant pallor of Noel Aragon.

Ali was obsequious, with quick darting eyes, a nervous laugh. He was obviously very apprehensive as to why he had been asked to fly back from Tokyo to attend a Sunday luncheon meeting in London at the command of John Salisbury.

When Salisbury had contacted him in Japan, he mentioned three words that got Ali quickly on his 737: "Gulf," "project," "urgent." That was enough for Ali. But unlike John Salisbury, who had descended on London from the West, Ali, who had sped through the skies from the Far East, had no idea what was urgent enough to bring Salisbury to London to see him. Neither had his sidekick, the ever-anxious Mr. Aragon, who looked pale and nervous throughout this luncheon, his intuition telling him that something very ominous was pending.

John eyed them coolly; his manner throughout the awkward hospitality of drink and food served in the living room on his suite was forbidding.

"Well, sir," said Ali, pushing his chair back from the table and lighting a thin dark cigar, "it's a pleasure to see you, Mr. Salisbury." He looked at the tip of his cigar as the smoke curled toward the ceiling. "I wonder if you could enlighten Mr. Aragon and myself as to why we have been honored by your visit?"

John looked at the dark eyes and could find no subterfuge there.

"Mr. Ageel—"

"Ali, please."

"Mr. Ageel, earlier this week I was subjected to two incidents which I'm unable to explain. I have reason to believe you can enlighten me.

"I was made aware of a taped conversation between that gentleman"—John nodded toward Noel—"and Mr. Dowding of our bank, recorded in your home on St. John. Mr. Aragon offered Mr. Dowding a five-million-dollar bribe."

An Arab turned gray; an Anglo-Saxon went from off-white to bleached bone.

"I'm afraid I don't understand, sir."

John's look was venomous.

"I think you do, Mr. Ageel."

Ali looked quickly at Noel. "But I assure you, sir, I don't know what you're talking about. What tape? What conversation?"

"Are you so contemptuous of my intelligence, Mr. Ageel, that you expect me to believe you don't know about the existence of this tape?"

Ali again looked at Noel, then back to John.

"Mr. Salisbury. I think there must be some mistake."

"I wish there were, Mr. Ageel, because the existence of that tape is all too real. It happens to be in the hands of the director of news for the NBT broadcasting company. He is going to release it this Friday at noon." John paused, looking first at Noel and then at Ali. "It will cause the resignation of both Mr. Dowding and myself."

Ali was absolutely dumbstruck. His mind raced to cover the spectrum of possibilities that John's disclosure had revealed.

What the hell was he talking about? Ali asked himself. Did Noel make a tape of his conversation with Dowding? Why? Who asked him to do such a crazy thing? What prompted him? How did the tape get out of Noel's hands? My God, thought Ali, this will ruin me. Salisbury's now an enemy, and from the look of things, a very dangerous one. Why? Why did Noel do this? More important, why did he not mention the existence of this tape? Noel's betrayed me, Ali said to himself, and looked murderously at his associate.

Noel Aragon through all this looked like a frightened man. Noel knew Ali as well as anyone on earth could know this son of the desert. Noel knew that for all Ali's Western education and background, he was still a Bedouin whose ideas of justice and retribution were not found in the institutions of parliamentary democracy; they were the curved sword and dagger.

"Mr. Salisbury. If what you are telling me is accurate, and I am sure you would not have come to London to indulge in such fantasies—"

"Unfortunately, Mr. Ageel, this is not a figment of my imagination; I wish it were. The tape was played for our edification in my office."

Ali turned to Noel. "What in hell is going on here, Noel? Is this true? Does such a tape exist?"

John was beginning to get the feeling that Ali wasn't acting; his surprise seemed genuine.

Noel looked as if someone had nailed his foot to the floor. He nodded his head affirmatively.

Ali's eyes flashed. "Who gave you the authority to do such a thing? And if you were stupid enough with your Anglo-Saxon passion for preserving information, how could you have been so inept as to let this tape get out of your sight?"

Noel's lips were compressed. He opened the palms of his hands slightly and shrugged his shoulders. He really didn't know how that tape had got out. He still had it in his safe at Belgrave Place.

"Well, speak up. You haven't become mute, have you?"

Noel was having difficulty just breathing. His voice was a low monotone. "Ali, I still have the tape. I haven't the faintest idea how that conversation was recorded. As far as I know, I have the only tape locked in my wall safe at home."

This was too much for Ali. He turned to John Salisbury. "Sir, if I didn't have too much respect for your intelligence and your position, I would say that you have accused me of initiating a vile, stupid ploy which is diametrically opposed to my own interests. Why would I choose to antagonize you, sir, when you're the one person whose help we counted on obtaining?"

"For what?"

"To use your considerable influence with my king on behalf of the Tennant Corporation."

"Mr. Ageel, I don't know what's going on here, but one telephone call to NBT will confirm what I've just told you. Do you want me to make that call?"

Ali took out his handkerchief and wiped the perspiration from his forehead. The sound of traffic outside, muffled by the heavily draped windows, was faintly audible.

John got up. "I have the impression you two gentlemen would like some time alone. I'm going downstairs to send some cables. I'll be back in thirty minutes."

John got up, folded his napkin, and, with a gesture of disgust, threw the heavy linen down on his empty plate. He walked out of the room.

Ali sprang up when the door had closed and began pacing about the large living room like a berserk panther.

"You son of a bitch! You stupid English son of a bitch!" He whirled to face Noel. "Why did you do such a thing? Did I tell you to tape anyone's conversation? And if you have the tape, how did someone else get it, especially someone in the media?"

Noel was a wet, torn paper bag. His voice was so low it could barely be heard.

"I don't know, Ali. I simply can't answer that."

"Can you answer this, you shit dog? You knew about that

tape, and you didn't tell me. You let me set up that account
for Dowding when you knew the sole purpose of that maneuver was to keep Dowding from going to Salisbury about
our little offer. But with someone playing a tape for Salisbury
of your conversation with Dowding, there wasn't much point
in my setting up that account, was there? And that account
indelibly marks me as having a hand in this affair. You knew
that, you English shit dog. You son of a whore. You betrayed me. I trusted you, and you betrayed me. You've ruined
the biggest deal of my career, and you've probably cost me
my relationship with my king."

Ali stopped in midsentence and turned toward Noel; his
eyes were two blazing coals straight from hell. "You're a
dead man, Noel," he growled from between clenched teeth.
"You're a dead man."

When John returned, he took one look at the two of them
and decided that Aragon was the one who had taped the
conversation with Doug, but he also knew that Ageel had
sponsored the bribe and had set up the account at the Gneist
Bank.

Ali's world had suddenly opened beneath his feet, reveal-
ing an enormous trench whose black maw seemed only to
wait for him.

"Mr. Salisbury, if you'll give me a little time, perhaps we
can obtain that tape."

"Mr. Ageel, there's no possibility of getting that tape
back, and even if there were, you couldn't be sure that they
hadn't made another transcription. It seemed easy enough
to record Mr. Aragon's."

Ali's face was wet with perspiration; little gleaming droplets
of jeweled sweat reflected the soft light of the yellow sconces
on the wall.

"Then what do you intend to do, sir?"

John looked at Ali with implacable hostility and contempt.

"You'll be aware of that soon enough, Mr. Ageel. And now, gentlemen, I have some things to do. If you'll be good enough to excuse me." John stood up. It was over. But not for Ali, or for Noel. This was a game, it seemed, where everyone lost something; there were no winners, but some would lose more than others. A lot more.

HENRY READ THE NOTE FOR THE TENTH TIME.

"This won't be any formal letter of resignation, Henry, because I don't feel very formal writing it. And I'm not just resigning from NBT. What hurts so much more, Henry, is that I'm resigning from us.

"I've thought about this over and over, and no matter how I feel about you, or you about me, there seems to be too big a gap in our values, for me at least, to think we could make it together.

"I know that you feel you must do what you have to do, and I can understand that. But I can't forget that because of me, and your own code of professionalism, we have ruined the lives of at least two men, not to mention their families.

"I haven't lived through the traumas you have, Henry, but I know I don't want to continue being a part of a profession that does this to people.

"The hell of it is, I love you.

"Joan."

He got up and lit a cigarette and walked to the windows of his office.

He looked out at Manhattan shut off from the sun by a high, gray, overcast sky.

He folded Joan's note carefully and put it in his breast pocket.

JOHN'S BODY CLOCK WAS NOT WORKING PROPERLY. HIS mind knew where he was, but his physiology refused to pay any attention. He slept with the aid of pills, and watched the hours turn into days and the days move pell-mell toward Friday.

John was reminded of that night at boarding school his first year. It was his first time away from home except for summer camp, and he was very homesick.

He recalled being taken to dinner by his parents, and sitting in the little movie house afterward, his parents on each side of him. He didn't really look at the movie, but, rather, at the face of the clock that was hung to the right of the screen in front of a wine-colored drape. That clock had always stayed in his mind as a symbol of the inexorable course of time; nothing could stop it.

He knew that when the movie was over, his parents would return to the inn, and the following day go back to New York. He would be left alone, in the hostile atmosphere so alien to most young boys. The feeling of loneliness that he had experienced so many years ago kept coming back to him now. He was alone. There wasn't the usual coterie of officers and aides, or the pressing schedule. There was too much time to think, too much time alone with the clock against the wine-colored drape.

He ate a leisurely breakfast of kippers and scrambled eggs, toast, and coffee in his suite. He became impatient with the solitude of the hotel and felt guilty because of the work in his briefcase that remained undone. For the first time in his life he was neglecting his duties, his obligations, but after Friday the bank would no longer be his responsibility. He would assist in the transition, of course, but that would only prolong the agony. It was a hell of a way to have to end one's career, he thought for the hundredth time.

He was depressed over having to wait until Wednesday to see the king, and the thought of another six-hour flight, taking him yet farther away from home, made him feel even more separated from what was left that was loving or familiar.

He got up to begin packing for tomorrow's trip to the Gulf. At least that was something that required physical activity. It would lead to movement and eventual escape from the solitude and loneliness of the hotel. He thought of the clock in the little movie house when he was a boy, and shook his head.

He had made the trip to Heathrow so often that it almost seemed like going down the East River Drive.

He thought of the time he had spent living in London as a student at the London School of Economics in 1948, and working at the bank's London office part time. He had been a good deal happier then. It all seemed a long time ago.

As he thought of his career at the bank, he could not escape the conclusion that his tenure had been flawed.

Everyone thought that his rise so quickly to the office of chairman was solely because of his family's connections and their ownership of a substantial block of stock in FMB. In part this was true, but those who worked with him saw the skill, determination, and intelligence he brought to each assignment, each new managerial role. His critics might have laughed at the idea that he was anything except an owner of the bank, but he was a great deal more than just an inheritor of position and title.

Unlike Doug, he had the intellectual capacity to do his job. What, then, had gone wrong? Where had he let everyone down, himself most of all?

Dutch, of course, had given him the answer to those questions not once but many times, but he had never accepted Dutch's analysis as valid. He sincerely felt that Dutch didn't understand the problems of multinational banking, and especially of this bank; but it didn't matter, it was all over.

As Hugh drove the Daimler skillfully through the mid-morning London traffic, it began to rain; heavy, fat drops splattered against the roadway. He looked up at the gray skies to see the endless flights of descending aircraft break from the mist of clouds like lazy giant gliding birds, seemingly suspended in midair. He thought of his own flight, from New York to the moderate temperatures of San Francisco, over frozen tundra near the top of the world to the wet gray of London, and now he was headed for the steaming humidity of the Gulf. His mind understood all this, but not his body. He knew from experience that when he returned to New York it would be the better part of a week before his biological clock was functioning properly; he knew the exhaustion he would feel. But then, he told himself it was the last time, and maybe it was for the best. Perhaps Jane was right. Maybe he hadn't been a very good father. He shook his head. If he had not been much of a success as a banker or a father, then the past twenty-five years had been pretty much a waste of time. Is that what his life had been —a waste of time?

As the Daimler moved into the general aviation area, he wondered how many people in the world would think of

John Salisbury as a failure. Not many, he thought, but he knew how a small coterie of intimates would have passed on that judgment—perhaps not as sharply or with the condemnation with which he accused himself, but there would still be those who'd give him very low marks.

He sighed as he followed Hugh to the officer who was waiting to take him personally through customs.

They had climbed through the dense layers of clouds to the clear blue skies of high altitude and bright sun.

They were crossing the Channel headed for France, then over the white spine of the Alps, across the Adriatic, over the edge of Greece, the Mediterranean, past the island of Crete, across the northeastern tip of Egypt, over the pie-shaped wedge of Israel, across Jordan, and then the long descent over the desert.

John looked at his watch and advanced it two hours. They had taken off from Heathrow at 12:35 P.M London time. The flight would take just under six hours. It would be almost 8:45 P.M. by the time they landed.

John thought about the king. A private audience had been arranged, but because of other commitments John wouldn't be able to see the king until Wednesday. It would give him a chance to rest, he thought, unless the vaunted hospitality of the crown prince precluded the sleep John so badly needed. If his past experiences were any guide, sleep would be the only luxury he would go without.

The Gulfstream streaked through the sky, hurtling its way toward the sixteenth-century paradox that substituted Mercedes for camels and oil for gold.

John knew this area of the world. He had been exposed to the 120-degree temperatures in the shade during the summer, to the sand of the desert that was able to infiltrate any clothing, any vehicle. He knew the people, their latent hostility and arrogance that were the legacy of colonial subjugation under the British, the French, and the Germans. He understood their suspicions, prejudices, pride, and generosity. He also knew of their terrible retribution for any serious violation of trust or honor.

John knew these people. Perhaps not as his grandfather did, but well enough, and the measure of their respect and affection for him was this private audience granted by the king.

The hours in flight passed slowly as they devoured distance. They were approaching the eastern end of the Mediterranean; below the Nile and then the Suez Canal, two tendrils of twisting strings splitting the sands of Egypt and the Sinai.

John realized they were losing altitude. It was dark on the ground.

As they made their approach over the hillocks of sand to the long black runway, John had the same impression he had had the first time he visited the kingdom.

The airport and everything else seemed to have suddenly appeared out of nowhere like the formation of a volcanic island. Hundreds of thousands of square miles of barren rock and scorched desert, and then suddenly an oasis of light, a modern airport with fluted arches that led into a terminal one might expect to find in New Orleans except for the babble of incomprehensible tongues. The blacks, who were not citizens of the kingdom but who did the menial labor, rushed about, chattering like monkeys. The blast furnace of heavy moist heat hit you like a wet hot towel when you stepped out from the air conditioning of the plane.

A Mercedes 600 limousine was waiting as John's plane taxied to the ramp.

John could see the well-fed figure of Prince Khalifa in a flowing black robe with gold embroidered borders waiting for him.

John had entertained the prince on several of the prince's visits to New York. He had also helped him buy an exclusive triplex apartment on Park Avenue that the prince was having difficulty purchasing. It took a good deal of persuasion on

John's part to talk the other owners into allowing the prince to buy into their building.

John remembered a nervous call from the State Department asking him to do what he could to assist the prince, and to prevent the other owners of the building from offending him. The prince had been very grateful; so had the king.

"John, my friend. How good to see you." The prince gave John the traditional Arab embrace, which was a sign of genuine friendship, especially toward an Anglo-Saxon. "Well, John, how is New York? I'm going to be there next week."

John felt the heavy, sodden blanket of the Gulf's night air.

They stood near the aircraft talking, catching up on old times. The prince confided that he would far rather see John in New York, where there was so much to do, than in his own country under the eyes of his watchful father, where he had to behave and set an example. This was somewhat constricting for the prince, who was known the world over for his love of women, drinking, and gambling, and in that order, but not in his own country; here he had to watch himself, and it was very confining.

"So, my friend. What brings you to see my father? It must be something important, no?"

John nodded. "It's quite important."

"You look so serious, John. Is it serious?"

John hesitated. "It's serious, yes."

"Ah. I see. Well, in that case let's go to the palace. My father has instructed me to bring you to him so that he can greet you. He apologizes for not being able to see you until tomorrow, but he had commitments he just couldn't break. Anyway, old friend, it will give us a chance to be together and catch up on old times, eh?"

The prince clapped John on the back as they walked toward the car. "I'll take you to the market after we see my father. You always liked that. You can buy Margret a present, my frugal friend, eh?" The prince smiled broadly at John. "This could turn out to be an expensive trip for you, eh, John?"

John nodded knowingly. His mind flashed to the marketplace as he had known it; he remembered the colors, the sounds, the smell of incense that cost two hundred dollars a pound.

John thought of this labyrinth of winding narrow streets, actually walkways whose stalls were open to the edge of the street without grate or protecting door. Not unusual in a country where they cut off a shoplifter's hand in the public square.

John thought of the stall lined from floor to ceiling with bracelets and ornaments of all kinds, all in twenty-four-karat gold. Here cultured pearl necklaces were thrown to silent waiting black attendants, who dropped them casually into brown paper bags.

John had avoided buying the gaudy diamonds and rubies that the prince was forever thrusting at him to buy for his wife. When John would settle on a relatively inexpensive bracelet or necklace, the prince would roar with laughter and slap his heavy thigh. It struck him as incongruous that one of the world's richest and most powerful Anglo-Saxons could be so conservative. That's how John became known as "the frugal one."

He thought of all this as he walked toward the car. He noticed two Arab soldiers with U.S. submachine guns who stood by the limousine. He was surprised by that.

"It's my father. Ever since the assassination he insists I have a bodyguard everywhere I go, including out of the country. These fellows create quite a stir in a nightclub, I can tell you."

They both laughed.

The long black Mercedes drove carefully out of the airport. One bodyguard was seated next to the driver, the other sat in the rear facing John and the prince. It was somewhat disconcerting.

KAREN HAD USED UP WHATEVER WILLPOWER SHE HAD to keep from calling him. She had used it up over the days and nights of wanting him, needing him, and then it was all gone. She couldn't believe it herself when she actually called Doug; she thought she was stronger than that.

He was drawn by the magnet of memory to her. Over the rough, craggy ground of his guilt and shame he came to her; dragged and bruised, but he came.

They had made love the way they always did, but this time there were no preliminaries; their desire was too great.

Now they lay in bed the way she always wanted him. He was inside her, her breasts close to his mouth, but what had come between them hung like a shroud waiting to bury what they had. It was their guilt, his now more than hers.

Doug was torn in half by his desire, his need for Karen that his body and mind demanded, and the guilt he felt in the betrayal of his wife, especially after Bardia's intervention. Doug knew that he couldn't continue to be stretched on this rack any longer; he simply didn't have the strength. Karen knew that too; she also knew that she would somehow have to get a hand on her own resolve or she would ruin her life as well as his.

They both understood it wasn't love that would leave when he did, when he went back to his wife. But they did know in the soft darkness of the room that whatever it was, it would call out to them again, and somehow they would have to find the strength not to listen.

"What are you thinking?"

He didn't reply for a long while. When he did, he spoke to her in an exhausted, husky whisper. "About us, about John, about Bardy."

She moved slightly, trying to get closer to him. Far down, where it was dark, she was weeping. But that was beyond his or perhaps even her recognition. Yet she did realize her sadness though she couldn't name it.

"I've thought about leaving New York," she said.

He didn't answer her. His mind wasn't functioning in any logical sense. It simply skipped from one thought to another, sometimes running everything together.

"You at least have Bardy," she said.

He remained silent, a prisoner to the anguish that would not let him speak.

THE RECEPTION HALL HAD BEEN CLEARED, WITH THE EXception of four robed bodyguards, who sat near the entrance holding submachine guns on their laps. They chatted quietly among themselves, stopping only to look at John, who was being escorted to the king by the prince.

They walked through the long room over the red fleur-de-lis carpet. Gauze hangings at the tall windows softened the harsh sunlight. Scarlet drapes framed the windows against yellow walls.

The king was seated in a wing chair next to the east wall at the opposite end of the room. His robe was black like the prince's, but around his head was wrapped the gold agal, or headband, which distinguished him from anyone else in the kingdom.

The prince bowed quickly before his father and withdrew. As he passed one of the guards he issued an order quietly, and the guard picked up a chair to place near the king. This was a signal honor for John and a sign of affection and regard. John was fully aware of the deference being shown him.

The king's face was thoughtful. In the tradition of many of

the men of his land, the king wore a short spade beard but no mustache. He had postponed his weekly *majlis,* or open meeting, where petitioners could be heard by their king. John was unaware of this, but had he known, he would have been very flattered.

John bowed to the king, who smiled and pointed to the chair.

"Well, Mr. Salisbury, this is a pleasure seeing you again."

"It is for me too, Your Majesty."

The king looked at him shrewdly; the black eyes were those of a hawk. He was used to peering into the minds of men, and his cunning, his quick intelligence, and his long experience gave him an uncanny ability to discern the motives of those who would seek his help.

"I am very grateful for what you did for my son. It could have been most embarrassing for us."

"Not at all, sir. I was delighted to help."

"You see, Mr. Salisbury, we are still somewhat sensitive here to the slights imposed on us by the West. There are many here who have spent time in British jails, and many who are not here because of the Germans and the Turks." The king looked away from John as he went back in time.

"Your grandfather was a great help to my father, Mr. Salisbury. He was a true friend to my father, at a time when we didn't have many friends.

"Today the world sees us solely in terms of our wealth, which of course is our oil. But as you know, there is a finite amount of oil under our sands and off our shores. Unless we build a technological capability that will let us become an exporting nation of capital and consumer goods, we are doomed when the West develops alternate sources of energy or when we run dry."

His voice was soft, and the concerned, troubled expression in his eyes revealed a monarch who was sincerely devoted to the welfare of his people.

"But you have not come all this way to listen to me talk

about the problems of my country. There is something I can do for you. What is it?"

Now that he was here, John wondered if the whole thing made any sense, if the king would perhaps feel imposed upon; but he went ahead.

"Your Highness, I assume you know of a Mr. Ageel?"

"Ali Ageel?"

"That's right, sir."

"Yes. Of course I know him. He has been very successful in helping us find Western interests who can assist in building our infrastructure."

The king motioned for John to continue.

"Suppose I told you, sir, that Mr. Ageel, through his associate, Mr. Noel Aragon, offered the president of my bank five million dollars in Swiss francs to get me to sponsor the American group that's competing against the German-Japanese consortium for the contract to build up the southern portion of your country?"

"You mean a bribe?"

"That's right, sir."

The king was well aware of the different attitudes in the West toward these things, which are perfectly acceptable, even expected, in the Middle East.

"You find this offensive, Mr. Salisbury?"

"I must say, sir, that I do, and more to the point, forgetting my own feelings, is the fact that this attempt to bribe the president of one of our country's major banks was recorded on tape by Mr. Aragon, Mr. Ageel's senior aide. That conversation somehow got into the hands of the media, and will be released this coming Friday at noon."

The king's face clouded. At the mention of the word "media," the king thought of what most Arabs regard as the "Jewish Controlled Media," highly biased in favor of Israel. The American media was no favorite of the king's.

"How did they come by this? Do they have actual possession of the tape?"

"They do, sir."

"And you say this Mr. Aragon is associated with Ageel?"

"He's Ageel's right-hand man."

The king's eyes grew cold.

"Continue."

"Sir, as you know, we've had a lot of unfortunate publicity in my country about this sort of thing, and our regulatory bodies have been pressing very hard to discipline this kind of activity." John paused. "I'm afraid, Your Majesty, that this is going to create a tremendous row in the United States, which will affect the relations between our two countries." John looked at the king closely. "As for me, sir, and Mr. Dowding, we will be forced to leave the bank."

The king was very sensitive about the quality of the relations between his country and the United States, and toward the obvious distress forced on the grandson of his father's old friend.

His government was the most conservative of the Arab countries, and the most stable. His subjects were encouraged to be relatively freewheeling capitalists, and his government had long ago decided to throw in its lot with the United States. They despised the Russians and were in ideological conflict with their atheism.

More important, the entire military posture of the country was based on American weapons systems, and they were dependent upon American technicians to train their ground and air personnel in the use and maintenance of this sophisticated weaponry.

It was extremely important to the king to have the goodwill of the United States government, and he could not afford to tolerate anyone who rocked the boat between the two countries.

As he listened quietly to John he became angry, although he was a master at concealing his emotions. This Ageel, no more than a common broker, a go-between, had offended—

no, jeopardized the career of one of the United States' leading bankers, and through the publicity that John spoke of, would create a scandal that would rock their two countries.

The king held up his hand. John stopped speaking.

"Is there any way that this disclosure can be prevented?"

"I'm afraid not, sir."

"What if I called the President?"

John thought carefully. "It's possible the President could prevail upon NBT, but my guess is that he wouldn't put himself in the position of being charged with abrogating our freedom of the press. I can see all sorts of political pitfalls for the President in this situation, Your Majesty. I don't think he'd be very anxious to help."

"You should have a monarchy, Mr. Salisbury. I've often told you that. In my country I could solve our mutual problem with one phone call."

"Unfortunately, Your Majesty, our system complicates life more effectively."

"I should say it does. You let a few Jewish businessmen control your media, and a handful of Jewish senators run your Senate. It's disgraceful."

John had heard all this before. He never understood whether informed Arabs actually believed this nonsense, or whether simply by repeating the same tired diatribe so often they had come to believe it. He certainly wasn't about to argue the point with the king.

John thought he could read concern in the king's dark eyes.

"So you will be forced to resign from your family's bank?"

"Yes, sir."

"And this group that Ageel represents, they are well known to you?"

"Yes, Your Majesty. The Tennant Corporation; it's one of the finest design engineering firms in the United States."

"You would recommend them?"

"If their proposal meets the requirements of your technical

people, sir, I would; they have a fine reputation worldwide."

The king looked concerned.

"I find it difficult, Mr. Salisbury, to sit here and do nothing, letting this catastrophe break over our heads."

"I don't know what else we can do, sir."

"I think I do."

"What's that, Your Majesty?"

"Suppose we threaten to withdraw our short-term deposits from all U.S. banks."

John was horrified. "That would be disastrous, sir. I would think that would cause a terrible strain in the relations between our two governments. I'm afraid, sir, that would strike our Congress, and perhaps even our President, as a most unfriendly and hostile act. I would suspect we would respond very vigorously to such a challenge, Your Majesty."

The king remained thoughtful.

"I assume, Mr. Salisbury, that you haven't come all this way simply to deliver a message."

"No, sir."

"Then you have a proposal?"

"Yes, sir. One that I think will have the approval of my government."

"Are you speaking for your government, Mr. Salisbury— unofficially, of course?"

"No, sir, I'm not."

The king pursed his lips, but remained silent, indicating to John that he wished him to continue.

"Sir, when NBT makes this public, it will cause a furor in Washington. Mr. Dowding and myself will be under severe criticism by members of the Congress and the press. There will be all sorts of pressure to create new legislation to deal more firmly with this kind of payoff. I believe, sir, we can circumvent at least some of this criticism if the disciplinary action comes from you, rather than Washington, and if it's initiated before this unfortunate affair is made public."

"You are suggesting I punish Aragon. I can do nothing about this Aragon. Isn't he a British subject?"

"Yes, sir, he is. But you can discipline Mr. Ageel."

The king began to smile. This was something he understood. It was revenge. So this pale American was not such a schoolteacher after all. He still had some of the steel of his grandfather.

"What would you suggest I do? Shall I have him beheaded? Cut off his hands? Have him stoned to death? What do you suggest I do?"

"I wouldn't presume to advise you as to that, Your Majesty."

The king looked at John with just the faintest trace of a smile. "But you do want blood, eh, Mr. Salisbury. You have come here for revenge, is that not so?"

John remained silent.

The king did not press the subject. He thought for a moment.

"Suppose, Mr. Salisbury, I forbid Mr. Ageel to receive any monies should we decide to award Mr. Tennant's company the general contract? If I recall the figures correctly, that would deprive Mr. Ageel of approximately a hundred and forty million dollars over a fourteen-year period. Surely not an inconsequential penalty." The king looked carefully at John, who remained silent.

"Suppose, Mr. Salisbury, that I recall Mr. Ageel to this country and strip him of all his assets held in this kingdom, and force him as well to dissolve his business? In any event, without my patronage he has nothing to sell." The king's gaze was steady. "Would that repay our debt to your family, my friend?"

John's eyes were cold and hard. "It would be a most useful way of handling this unfortunate affair, Your Majesty. One that I think would find favor with my government as well."

"It will be done tonight, Mr. Salisbury."

The king rose. "And now, Mr. Salisbury, I have kept my

people waiting long enough, I'm afraid. Please convey my respects to your President. I hope our two governments can continue to pursue peace in this troubled area." The king shook his head. "If only your government were not so unduly influenced by a handful of Jews."

John said nothing. He smiled politely, bowed to the king, who extended his hand. It was a signal honor.

"You know, Mr. Salisbury, we Arabs have a taste for revenge. You would have made a good Bedouin." The king laughed. The audience was over.

A PALE MOON HID BEHIND DARK, SWIFTLY MOVING clouds whose edges were tinged by its dead light. The bright glitter of stars occasionally flashed blue fire at the sleeping city.

The crescent of white-fronted porticoed doorways that was Belgrave Place stood like a row of gravestones in the feeble glow of the electrified gas lamps.

The figure in the dark coat and bowler hat carried a black medical bag. He mounted the steps of Noel's house with accustomed assurance, inserted a key in the lock, and carefully opened the heavy door that he knew would be held by a chain. He withdrew a pair of chain cutters from inside his coat. He stepped quickly into the hall.

He ascended the stairs quietly without hesitation. He might have been a doctor making a late-evening house call unless you saw his eyes. Mad, burning pools straight from the fires of hell. A look in his bag would have further changed that impression.

There was a curved knife, whose edge was sharp enough to sever individual human hairs, and a stainless-steel surgical bone saw.

The bedroom door opened silently. A damp breeze crept

272 /

through the crack of the window by the side of Noel's bed.

Noel Aragon tossed fitfully in disturbed sleep. He was dreaming that something was in his room, a shape he could not recognize, a presence. In his mind he felt it as a cold, diaphanous mist. It was something that moved with a menacing precision, something that threatened him. A black force that had come to destroy him.

He moaned loudly in his sleep, his terror finally piercing the veils of his unconscious. He sat bolt upright in bed. He was wringing wet.

His eyes caught sight of something hovering over him in the darkness.

He started to scream but never emitted a sound. The knife that cut his throat was so sharp he felt little pain. He was only aware for perhaps two seconds of the warm, thick liquid that ran down his chest.

When the Yard was called in in the morning, they found the bed drenched in blood. His right hand had been cut off, his testicles stuffed in his mouth.

It was obvious that someone had been very displeased with the Honorable Noel Aragon.

John couldn't sleep. His bioclock was so mixed up because of the different time zones that it was hard for him to remember he was back in New York, in his own bed, beside Margret. That tomorrow before noon he would announce his and Doug's resignations.

He lay staring up at the soft darkness of the ceiling. Margret was close to him, wide awake, letting him talk, trying to give him whatever comfort and support she could, including a silent prayer that he might be spared some of the anguish and humiliation she knew he would be subjected to tomorrow, and in the next several weeks to come.

"Well, darling," said John, "at least Ageel is through. The

king will strip him of his assets. Without the patronage of the king, he's finished. I'm sure he has enough squirreled away so he won't exactly starve in the street. But the king has taken away the essence of that fellow's ego and, worst of all for that part of the world, exposed him to public shame."

John moved his arm slightly so that Margret's head, resting upon it, would be turned so that he could kiss her.

"Darling, I've never knowingly hurt another man in my life, but I deliberately destroyed that one."

She put her arms around him. He could feel the warmth of her body close to him. Even after all these years she was still attractive to him, her body still firm and appealing. But he was so exhausted that his momentary desire for her subsided; just a trace remained to remind him of how much he loved her, and how thankful he was that when all this broke and spilled over the family, she would be there beside him, unwavering and fiercely protective. What really haunted him more than the trials that awaited him was the thought of Jane. He felt this as his greatest loss, his real failure. Margret interrupted his sorrow.

"What about this fellow Aragon?"

"I don't know what will happen to him. If I know the Bedouins, though, I'm not so sure I'd want to be the Honorable Noel Aragon."

It was eight o'clock in the morning in London. John could not possibly have known the fate that had so terribly mutilated Noel.

At that moment Noel's butler had come to awaken him. When there was no answer to his repeated knocking on Noel's door, he thought it peculiar. When he opened the door to the bedroom, he saw Noel sitting up, propped against several pillows. Noel's eyes were wide open, almost popping out of his head with terror.

The butler took one look at the ghastly scene and vomited.

THE WEATHER WAS LIKE HENRY'S MOOD: FOUL. HE SAT in the anteroom of Lionel Emden's office, half seeing the rain that fell past the windows of the fifty-fifth floor.

As president of NBT, Lionel was known as a hard worker. His day began at 8:00 A.M., and for a man who was nearing his sixty-fifth birthday it was a pace that his associates found both intimidating and frightening.

Lionel had been plagued for years with back problems, and wore an orthopedic brace to keep him vertical and ambulatory. He was a fixture in the industry, highly regarded for his accomplishments and for his character. He was tough but fair, demanding of himself as well as his subordinates.

He was slightly on the portly side with thin sandy hair, quick, appraising brown eyes, and a ready laugh that didn't disguise a "bottom-line" attitude.

Lionel's door opened and Betsy Wright, his secretary for the past fifteen years, smiled at Henry and asked him to come in.

Lionel was genuinely fond of Henry and rose to greet him, his hand outstretched in a gesture of affection and respect.

"Well, you old hound, what brings you to my door when

you should be planning on how you'll spend the weekend with Miss Hopkins?"

Lionel raised an eyebrow in mock rebuke.

"Don't tell me, you old dog, that you think your attentions to your assistant producer haven't reached this office. You should know by now, Henry, that in this business everybody knows what everyone else is doing, or at least thinks he does."

It was supposed to be just light banter between two old friends, but Lionel could see that Henry's mood was far from trivial.

"Henry. For Christ's sake. I was only kidding. Don't look so serious. It's Friday."

Henry sat down on the sofa and took out a cigarette.

Lionel could see now that Henry was very upset.

"O.K., Henry. We've known each other for twenty years. You've got something on your mind. Let's have it." Lionel looked directly at Henry. "Come on. Give."

Henry exhaled cigarette smoke through his nostrils and mouth simultaneously. It was as if he were uttering a visual sigh.

"I'm quitting, Lionel."

Lionel Emden felt a tight knot form in his stomach.

"You're what?"

"I'm resigning as of this morning."

"You are like hell. You've got a contract with us, Henry, and I'll sue your balls off if you quit on me."

Henry shook his head. "I'm doing it for you, Lionel. We've known each other too long for me to stick around when I'm not the man you think I am."

"What the hell are you talking about?"

"You want a pro to run your TV news department, not someone who's lost the guts to do his job without letting his own sense of values interfere. No, Lionel, I've had it. I've been around too long, seen too much blood on the floor, and I'm tired, damn tired."

Lionel knew this wasn't Henry Cannon. Not the Henry Cannon who had covered three wars, who was one of the most respected newsmen in the business.

"Henry. You have me at a slight disadvantage. Will you please tell me what the hell you're talking about?"

"I've just told you. I've got too much respect for this business, for you, and quite frankly for myself, to continue in a responsibility that I can't measure up to any longer."

Lionel leaned back in his leather chair with the built-in headrest. He looked at Henry long and searchingly. If this had been anyone other than Henry Cannon, Lionel would have thrown him out of his office with an angry "Don't waste my time. If you're not happy, get your ass out of here." But this was not just another neurotic executive whose ego Lionel habitually had to soothe; this was Henry Cannon, and Henry didn't have a phony bone in his body. If Henry was disturbed about something, it was important, and if it was important to Henry, then it was damned important to Lionel Emden and NBT. There was only one Henry Cannon, and Lionel couldn't afford to lose him.

Lionel got out of his chair and walked over to Henry. His voice and manner were concerned and sympathetic. He put his hand on Henry's shoulder.

"Now look, Henry. You don't have to crap around with me. We've shaved in a helmet together in Reims, remember, and picked mud out of our teeth in Cologne. If something is eating you, Henry, we've been friends long enough so that you ought to be able to let me in on it."

Henry was only half listening to Lionel. He was looking out the window, thinking of the winter grass on his father's farm in Lancaster, Pennsylvania. Of the stand of hemlocks and evergreens that stood on higher ground, and sloped down to a running creek.

John looked drawn from the fatigue of his trip.

An hour and a half before Henry releases the story, he thought.

Doug was sitting in John's office smoking quietly, resigned, almost insulated from what the day would bring. He felt numb, really not caring any more. A vague thought surfaced in Doug's mind.

"Should we try Cannon one more time? Maybe he's changed his mind, or is willing to listen to reason."

John leaned back in his desk chair looking out the window, thinking that soon this view would no longer be his. "We can call him," he said, and buzzed his secretary to place the call.

They sat silently waiting for the call to go through.

Then John's intercom buzzed. "I'm sorry, Mr. Salisbury, but Mr. Cannon is tied up in a meeting with Mr. Emden."

"Can he be interrupted?"

"No, sir. Do you want me to leave word for Mr. Cannon to return your call?"

"Do that."

"Yes, sir."

"Look, Lionel, I'm not subjecting you or myself to this because of some whim. I've thought about this very carefully. I simply can't continue in a job where I can no longer meet my responsibilities either to you, or NBT or to myself. When a man gets to that stage if he has any self-respect he has no alternative but to resign."

Lionel was now walking about his office, his whole manner reflecting his concern over what Henry had been telling him. The only problem was that Henry hadn't told him a damned thing.

He turned to look at Henry.

"You're not being exactly explicit—you realize that, Henry."

Henry remained lost in thought. He couldn't tell Lionel about the tape or about Joan. Once he started to unravel this thing it would never stop. He would lose complete control over everything, and events would assume a momentum of their own.

He was bothered most by his lack of professionalism, and his breach of trust toward Lionel and the network. But even more corrosive was the collapse of his own standards as a newsman, which he had followed under the most arduous of circumstances for the last thirty years.

"Henry, are you in some kind of trouble? Is it a woman? Do you need money? Have you got the clap? For Christ's sake, what the hell is it? One of the best and most respected newsmen in the business sits in my office and suddenly ends his career and won't tell me why. That's bullshit, Henry. That's not the Henry Cannon I know."

Henry rose and looked at Lionel. He went over to him and put his hand on his shoulder. The expression in Henry's eyes was one of acute pain in letting an old friend down—but even more important, letting himself down.

" 'Virtue refuses facility as a companion,' Lionel."

"Who the hell said that?"

"Montaigne." Henry patted Lionel on the shoulder and left him standing in the middle of his office with his mouth open like a feeding fish.

When Henry returned to his office, he saw the telephone slip on his desk indicating that John Salisbury had called.

He placed the return call himself.

"I'm sorry, Mr. Cannon, but Mr. Salisbury has just gone into a meeting and I'm afraid I can't interrupt him."

"Thank you. Just tell him I returned his call."

Henry hung up the phone and took out the tape recorder from his top desk drawer and began to play it.

He was startled to hear Joan's voice: "This is the worst thing I've ever had to do, Henry, but I've erased the tape. I simply couldn't be responsible for ruining Doug's life, and John Salisbury's as well." There was a long pause on the tape.

"I did it the night I left you my note, Henry, and if you have any respect left for me at all after this, I cried the whole damn time I was doing it. I know this probably will kill anything that might have been left between us, darling, and that, of course, is what hurts most of all. Forgive me, Henry, if you can, and remember—" Here the tape trailed off. After a long silence the voice, tremulous now, came on again. "I love you, darling."

That was it.

It was also "it" for Henry. He picked up his hat and coat, and with a look of grim determination mixed with a great deal of personal anguish, he walked quickly from the room. As he passed his secretary, she saw that he was deeply troubled.

"Will you be back, Mr. Cannon?"

He stopped and looked at her. "I've got to get the hell out of this business," he muttered, and walked out of his office.

On the street, in the damp, penetrating wind that was more chilling because of the shadow of the NBT Building, he stopped. He felt for the note from Joan that he had carried in his breast pocket ever since he had received it. Somehow it made him feel closer to her. He shivered in the wind, and then began to smile. I think I know where I might find that girl, he said to himself, but this time I'm bringing my long underwear.

"Let's try and get Henry one more time, shall we?"

Doug nodded.

John buzzed his secretary. "Try and get Mr. Cannon again."

They both waited, their stomachs in knots, hoping they could reach Henry.

"I'm sorry, sir. Mr. Cannon has left the building."

John frowned. "Let me speak to his secretary."

"She's on the line, sir."

"Hello. This is John Salisbury. You say Mr. Cannon has left?"

"Yes, sir."

"Didn't he try and return my call?"

"Yes, sir. But you were in a meeting."

John's patience was going quickly.

"Your secretary said you were in a meeting, Mr. Salisbury, and couldn't be disturbed."

John wanted to swear, but that was not his habit. "Did Mr. Cannon say anything, or give you any idea where I might reach him?"

Henry's secretary hesitated.

"Well, did he?" John's voice was unusually sharp for him.

"Well, sir, he did say something, but I'm not sure he'd want me to repeat it."

"What was it?"

She hesitated. "He said, 'I've got to get the hell out of this business.' "

John's stomach developed one more knot. "Thank you," he said, and hung up. He turned to Doug. "I guess that does it, Doug."

"You can't get hold of him?"

"No. He's left the building. Said something about wanting 'to get out of this business.' "

"Then it sounds like Cannon's going ahead with the release."

"It seems that way to me," John said.

John buzzed his secretary. "Would you come in here, please?"

John got up from his desk. He held a yellow lined pad in his hand. His secretary came in with her dictation book.

"Please take this down. Mr. John Vincent Salisbury III and Mr. Douglas Dowding wish to advise the board that they are resigning their posts as chairman and president of the First Manhattan Bank. They will present their joint resignation for formal acceptance by the board at a special meeting to be held in the directors' room of the First Manhattan Bank on December seventh. Mr. John Vincent Salisbury at that time will place in nomination for the office of president of FMB Mr. Daniel Bernays."

John turned to Doug. "December seventh. A fitting date, don't you think?"

Doug smiled without humor, and nodded.

"Send that out immediately by telegram to the entire board, and a copy to our publicity people for release to the press."

It was done.

They both looked at each other. Doug got up slowly from the couch. "Well, John, as I've said to you before, it's been a long war."

John brushed the hair back from his forehead, his face white with fatigue and frustration. He looked at Doug.

"If Bardy can make the trip, why don't we fly up to Dark Harbor and get away from all this at least until Monday?"

Doug shook his head. "I appreciate that, John, but Bardy couldn't do it. I'm going to go home and take the phone off the hook and simply try and rest up for the hell that's going to break loose around here next week."

John looked at him carefully. "Doug, I know how hard this has been on you. I've got some ideas that include you. Maybe we can even find something to do that's fun for a change. That would certainly be different, wouldn't it?"

"It sure as hell would, John, but I doubt if anything like that exists."

Doug returned to his office. He sat at his desk not seeing anything, looking inward, almost anesthetized by the events of the morning.

The light on his private line caught his attention. He stared at it, almost unable to move. He finally lifted the receiver. Her voice came to him as if out of an old dream.

"Doug?"

It took him a long time to answer. Even then his reply was almost inaudible.

"Doug, are you all right? You sound so strange."

He could hear the anxiety in her voice.

"I'm O.K."

"Doug, I know something's terribly wrong."

He sighed audibly. "Karen, the whole damn thing has blown up. It's all over."

"Oh, Doug, I am sorry."

He sensed her hesitation, and was aware of her concern for him.

"Well, it's not the end of the world, Karen. Life goes on." He paused. "I've been thinking about you, too."

The lump in her throat was choking her. It took every ounce of will she had to keep her voice from breaking. Why? What had they ever really had together? When was it ever that good? She didn't know. She didn't know why cutting this tie hurt so damn much, but it did. "I didn't want to leave without saying—ah, without saying good-bye."

He was simply too numb to react.

"Where are you going?"

She hated to add to his problems. She was sorry she had picked this time to call.

"Doug. I'm going out to Stanford. I have an interview with the head of their department of internal medicine. I'm going to stay on the Coast and look around, in case Stanford's not too encouraging."

He heard what she was saying, and he realized that the implications of what she was telling him would hit him later. Right now his emotions were too insulated by the battering he had taken. He was like a punch-drunk fighter.

"Doug. There's no reason why—we have to lose touch. I'll let you know where you can reach me." She fought to keep control. "Thank you for Oxford, Doug." She couldn't continue.

"Karen, I—"

"Good-bye, darling."

He could hear her trying not to break down.
Then she hung up.

He sat there holding the phone in his hand, looking at it as if it were the severed cord of a part of his life, which it was. He put it back gently. The whole room was now misted light. He couldn't talk. He couldn't make a sound. Slowly he got up, managed to get his hat and coat, and like a sleepwalker moved toward the elevators. He was going down.

MIKE HAD FLOWN TO SEATTLE TO GIVE DUTCH HIS preliminary report. They were sitting in Dutch's living room with its vast angled beamed ceiling. Skylights let in the new morning sun on polished redwood and stone and on hand-crafted flame maple furniture with red-clay-colored cushions.

The lines of the room were the straight, uncluttered planes of the Japanese. The scattered Indian rugs on the polished flagstone gave the room a masculine look. They sat on op-posite ends of the enormous rust-colored L-shaped sofa.

"Mike. Just give it to me clean and simple. What the hell is going on at that goddamn bank?"

Mike's posture as usual was that of an uncurled question mark, half reclining, his long legs stretched in front of him.

"Dutch, you have to realize that in the short time I've been looking at FMB, the only impressions I could have would be very superficial—"

Dutch raised a beefy hand. His voice growled. "Forget the introduction. Get to the chorus."

Mike smiled and shook his head. He had a quick sense of humor, and he needed it with Dutch.

"Dutch, if I had to answer in one sentence what I thought

the main problem was with FMB, I'd say lack of leadership caused mainly by a breakdown in communication. The place has the intrigue of a seventeenth-century Italian court. So much energy is wasted on the part of their senior people in political game playing, in subtly maneuvering to improve their own personal positions, that they don't talk to each other. The sixty-seventh floor is a warren of executive spaces separated from each other by closed doors. The atmosphere is secretive and suspicious. There's a lot of talent there, but it would take a strong man with a clear mandate of authority to open that place up—blow some fresh air in there and get everybody pointed and moving in the right direction."

Dutch was listening to Mike intently, his face a study in grim concentration.

The light on the phone beside him preceded its jangling ring.

Dutch held up a hand toward Mike, and picked up the receiver. It was his secretary.

"I'm sorry to disturb you, sir, but this telegram just arrived from Mr. Salisbury. I thought you'd better hear it."

"Go ahead."

She read Dutch John's telegram. As he listened the color drained from his face.

"Jesus Christ!" He hung up. He turned to Mike.

"That fucking Salisbury and Dowding are resigning!"

Mike stood up. He was incredulous. "You can't be serious."

"You're goddamn right I'm serious."

"But why?"

"How the hell should I know?"

Dutch thought for a moment, then started punching savagely at the buttons on the phone to call John Salisbury. He glared at Mike and clamped an unlit cigar between his teeth.

"I'm getting the hell off the board of that fucking turkey," he growled, and waited with volcanic impatience to be put through to John Salisbury.

＊ ＊ ＊

Doug walked solemnly into the apartment. His thoughts seemed far away.

Bardy was eating lunch alone. She looked up at him as he came into the room, her eyes soft with compassion.

He noticed that she had on a new suit that he hadn't seen before. She was wearing a touch of lipstick, and her hair had been carefully set.

He stopped and looked at her, his face reflecting his disappointment.

"Are you going out?"

"No," she said.

He was puzzled. He still had on his coat. He had put his hat on the hall table. He was holding a small box wrapped in brown paper. His hands were shaking.

"You're all dressed up."

"Am I?" She smiled. "I didn't think you'd notice."

She got up and came toward him, then stood just a little apart.

"Was it very difficult?"

"Nope. Easy. John and I just blew twenty-five years."

Her lips trembled slightly. She went to take his coat.

"No, I'll do that. Here. I've got a little present for you." His lips compressed as he handed her the box.

She removed the cheap brown paper and opened the thin paper box that was packed with tissue. She carefully took out the cup and saucer from her mother's set that he had accidentally broken what seemed like such a long time ago. It had been repaired perfectly.

"You said we couldn't put back the pieces, remember?"

She nodded. Everything in the room seemed to blend into soft colors and light.

"I thought I'd try," he said.

She touched his sleeve. She knew him so much better than he knew himself. She understood what he needed and what she couldn't give. She knew what time would do to them.

She looked down at the cup and saucer that rattled gently in her hand.

"You know, this will never last in hot water," she said.

They both looked at that truth, and it hurt like hell.

John hadn't said a word throughout dinner. He had hardly touched his food.

They sat close to each other in the small family dining room at right angles at the end of the table. The room was so quiet Margret could hear the sounds of her own breathing.

Her heart had broken for him. She looked at him, at the bowed head that seemed to stare at his plate without seeing anything—not in defeat, but in concentration, with purpose.

She sensed that he was resolving something and she wanted to be a part of that. She leaned forward looking at him, wanting to give him whatever she could.

He clasped her hand tightly; his face had softened as he looked at her. The stranger in his eyes had gone.

She tried to speak. Her lips were trembling and her voice was choked with love and heartbreak.

"Don't worry, darling. You have so many interests. You'll find a new direction. You'll know which way to go."

He met her love with his.

"I already do," he said. His smile was slight but determined.

Her eyes seemed surprised, even through their mist.

He leaned toward her and kissed her with great tenderness. His voice was husky. "I'm going to find Jane," he said.

She looked at him for a long time. They were holding each other's hand hard. Something new told her that she would have to learn how to let go—a little.

B/03
4/

DATE DUE

SEP 1 9 1979 E. MKW		
OCT 2 4 1979 MY 7 '83		
NOV 2 8 1979 OC 24 '83		
JAN 2 4 1980 JUL 1 3 1988		
MAR 4 1980		
APR 9 1980		
JUL 1 6 1980		
FE 5 '81		
MY 7 '81		
JY 23 '81		
NOV 19 81		
JA 11 '82		
MR 9 '82		
MY 3 '82		
JE 7 '82		
AG 3 '82		
NO 23 '82		
NOV 9 1982		